ISLE OF DARKNESS AND LIGHT
1862: MAROONED WHERE PIRATES LURK

BROTHERS IN PERIL TRILOGY
BOOK TWO

Elizabeth Ann Boyles

Published in the United States by Promise House Publishing, Colorado Springs, CO
Library of Congress Control Number: 2025911633
ISBN: 978-1-7345011-4-8 (Paperback)
ISBN: 978-1-7345011-8-6 (Ebook)

Scripture quotations are from the King James Version of the Bible.

Cover design by Kim Killion/The Killion Group, Inc.

*Dedicated to My Critique Mentors I'm
ever so grateful for your encouragement,
guidance, and most of all—friendship!*

CHAPTER 1

Uncharted Pacific island
Mid-October, 1862

A lightweight object, like an acorn, grazed Tom Ballard's arm. Startled to see the morning sun, he brushed off leaves and leaned up against the trunk of the tree he'd slept under. The quick movements were a mistake. His body hurt like he'd had another bruising fight with the eighth-grader who tormented his younger brother years earlier. The next second, a pebble, not an acorn, bounced off his arm. He swiveled slowly to view the pebble's source, preparing to spring up if a fight were imminent.

The Japanese girl who helped rescue him off the cliff's ledge the previous night stood next to the jungle-like forest. When he stood and their eyes met, she bowed, her glossy hair sweeping over the shoulders of her faded green robe.

"You've come to help me?" He stopped himself from adding a complaint about how she and her brother had left him alone, once they'd gotten him off the ledge, exposed to whatever prowled the island at night.

She put her fingers to her lips and beckoned for him to follow her.

When he strode quickly forward, she held up her hand for him to halt. Getting her meaning, he kept several paces behind her, wanting to argue that the "deal" he'd accepted with her brother—to live separated from them, not bothering one another—didn't say he couldn't come *near* her. What's more, he hadn't been given much choice in the matter. Either accept the agreement or be left where he'd fallen, which would have handed him over to the pirate cursing on the beach below him.

He followed her as she turned into the forest, or jungle, and wove through umbrella trees, island pines, unfamiliar tropical trees, and the undergrowth of huge ferns, shrubs, and vines. She moved smoothly along a barely discernible path, seemingly unperturbed by the possibility of venomous snakes. When he'd crept through the same kind of growth before his accident, hunting for fresh water for the ship, he'd thanked his lucky stars for the small protection his tough sailor trousers and thick boots provided.

After about twenty yards, his will-o'-the-wisp guide finally led him out of the trees. As they stood apart on the far side of the ridge, the girl glanced back at him, as though a hen checking on her chick, despite being more than a head shorter and probably younger than his nineteen years. Apparently satisfied, she started down the incline, edging past dark boulders.

Tom paused to take in his first good view of the oval valley below—the small island's centerpiece. Two connected ponds glimmered in the distance, surrounded by marsh-like grass and possibly cattails. A bamboo grove grew at one end of the oval, explaining the homemade ladder her brother had used to get him off the ledge. No sign of human occupancy dotted the valley or rocky hillsides, so the island's only inhabitants appeared to be the Japanese pair and the pirate.

A hermit might like the emptiness—no chimney smoke, no clatter of wheels, no children's cries. A monk might value the chance to commune with nature or a god without interruption. For him, it looked a desolate wilderness.

The girl stopped and waited for him to return his attention to her. She pointed toward the ponds, cupped her hand to her mouth, and shook her head.

Tom nodded. Brackish water, he guessed. The valley had probably been a lagoon ages ago, ringed by a coral reef. Good thing he hadn't led the other sailors in the skiff to the ponds, only to be razzed for his ignorance or accused of trying to poison them.

The incline became steeper halfway to the bottom. "Can I help you?" Tom called. Aiming to catch up with the girl, he hurried around boulders while dodging brambles the best he could.

His guide shot her hand up again for him to keep his distance and forcefully shook her head, obviously a true-blue follower of her brother's commands.

He huffed a breath and shrugged.

When his guide had come within nine feet of the plain, she stopped and pointed to a small opening in the hillside.

Approaching with a turtle's speed so not to alarm her, he was tempted to ask if the cave was what her brother had assigned him in his island "kingdom." But instead, he pointed to himself silently.

She nodded, bowed, and left him. She gracefully covered the distance to the bottom of the hill, like part dancer, part mountain goat. He watched her slender form until she entered another cave farther along the valley's arc. Her brother might be an uncompromising recluse, but from the look of things, the girl herself was more like a dark-eyed angel, although an unapproachable one, subject to her brother's whims.

Tom poked his head into the cave's entrance to see what he might have to endure until his ship's search party found him. He wouldn't, couldn't, entertain the thought that his shipmates had left him for good, on purpose, no matter how many of the merchant ship's devils would have favored marooning him at one time or another.

The cave's ceiling exceeded his five-foot-eleven height by half a foot or so. In the dim light, he made out a pile of bamboo stalks and leaves against the back wall, probably courtesy of the girl. His two buckets from the ship were closer to the entrance, undoubtedly also put there by the girl, who had been honest enough not to keep them. He stepped inside and found the buckets no longer held the clams he'd dug for the ship's cook, but were full of water—fresh water.

After taking long, life-giving draughts, he brought one of the buckets outside and washed the wound where the back of his head had smashed onto the rocky ledge. Then he rubbed water over the scratches on his arms and one on his cheek. He emptied the bucket's remaining water onto the top of his head and shook his hair like his mongrel dog Tuffy did after a swim in the creek behind their New York home.

Glad of no fresh blood and only a faint headache in addition to his bruises, which hurt but weren't debilitating, he headed to the top of the ridge that encircled the island. Having learned the hard way not to get too close to the rim's unstable edge, he viewed the ocean from several steps back. The crashing waves and geysers of spray against the rocky shore didn't resemble what he'd faced with five other rowers the previous day. They had managed to skirt hazardous reefs and enter quieter waters of a lagoon, separated by cliffs from where he'd fallen.

Captain Madison would order the *William Parton* to circle the isle until he found the best place to send larger search parties safely to shore. Clearly, the area below him was not a possibility. Tom set out for the rim above the lagoon, staying on the narrow strip between the trees and cliffs. The sunshine grew in intensity. The dark forest blocked much of the south wind, but he didn't mind the sweat trickling down his back or his renewed thirst. In the next few minutes, he'd see the merchant brig's glorious sails and boats coming for him, with his brother Terry among the group.

Reaching the area above their first landing spot, he peered at the lagoon, then at the ocean beyond. A vast emptiness greeted his eyes. He tamped down his disappointment. A more favorable inlet had to exist.

Three hours later, by his best estimation, he had completely circled the island. He squatted and used his shirt to wipe the sweat stinging his eyes. The rough seas had to explain his rescue's delay. Despite the knot forming in his gut, he would not think otherwise. His brother would never allow the ship to maroon him. And there were seamen's rules too. If a sailor fell into the sea from the highest royal yard and it was known he couldn't swim a lick, the ship still dispatched rowboats to search for the fellow. Surely Captain Madison would assume his missing sailor was much more likely to be alive on the island—just somehow incapacitated.

He hadn't eaten for over twenty-four hours except for the raw mackerel the Japanese pair had lowered to him while he was still stuck on the ledge. But he couldn't take time to catch a fish or trap one of the birds near the ponds. He would just keep circling on the ridge in case the sea's condition improved enough for the search party to land elsewhere.

Two rounds later, Tom stopped when he again reached the ridge's section fronting the lagoon's quieter shore. No other spot came close to being as accessible. The captain had been plain lucky the previous day in his choice of anchorage.

The wind caused the trees' lengthening shadows to flicker close to his feet. The thrum of locusts announced the late afternoon. He steeled himself for another night on the blasted island and increased his pace until he came to the crooked path through the undergrowth. Keeping an eye out for anything dangerous, he wound through the entangling vines and brush. At last coming out of the trees, he stumbled down the incline.

Three-quarters down, he stopped. Where was the wretched cave? The protruding rocks' black shadows kept tricking him to check one deception after another. The low red sun was casting its final beams over the trees. He gritted his teeth. He couldn't bear another night outside, unprotected from whatever wildlife inhabited the island. He moved toward another shadow and huffed a puff of relief when he stood in the entrance of the dark cave.

Just then, a creature flew right over his head. He ducked as several more buzzed past. Looking up, he gasped as a dark cloud winged straight down from the trees lining the ridge above. "No, no! Go away! Get outta here!" he yelled, waving his arms. The monstrosities whizzing by him had faces like foxes. The final one in the group flapped back and forth above him, as if scrutinizing him for a meal, then flew on.

He shuddered. Not foxes. Bats. Giant bats! He'd gotten a better look at the last one. Its wingspan had been a good three feet. Were they vampire bats? Or the harmless fruit bats he'd heard reports about? Another undulating cloud flew out of the woods, and he dove into the cave.

Taking half of the bamboo, he covered the entrance the best he could, twisting the stalks into the ground and scraping rocks from outside to lend support. If the bats weren't aggressive blood suckers, he'd make it through the night. First thing in the morning, he'd corner the Japanese pair, get information, demand the return of his knife the brother had apparently taken while following Tom up the ladder, and then kill something to eat, even if he had to eat it raw.

He rearranged the remaining pile of bamboo into a pallet and lay down in the thickening darkness, wishing he'd examined the cave more carefully when he first entered it. He should have checked the small opening in the wall to the right of the entrance. Maybe the hole opened into a giant cavern, one with more bats and revolting creatures, and he lay in its vestibule. He hugged his arms to his chest. If creatures shared his cave, it'd be really helpful if they'd already had a feast fit for a king.

The bamboo rolled under him. Twigs poked him. On the ship, he'd missed his home's feather bed. Now he missed the too-short cot in the crew's forecastle. More than that, he longed for the ship's cardboard-tasting food to quash his hunger pangs. And then there was his brother. Terry could be a pain, but they understood each other. They could count on each other. His brother was his buddy.

A lump caught in his throat. What if he were truly stranded on this god-forsaken island with no people but a rascal of a pirate and the Japanese pair, who were dead-set on isolating him? If he had no one to joke with, or argue with, or even think about things with, he'd go stark-raving mad.

He drew in a sharp breath. If by some unimaginable misfortune, he was stuck on the island for longer than another day or two, moaning over his loneliness would get him nowhere. First off, he had to achieve a new agreement with the brother and sister. That would be harder than he'd anticipated in the first minutes after the pair rescued him. But surely not impossible. Although Japanese people most likely had a whole different way of thinking, it wasn't like the three of them had nothing in common. The harsh wilderness obviously affected anyone trapped on the island. Also, they had a common enemy in the pirate, and most likely, the pair wanted to escape their rocky prison, too.

He felt a flicker of a smile. When the rescue party came, he could repay the brother and his kind sister for getting him off the ledge. Captain Madison's pride in his reputation wouldn't let him refuse passage to marooned unfortunates.

If only the rescue would happen exceedingly fast.

CHAPTER 2

Ogawa Daisuke watched his sister Sara preparing the mackerel next to the modified metal bucket that served as their charcoal burner. The knife barely missed her nimble fingers. "Pay attention your work," he grumbled in English, then switched to Japanese. "What is wrong with you tonight?"

She jerked her head as though waking from a dream. "Thank you for your concern. I am all right." As always, she'd used the Japanese phrases showing her respect.

"Your preoccupation bothers me, especially while using a sharp knife. There's an ocean between you and a doctor."

"Forgive me for disturbing your harmony." She made a couple of tentative slices.

"Since you already have, you might as well disturb it further. 'What is wrong?' I ask again."

"Begging your pardon, I feel sorry for the foreigner. He knows nothing." She blushed.

"We knew nothing when we were swept ashore."

She nodded and bowed.

"We learned."

She bowed again.

"He is a barbarian. Not so bad as the pirate outwardly, but maybe more dangerous covertly. Dangerous for you. Maybe we shouldn't have helped him off the ledge."

"He circled the ridge several times today, probably watching for his ship. My heart hurt to see him suffer. Forgive me, but does not Jesus tell us to help others?"

"Who knows the full meaning of those hard teachings? But I *do* know you were wrong to check on the barbarian so frequently, Sa-*chan*."

She bit her lip with a sigh, then wrapped the fish in boiled bamboo leaves for heating.

"What is it? You didn't *talk* to the barbarian, did you?"

"I didn't utter a word, but I thought aiding him a little would be all right." She hurried on, as though she expected a storm and had to say everything before the thunder boomed. "This morning, I emptied his buckets of clams, fearing they had spoiled, and filled the buckets with fresh water so he wouldn't get sick on the bad pond water."

"Where did you put the buckets?" He clenched his fists, hardly believing Sara's rashness.

"At the entrance of the cave, and … and I led him to the cave, but I didn't let him approach me, and truly, I didn't speak to him."

Daisuke sprang up and stomped his foot. "I didn't expect my sister, the daughter of six generations of honorable samurai, to sneak behind my back. To shame herself!"

She knelt with her forehead to the ground. "I didn't mean to bring shame. I tried to obey both you and our Master. I am deeply sorry."

"I forbid you to help him further. I order this as your elder."

Although no doubt aggrieved, she touched her forehead to the ground again.

The meal was a silent one. Sara kept her head bowed as she ate. He berated himself for his permissiveness—allowing Sara to eat with him in order to ease his loneliness and cheer her up and, more harmful, letting her hunt with him to supplement their supply of duck and pigeon meat. He'd shown her how to aim better, and after practicing with her bow for days on end, she'd become as skilled as he. This laxity in maintaining a proper relationship must have led to her boldness in expressing opinions, in acting on her suppositions.

What would happen if they ever escaped the island and she married? He might have ruined her. The man she had been promised to since childhood would surely have ended the betrothal contract after she had been missing from their homeland for so long. Now that she was nineteen years old, and would only get older, any prospective husband would worry about her advanced age. The man would certainly be shocked if he knew of her island behavior.

He sighed. What was done was done.

When the glowing embers had mostly turned gray, Sara retired behind the bamboo-and-palm-frond partition dividing the cave. Daisuke checked on his number two *yukata* robe for the next day, then lay down. After the last of the embers winked out and the night air cooled the cave, he still couldn't sleep, bothered by a nettlesome pity for the barbarian. The sailor had suffered a hard fall and was alone, most likely marooned like them, with no end in sight. Despite his bizarre looks—scraggly hair the color of pears and startling blue eyes—the barbarian surely had some feelings similar to his own.

Maybe Sara was right, and their new master, Jesus, did require them to help even a barbarian. He would look into the bulky Bible they'd carried with them on their disastrous journey.

Getting any guidance, however, could take a long time. After reading only a page or two in English, his mind always refused to continue the grueling exercise. In the meantime, he hoped Jesus would excuse his ignorance.

A low rumble came from the earth. He turned to get more comfortable, ignoring another one of the almost weekly tremors.

All at once, the floor of the cave jerked sideways, then jounced up and down. Before he could grab hold of anything, the floor shot higher up, paused, and crashed down with a thunderous boom.

Sara was screaming.

Struggling for breath, he picked himself up from where he'd landed. No sooner had he steadied himself than a massive jolt knocked him over again. He threw his arms over his head as a roar of boulders pounded down outside the cave's entrance, drowning out his sister's cries.

Thick dust filled the cave. He covered his mouth and nose with the crook of his elbow, bracing for an onslaught from the cave's implosion. Was he really ready to die as he'd bragged to his samurai companions—friends in another lifetime? His hammering heart said *no*.

The earth groaned as if in agony. Then all became eerily quiet except for his and Sara's fits of coughing. When the stillness continued, he spit out what dust he could and once again pushed onto his feet.

Sara, mumbling prayers interspersed with sobs, bumped into him in the dark and gasped. "Are we buried in here?"

"Of course not. Go lie down before you trip over something. We'll work our way out when it's morning." He doubted she had confidence in his assertion, but she obeyed.

He lay awake the rest of the night, trying to imagine their true situation. When a sliver of dim light seeped through a crack in the blocked entrance, he called Sara. "Help me push."

Their grunts and shoves didn't move the wall of rock even a hair. The boulders were like an impenetrable mountain.

His sister began sobbing, louder this time.

"The cave's intact, and it seems you're not hurt. That's what matters." He took her arm and turned her toward her part of the cave. "You belong to a long line of samurai. Go lie down until you can control yourself. We'll push again after a while."

"Nothing budged." A sob made her hiccup.

"Obey me."

She drew in a sharp breath and shuffled away.

He crawled to his pallet and lay down too. He needed all his strength even if their fate was to die a slow death.

From behind the cave's divider, Sara began softly reciting a psalm the Christian *sensei* had taught them. His heart's wild thumping slowed. Undeniably, the words had a power of their own. Drawing on his samurai training, he focused his thoughts on the psalm's simple image of a sheep in a green pasture. He rejected each encroaching desire, including his persistent yearning to escape the miserable island itself.

The psalm's words about "a table before mine enemy" interrupted his concentration. The barbarian was undoubtedly a true enemy, but the Christian God had allowed him into their lives. Sara even claimed to have prayed for a companion if they were marooned indefinitely. Maybe his sister's shameful contact with the sailor hadn't been so shameful after all. If the tall foreigner had survived the quake, he would have to repay the aid they had given him if he had any sense of honor at all.

Was Jesus giving him a message? Was he so hardheaded it took an earthquake to get his attention? Or was he being unduly influenced by Sara's naivety?

CHAPTER 3

Tom squinted one eye at the dim morning light. He ran his palm over the ground next to him and raised his head for a cautious inspection. No rubble, and the thick dust had settled. But was the quake over? He curled back into a tight ball with one arm protecting his head, listening for any more murderous rumblings.

When full daylight entered the cave and the ground had clearly stopped acting like a stallion gone wild, he uncurled and looked for the remaining bucket of water. Seeing it on its side against the left wall, he let out a curse his grandparents' parson would despise. He slurped a little of the water that hadn't escaped, but instantly spit it out—muddy slop not fit for a pig.

Venturing outside, he ran his eyes around the rim of the ridge. No sign of the bats, which probably slept until dusk. Although a few brown birds, maybe warblers, flitted over the trees, the island was quieter than the prior day, as if the wildlife had to recover from the jolts too.

But how could anything with half a brain *recover*? Next time, he might not be tucked away in the cave. The ground could open up under him. Swallow him up. The crew had better show up soon. Leaving him without carrying out a good search was criminal enough, but subjecting him to an island plagued by midnight earthquakes was evil at its rankest.

He headed down to where he would have a better view of the brother and sister's cave. At the foot of the hill, he skidded to a stop. A jumble of boulders and torn-up bushes covered the pair's area. The cave had become invisible.

Had the cave collapsed? Were the two dead? He shivered, imagining the horror of being crushed.

But since his cave had held up, theirs probably had too although they might be trapped inside. Despite the deal, he ought to see what was going on. He skirted the hill to where he guessed the other cave was located.

"Hey! Anybody there?" He picked up a rock and knocked on the boulders as he worked his way forward, shouting every minute or two. If the devil had wanted to disguise the entrance, he'd done a superb job. He expanded his range, while worry ate at him. What if a search party came and it included the same five villains who had left him? They might make a quick pass along the other side of the island and talk the whole group into taking off, their distasteful duty done.

He paused to wipe the ever-present sweat from his forehead. Should he give up looking for the cave for now, try again later, maybe with the help the captain could deliver—if the man was in a decent mood?

But the two had to be scared to death, and another few minutes in the hill's shadows wouldn't hurt. Besides, hunger was renewing his dizziness. They probably had extra foodstuff—a catch from the ocean or at least berries—to tide him over. A fleeting vision of sizzling bacon, fried eggs, and a pile of his grandma's fluffy biscuits, so light they nearly floated, made his mouth water and his step falter. What he wouldn't give to be sitting at that farmhouse table, or better yet, feasting at his Albany home.

"Help!" came a faint cry from rocks ahead of him.

"Coming!" Tom climbed to the top of the pile of stones and dirt that muffled the continuing calls. After pushing away the hillside's debris, he reached the massive boulder resting on lesser boulders that barricaded the entrance. The giant sealed the cave, as if demanding Ali Baba's magical words.

He raised his hands to push, but hesitated. He could leave the two alone, like the deal dictated, couldn't he? He wouldn't be killing them. They might get out. But if they didn't, and if he were marooned—purely hypothetically—he'd have the run of the area. *He'd* be the ruler.

No, by jingoes! He wasn't a paragon of goodness. Shame still haunted him for how close he'd come to killing his enemy on the ship. But he sure wasn't so coldhearted that he wouldn't help his rescuers. Even if a fraction of the reason to aid them was to avoid being completely alone, the New York parson couldn't accuse him of being vile like his shipmates.

However, here was his chance to demand a new agreement, to improve his situation a lot—if, by any chance, the ship didn't come for a number of days.

Gathering all his strength, he pressed his hands and chest against the monster, shoving it as though he himself were its victim. It grated, tipped, then rolled and bounced down the slope, slamming onto the level ground amid a spew of sand and dirt.

A large slit showed above the newly exposed boulders. Putting his face close to it, he found the boy's dark eyes searching the outside situation, then settling on him.

"We need a new deal," Tom said, once he had regained his breath.

"No new deal." The boy drew his face away from the slit.

"*You* made the agreement when you helped me. Now, *I'll* make the deal since I'm helping you. If you don't take it, you won't see me again." The pair wouldn't know it was an empty threat.

"What is the deal?" The boy's irritation came through loud and clear.

"As long as we're stuck here on the island, we become a team, help each other, talk together."

Silence greeted Tom. Then, a different sound. Was it the ship's horn? "I'll come back. With more help!" he shouted, as he clambered up the hill. Scarcely able to contain his joy, he tore through the forest, not caring when a vine's thorn ripped into his shirt. Wheezing, he raced around the ridge to the initial landing area.

Peering as far as the horizon, he searched for sails. Even if a jolly-boat or cutter was on its way back to the ship, the *William Parton*'s sails would still be in sight.

Only the shimmering sea met his eyes. Had he imagined the horn? Normally there would have been shouts as well as several gunshots. He'd heard only the one signal. The sea below was quieter, permitting a landing, but there wasn't any. He gazed long and hard into the distance, his chest rasping, his throat constricting. He was—as far as he knew—really and truly marooned!

Falling to his knees, he pounded the ground. Already he was hearing things. Going crazy. He rolled over on his side, mortified to hear himself wail.

When he'd finally gotten ahold of himself, he lay still. The tall cliffs fronting the ocean came to mind. How about a quick leap into nothingness, instead of dying day by day, or month by month, or year by year on the island, slowly turning into a gray-haired scarecrow?

But then, he'd be deserting Terry, who'd keep searching for him. And what about their parents and grandparents? And the two still entombed below? He huffed a breath. Why be so lily-livered? He clenched his jaw and stumbled to his feet. Either he would be rescued, or he'd find a way to rescue himself.

Arriving back at the sealed cave, he called, "You still there?" realizing a second later how asinine that sounded.

"I take deal," the answer came, a little husky. "Except one. You cannot talk to my sister. This is good for her. Good for you, too, I think."

Tom hesitated, hating to yield to any demand, but he had to have someone to connect with. One bossy fellow was better than no one. "All right," he conceded. "Maybe it's better that way." The sister was pretty, but his friend Peg—if she hadn't given up on him—would be happier for nothing to develop there. Besides, even if the sister's English was passable, what on earth could they talk about?

He told the pair where to push from the inside, and together they maneuvered the rest of the boulders. A narrow passageway opened up. He peered inside the cave, then blinked as a dark shadow blanketed him. He fumbled for the rock next to him. Hands caught hold of him as his legs gave way.

When Tom next opened his eyes, he was on the ground, leaning against a rock. The world spun as it had when he lay on the ledge.

The boy held half a coconut shell to Tom's lips. "Drink," he said.

Tom sucked in water and nearly gagged on something long and slimy. "What the—"

18

"Seaweed is good. Chew. Swallow."

The orders were exasperating, but he hadn't the strength to object.

"The sailors not come?" the boy asked after Tom finished a third cupful.

"Not any yet." He leaned his head back, unwilling to reveal his desperation. Only a fool would show weakness to a tyrant. "My brother won't forget me. If the ship left me, Terry'll get another one to come, somehow. We're thicker than ... most brothers." *Thicker than thieves* wouldn't give the best impression. Then he remembered his knife, too late for negotiation. "I want my knife back. You left me outside the night before last with no protection at all, while I knew nothing about what I faced."

"My people call you barbarian. You get angry or greedy, you want to kill us when we sleep."

"If we're a team, we have to trust each other. If I wanted to kill you, I'd have left you in the cave. I'd have watched for my rescuers early this morning instead of searching for you. I need my knife. I swear on my sister's grave, I'll never use it against you."

The boy reached under his robe's sash and drew out the knife in its worn sheath. "If you hurt us, our spirits join your sister. Haunt you into next life."

Tom took the knife, wondering what else the two believed in besides ghosts.

"I'm Tom," he said.

The boy asked, "Tamo?"

"No, Tom-m, but that's close enough. What's your name?"

"Ogawa Daisuke."

"Oagwa Die-ski?" Tom waited to see the reaction to his errors.

"Close enough." Daisuke frowned.

"How about I call you Dice?"

Daisuke shrugged with a slight roll of his eyes.

"And your sister?"

"You not need her name."

"So, *sister* will do?"

He scowled at Tom. "You can say Sara."

That's her name?"

"Her name is Ogawa Sara. For foreigner like you, you can say a little different, like in Bible. S-a-r-a-h."

"Oh, Sarah." He hadn't realized the name came from the Bible, but he guessed a lot of names had their origin there. "Your pronunciation isn't hard for me. It rhymes with the English name Laura. Sara, Laura." He rubbed his face, still not feeling right in the head.

"Come inside our cave, out of sun. You rest. We can talk later." Dice helped him stand and led him through the entrance to a pallet of bamboo—higher than Tom's and smoother because of a covering mat of woven fronds. The boy motioned to his sister to go behind the cave's bamboo-and-leaf screen.

After her uncomplaining obedience without so much as a frown, Dice squatted close to Tom's ear. "Now we are team. We need to protect her and us. Maybe more pirates come. Angry, cruel ones. Worse than one on beach, who is evil, too." He drew back and straightened. "Now rest. We shall talk later."

Rest? Tom snorted. What a ridiculous thing to say after such a disclosure. Was there even the slightest chance of their defeating a pack of bloodthirsty ruffians? Daggers would fly. Swords would whack off limbs. The air would be full of groans and curses.

He wasn't close to sleeping when a rumbling shudder from the depths of the earth wiped out all other thought. Rocks clattered outside. Dirty air swept into the cave. Another aftershock—with all three of them trapped inside!

Dice rushed to the entrance. "Not too many rocks," he reported. After ordering his sister to go back to her partitioned area, he returned to Tom, who had sat up. "Not like last night. First very bad quake after we come here. Hope it is last one."

"A bad quake or a not-so-bad quake—*any* quake—is one too many in my book." Tom lay back down, waiting for his nerves to ease. He looked up at Dice's stoic face. "My ship better come back double-quick before this place serves up more horrors. If something awful happens once—like last night's quake—it can jolly-well happen again, you know."

"Of course, I know. Maybe *you* do not know my country has much earthquakes." Dice turned on his heel and walked away.

Tom swung his arm over his eyes. Dice wasn't good company by a long shot. Besides handing out warnings and orders like Christmas candy, he would probably take issue with everything else they discussed. But he and Sara were living, breathing people, and *beggars couldn't be choosers*.

CHAPTER 4

"Sail Ho!" came from the lookout in the crow's nest high above the *William Parton*'s deck.

Terry sprang up the forecastle's ladder and banged open the hatch cover.

"Take it easy, Turd," a sailor grumbled.

Finished with worrying about the two-legged rats surrounding him—the five rats who'd left his brother to rot on the island in particular—Terry dropped the cover with a bang.

When he reached the starboard railing, the sails of a whaleship were already visible, and the ship was headed in the right direction. East. East toward the island and Tom.

Terry sprinted toward the ladder leading to the quarterdeck, where the first mate was pacing. Striving to be heard above the slapping sails, creaking blocks, and spraying waves, he hollered up, "Mr. Talbot! Mr. Talbot, sir!"

First Mate Talbot peered down at him. "What the dickens now, Ballard? Still ranting about that fool brother of yours?"

Terry climbed halfway up the ladder, not daring to get closer to the officers' privileged sanctity. "Sir, please. Could you ask the captain a great favor? One that will someday be rewarded."

"No doubt. With your one-twelfth of the jack-tars' payout." Talbot snickered. "Captain's busy. He's got duties more important than listening to every sailor's bellyache. Now get on with you unless you want double watch. My larboard watch's short one man."

"Sir, I can't bear it." Terry glanced toward the whaler. "That whaler's a chance for my brother! I swear, I'll climb up there and ask Captain Madison myself if you won't do it."

"I'll show you what threats like that get you." Talbot straightened and strode toward the rail where the captain was watching the whaleship with his spyglass.

A minute later, the captain motioned Terry onto the quarterdeck.

Terry climbed the remaining rungs, his mouth dry as a desert.

"Let's hear it, sailor." Captain Madison's steely eyes could have frozen furnace fires.

"A simple thing, but means more than life to me. Please sir, please tell that ship's captain about the island with the turtles and my marooned brother. Only that, sir."

Captain Madison turned to the first mate. "Didn't you say the men made a thorough search? That his brother Tom either deserted or was dead?"

"Aye, a broad search everywhere, Captain. The men didn't hanker to leave one of their own on a god-forsaken island."

"Sir," Terry interrupted, "Tom would never desert and leave me. He could have gotten lost in the thick jungle or have a broke leg." His voice shook, but he didn't care. "Just a quick message to the whaler. Please!"

"Wouldn't do any good," the captain huffed. Seeing Terry open his mouth, he held up his hand. "That ship has more to do than go off course. Squall during the night took us by the island. My chart didn't place that hunk of rock where we found it. Miles off, wasn't it, Mr. Talbot?"

Terry dropped to his knees. "I beg you, sir!"

Captain Madison pivoted sharply, a pant leg brushing Terry's face. "Take care of him," he called over his shoulder. "Needs to learn a captain's *no* means *no*."

"It's the brig for you." The first mate rapped him on the head with his bullhorn, like a harsh schoolmaster might a slow student. "Fasting two days in the dark gets through thick skulls. You can climb down and go peaceably, or argue and triple your time." He called down to Zeke, one of the shipmates who had left Tom, to bring the irons. Turning back to Terry, the mate leered at him. "In case they're needed."

Terry climbed down the ladder, his face burning with fury and shame. Ignorant of how it could rescue Tom, the ship would pass less than a quarter mile away. He turned to view the whaler just as it saluted the *William Parton*. The ocean between the ships sparkled in the sunshine as if welcoming the brave to cross over the short distance.

Terry shoved Zeke and the chains away, then stripped off his shirt. While loosening his trousers, he headed toward the side of the ship.

Balanced on the bulwark, he had one boot partway off when rough hands jerked him down. Kicking at his assailant, he struggled with all his might to get loose. A sudden chokehold cut off his breath, forcing him to yield. Seconds later, Zeke grabbed his arms and locked his wrists in the handcuffs, then put a thick chain around the neck of one boot.

"I'm holdin' him here." Zeke grinned at their shipmates, gathering like circus goers viewing a two-headed dog. "Captain Madison'll have a few words for the turd."

Struggling to keep from spewing obscenities at the men heckling him, Terry stared straight at the passing ship, within hailing distance. *One minute,* he raged to himself. All he'd begged for would have taken the captain one puny minute. Couldn't the man have scraped up that much sympathy? Common decency?

Bosun Gates' voice rose above the others' taunts. "Wouldn't want to be in your boots. Insubordination for sure." He ordered all back to work except his assistant Bick, whom he appointed as guard, and Zeke.

"N-No, no!" Terry stammered, dread replacing his fury. "I just wanted to tell the whaler about Tom. That's all!"

But the bosun was already out of earshot.

Zeke laughed. "Always an idiot."

The captain's message came all too quickly. "Keep him in the brig till Nagasaki. He'll be tried there for insubordination and enticement to mutiny under maritime law."

Terry's insides tumbled along with his descent into the bowels of the ship. How could a charge of encouraging mutiny be based on what he'd tried to do? Impossible. But the charge of insubordination wasn't farfetched. The bosun had been right about that.

He could never rescue Tom if found guilty and imprisoned. And a third of the crew had witnessed his rash act.

CHAPTER 5

A short-lived tremor interrupted Tom's dream of swimming through towering waves to a fishing boat, only to be shoved away by thugs. He jerked up and was confronted by Dice and Sara's stares. "What?" He glanced around at the shadows and back at the pair, orienting himself. "Am I bothering you?" He edged his legs off the pallet.

The girl, blushing, moved toward a corner.

Dice squatted near him. "No bother. You only lying there. You slept above two hours. You feel better?"

"Better? Yes, seems so." He wasn't dizzy even though he'd sat up quickly. He ran his fingers over the scab forming at the back of his head. His body was recovering despite the despair that had almost suffocated him.

"We go to check on the pirate. You want to come?" Dice waved his arm toward the cave's entrance.

"Who cares about that pirate, so long as he stays in his cove and leaves us alone?"

"You need care. If the earthquake gives him a way out, he attacks us—maybe middle of night while we sleep."

"Then by the stars above, let's get him first! You have a

ladder. There's two—or three—of us and one of him." At least they could get one peril out of the way.

"I cannot kill him. He saved lives. I shall tell you more after we check on safety."

Tom rose and found his legs steady enough to support him. "Let's go then." He would reason with the two about self-defense later.

Dice led the way with Tom on his heels. Sara—rhyming with Laura—followed four or five paces back. They took the familiar jungle path. At its far end, near the cliff Tom had tumbled from, they climbed over thick branches of a tree uprooted by the quake.

Tom checked the tree he'd slept under. Small branches littered the ground, but his tree still stood intact. Nevertheless, a similar earthquake could have finished him off. A sailor could fight against a storm or an enemy ship or a hostile native. No one could fight an earthquake. The crouching giant held all the cards. And most likely, the island held another unknown deck chockfull of misery.

Dice motioned to his sister to stop and whispered for Tom to crawl behind him and stay hidden. After they came within two yards of the edge, Dice stood.

The pirate walked out from a driftwood shack at the far end of the strand and limped in their direction. "Worried, are ye? You should be, desertin' me, who saved yer sister's worthless life. One more good quake an' I'm outta here. Gives cause for sleepless nights—heh?" He took more steps, while running his eyes along the ridge. "That sailor boy take off without you? The two deserters themselves deserted? Once you told me, 'What ye sow, ye reap.' True nuff." The pirate pointed back at his shack. "Heh, heh. Don't forgit me pet. Sleepless nights."

Not answering, Dice shuffled backwards, away from the cliff.

Tom stood up. Dice wasn't going to be the boss of everything. And the pirate wasn't going to get the last jeer. He swaggered up to within a yard of the edge. "Guess you're the one to lose sleep," he called. "You're outnumbered, and we have a ladder. Heh. Heh. Heh." While the pirate ranted, Tom walked away. He couldn't threaten an earthquake, but he could put fear in a man.

"Not smart." Dice glared at him.

"You don't run everything. We're equals on this island."

"Not smart to show enemy all your power. Samurai code says, 'Some things better kept secret.'" Dice swept past Tom and his sister, heading for the trees.

"Code, shmode," Tom said as he came to Sara. He offered her one of his best smiles.

She ducked her head without a flicker of a smile in return and motioned for him to pass.

Following Dice, he reminded himself the untouchable girl and he were worlds apart. But the pirate and his *pet*—whatever it was—were all too close. If the scoundrel got out of the cove, he could ambush his victim from a thousand hiding places—boulders, trees, marsh—day or night. Even a short time on the island would turn into an even worse nightmare.

When they got back to the cave, Sara started a fire in a vented bucket containing charcoal. Behind the makeshift stove, stones had been piled together, making a low, curved table. On the far side of the table, flat stones formed a semi-circle, resulting in seats four inches off the ground. The girl knelt at the table and busied herself, slicing dried fish into a large clay pot.

Tom glanced around the cave while Dice rummaged in a basket. The cave's interior was twelve or thirteen feet deep, the same as his, but maybe twice as wide, depending on how uniform the other side of the partition was. Woven baskets lined the foot of the bamboo divider. The far corner held more clay pots, homemade bows and arrows, a hatchet, and bundled ship lines. Halfway up the back wall was a ledge, made into what looked like a water trough. The smart pair had started with a cave bigger and better than his and had made it halfway livable—an impressive feat.

Dice laid two woven bamboo mats on the flat stones. He knelt back on one of them with his sandaled feet under him. "Sit. You eat with us today. You tell how you came here. Then I tell you."

Overlooking the abrupt commands in light of the offered meal, Tom sat cross-legged on the other mat, amazed that Dice, or anyone, could endure bending his legs and feet under him on a barely padded stone surface. Was the fellow trying to show how tough he was? Nevertheless, they were sitting side by side. Having someone to talk to—even argue with—about fairly normal things promised to ease a gnawing ache.

Tom started with a description of how he'd almost kissed his girlfriend Peg, but her father had not only interfered, but complained to Tom's parents. Sara let out a small gasp at the mention of the kiss—apparently an act frowned on in her background. When he went on to tell about the two deals he'd broken with his father, resulting in his unwise decision to run off to the sea with his brother, the two had stared at him as though he were a freak of nature. He didn't tell how his failure to admit a small theft on the merchantman led to another man's whipping—a memory that always pained him and might even have caused his fellow rowers to leave him on the island. That incident was best left alone. The pair already looked shocked enough.

"America custom is strange, very strange," Dice said when Tom finished.

Sara looked downright frightened.

"How so?" Tom ran his story through his mind, ready to defend himself, but seeing nothing so earthshaking.

"If I disobey father twice like that, he not only make me leave home. He never allow return. Some fathers kill their son."

"*Our* customs are strange? What about yours? I heard Japan was a bloody country. Now I believe it."

"Honor father and mother in the Holy Bible too."

"Yes, but killing a son for trying to kiss a girl and then failing to stay far enough away from her would take that way, way too far. Besides, there are lots of commands in the Bible people can't keep. Far too many 'thou shalt nots' to suit me."

If possible, the two looked more shocked. "You come from the Christian country. Yes?"

Tom nodded.

"So, barbarians do not believe religion. That tells why they barbarians."

"There are a lot of Christians who do believe those old dogmas. Everyone in my family is a Christian except an uncle and me ... and maybe my brother. He's always trailed after me, looked up to me." He dragged his mind away from Terry. "But I heard the Japanese follow a religion with stone gods. From what I heard growing up, that's a huge taboo."

"Many believe Buddha or Shinto or both. But I and Sara changed to Christian. Our belief is secret. I tell you the story after we eat."

Sara served her brother and Tom fish-and-gourd soup in coconut shells like the one Tom had drunk from earlier. Then she took her shell and retired behind the bamboo partition.

Tom glanced at Dice, who didn't look surprised. "Your sister doesn't want to eat with us?"

"Not a Japan custom. On island, our custom is different. But she is shy. That is good."

Tom copied his host's questionable manners in slurping the soup while thinking that shyness might be well and good in Japan, but with earthquakes, pirates, and a dismal future, she'd have to have guts to survive. The soup was worse than bland, but he was ravenous enough to have swallowed a whole bucketful if it were offered.

When no soup was left, Dice set a shell full of dried seaweed between them. "We talk here," he said and knelt back on his feet again. "That way, Sara can hear."

He nodded at Tom's mumbled *if you say so*.

"I begin at time our lifes changed." He handed Tom one of the dark green strips from the shell and took several bites of one himself. "In month of hare—maybe twenty moons, or months, before now—my family left Nagasaki. We go to visit our mother's parents in the Chōshū domain. Fog stopped ship at Shimonoseki Strait. While we wait, I and Sara hunted seashells for her. Pirates came out of mists like ghosts. My father and three more samurai fought six pirates on the beach. But other pirates dragged Sara and me away fast."

"Couldn't the ship you were about to board chase the pirates? Surely your father would keep trying to rescue you. Even in Japan," Tom added, intending the jab. He nibbled a little of the seaweed. The aftertaste was strong, but otherwise it wasn't bad, so he ate the whole strip.

"Of course. We not barbarians. Pirate ship has cannon. Other ship no cannon. Pirates made me and Sara slaves. Sara was small for seventeen-year-old girl—sixteen years old, your count. They think she like a child. That was lucky."

"So your sister must be about eighteen now, my count?" Hearing an intake of breath from behind the partition, he added, "It's tricky to judge a girl's age." Then he asked, "How old are you?"

"Maybe I am the elder."

"I'm nineteen." Tom assumed a superior tone, certain Dice couldn't be older.

"Twenty-one, by my country's count. Twenty, by barbarian count."

"Look, I think Japanese fathers who kill their sons are barbarians. You think sons who disobey are barbarians. Let's leave the 'barbarian' word alone. I am American. You are Japanese. All right?"

Dice frowned. "You want to hear rest of the story?"

"Go ahead."

"For four months, pirates made raids. Attacked ships. Murdered. One day they anchored off Naha in Okinawa. That town at end of Loo-Choo Islands. Okinawa island belong to China and Japan. Pirate ship flew Chinese flag, not pirate flag. They plan to raid Naha that night. I and sister hid in one of small boats behind ropes. When they unloaded their two boats at beach, they saw me. Tied me up. But they not see Sara. After they left, she freed me."

"Thunder! You and your sister lucked out there."

Dice shrugged. "When high tide came, we pushed boat off wet sand. Rowed to where the trees met water. Found a temple between the woods and town. Its priest not Loo-Choo priest. He was white man from a place called England. We very amazed to see pale skin, to hear strange language. The priest hid us. The pirates in hurry after raid, so they not hunt us. But if our country people find us, they arrest us. Not legal to leave land of gods."

"Ah, while at one of my ship's ports, I heard about your country's law from an American trader. He had acted as an agent for a Mr. Bartholomew. And by golly, he mentioned a sister and brother." Tom stared at the boy, hardly able take in what must be coming next.

"Chari Masutasu?"

"Yes, Charlie Masters. My stars! How unbelievable to actually meet you! Here, miles from everywhere. And what a life you've had! If you go to your home when we're rescued, you'd take a big risk—right? What will you do?"

"I let no one see me return. I shall greet my parents. Then become masterless samurai, called *ronin*." Dice shook his head and sighed. "Maybe Sara pretends she is my young brother. Do same. But if we stay here a long time before return, the laws can change because of treaties with foreigners."

"For now, you are in a tight spot."

"Tight spot not bad in Loo-Choos. Our sensei—teacher—wanted us to stay one year. I taught him Japanese and cleaned house. He taught English and Bible to me. His wife taught Sara English and Bible too. Maybe wife was better teacher."

Aha. Tom smiled to himself. Apparently, the silent Sara became a better English speaker.

"We stayed most of a time inside house," Dice continued. "Bartholomew-sensei told town people we his new Chinese servants."

"Guess acting as servants was lots better than life with the pirates, even if you could have discovered their hidden stash of treasure." Tom lifted a questioning eyebrow. Maybe the agent, Charlie Masters, had told Dice about the treasure map he'd described to Terry and him.

Dice harrumphed. "*Any* life is better. And no one can hope

for treasure. Maybe this island hide riches, but no hope to find. None. It—how say?—ridiculous notion."

Tom felt his ears redden. Given it had been a stupid thing to say, Dice needn't have rubbed it in.

"After one year, we knew much English, much Bible. We took Jesus as our new liege. It big secret. To be *Kirishitan* is against my country's law."

"Just like that? You became Christians? Even though it's illegal in Japan? Why would you *do* that?"

"I tell you why. One day on pirate ship, I thought about name *Yesu*. I knew name is in 'Evil Religion.' But I heard name has power. After four days, we escaped with the Christian sensei's help. So I thought much about Christian God. Also, beginning of world in Bible sounds right. World not come from sword drips."

"Maybe there was no beginning. The Earth, sun, stars might have always existed. Did you think about that?"

"If world always be, how we can have today?"

Tom rolled the question around in his mind for a second. "Gads. I'd have liked you on my debate team." *Unless you tried to take over.*

"Debeito team?"

"A school team that debates a proposition. Like, for example, two teams argue about whether or not an evil pirate should be killed before he *murders* innocent people." He paused, but when Dice remained as silent as the stone sphinx, he asked, "Is this island's pirate connected to the ones that kidnapped you?"

Dice moved his head a little closer. "No," he said in a loud whisper, "but he—we call him Bolt—says other pirates come again. Bolt was on pirate ship with much, much treasure. They hid the treasure on an island. Then ship sank. Only three survived—Bolt, another man who disappeared, and boy called Zeke, who swam away. New pirate ship picked up Bolt. Those pirates thought first pirates' treasure here. Bolt said not true. He said treasure in cave on different island. Maybe he lied because now he very afraid of second crew."

"So, Bolt knows where there's a stash of gold." He matched Dice's whisper. "Do you think it's in his cove?" Maybe a "notion" about treasure wasn't so "ridiculous" after all.

"Treasure may be anywhere. Any island. Only he knows where."

"But a young pirate called Zeke might know the place too? There's a sailor named Zeke on the ship that left me here. And Charlie Masters talked about a hermit with a treasure map who was hiding out in the island Guam."

"Bolt thinks pirate Zeke drown. He not talk about third pirate, except he disappeared."

"That's interesting. So, pirates who are foaming at the mouth for gold and angry with this island's pirate you call Bolt could show up at any time. We better be rescued first."

"His real name, Benjamin Bolt. He thinks Benjamin not a good name for pirates."

"I see. Go on." Dice narrowed his eyes, and Tom mumbled, "If you have more to say."

"After one year, Sensei gave supplies for our boat trip to south Japan island, called Kyushu. We still had pirate's small boat. Sensei helped add sail. Also, he gave hatchet, buckets, ropes, food, Holy Bible, cheap robes each—called *yukata*—and mirror for Sara."

"Not a bad haul."

"Hall?"

Tom shook his head. "Go on … if you please," he added with a tinge of disgust.

"First days, good weather. Third day, big storm pushed us into great east ocean you call Pacific. Storm pushed us away from our country for six, seven days. Our boat crashed on rocks. Bolt dragged me farther onto the beach. Next saved Sara. I and the pirate unloaded the boat before waves broken it. We thankful to Bolt. I helped him make a raft from old boat. But after three weeks, Bolt said Sara becomes his wife that night. I say, 'No!' I use jiu-jitsu to knock him down."

Tom tucked that piece of information away. If he ever had to fight Dice, it couldn't be straight-on wrestling.

"I and Sara climbed to ledge. Bolt cannot climb steep rocks because of limp leg. When Bolt asleep, we got raft and rowed around far point. Raft hit rocks and fall apart. But we reached shore where hill has no cliff—the same place you landed to get clams. Few days later, I made a ladder. Then in the night, we took back all things we carried from the Loo-Choos."

"How long ago?"

Dice's fingers moved in an unusual style of counting. "Maybe two-and-half months."

"All this time old Benjamin Bolt has been making threats? I don't see why you think you shouldn't kill him."

"He saved Sara. Maybe my life too."

"But now he wants to *kill* you, her, us!"

"I die before I break samurai code. Code says, 'Be not negligent all your life toward one who does great favor.'"

"Well, I don't have to follow the code. But I'm not eager to take on Bolt alone."

"It hard by self. He is tough. You throw away life. He still trapped in cove. Best to wait."

"All right." Noticing the lengthening shadows, Tom stood. "I can wait for now. But before I go, I need to know about the bats with heads like foxes. Are they dangerous?"

"No, they are like friends. Eat berries. Some bugs. Help island not have much mosquitoes."

"That's one piece of good news although they're nauseating-looking *friends*." Tom shuddered at the memory of the bat circling over his head. "How about poisonous snakes? Any here?"

"One poisonous snake, called *habu*. Angry pirates in second ship put the snake in wood box. They opened box on beach when they left without Bolt. But Bolt closed the box with snake still inside. He feeds it live food, like frog, each week."

"So that's his *pet*? Is a habu very poisonous?"

Dice nodded grimly. "If bite leg or arm, must cut off fast. If not, you die."

"And Bolt likes the snake?"

"Maybe he thinks it guards his shack."

Or the treasure you're not mentioning. Tom yanked his mind back to the reptile threat. "But you're sure that's the only snake on the island?"

"How I be sure? I not look under all rocks." Dice sounded like he was talking to a nincompoop. "Saw scorpions. Geckos. Snails. Snails here bad to eat."

"How about animals? Not any at all?"

"Only one animal. Maybe he likes you. Prob'ly not. But not danger like the snake. When you see it, you know."

"Well, I'm glad the place isn't crawling with lions and tigers." He forced a chuckle and let the topic drop so he could be on his way. "Mind if I take a burning branch with me? I want to check the cave. Make sure I'm alone there."

"Here is a better thing." Dice reached into a basket and picked up the cigar-shaped head of a cattail, with its stem threaded into a bamboo stalk. He lit the head's tip with the coals and handed the glowing torch to Tom.

After murmuring his thanks, Tom headed toward his cave, stretching the torch out in front of him to ward off any early-bird bats.

Inside his cave, he squatted and stuck his torch through the wall's hole, poised to jump back if something scurried or slithered out. Nothing moved. He scooted up to the hole and edged a little of his head inside. The air felt cooler, but not damp. The small enclosed area would be ideal for storing foodstuff—berries, fish jerky, cattail roots, whatever else wouldn't rot. Maybe Dice would loan him one of their clay pots until he could make one.

He snorted and jerked his head out of the hole. What was he thinking? He sure didn't plan on settling down on any island, let alone this hostile one. Turning away, he stood still, surveying the cave's flickering shadows. Other than the distant, monotonous roar of the sea, rustling leaves, and the muffled hoots of an owl, the silence was absolute. No sailors' snide remarks to irritate him or sea chants to lift his spirits. No teasing whoops from his brother. No urgent calls from his parents. Of course, no girl's giggle.

Just a graveyard of silence.

Swallowing the acid rising in his throat, he gazed back at the hole. Dice and Sara had made good use of their time while marooned. If he had to survive any length of days like them, he'd better copy the fable's sensible ant rather than the foolish grasshopper. The grasshopper's situation didn't fully match his. It had a good-time option. But that was beside the point. He'd ask to borrow a pot and store what he could.

He stuck the torch in a crack in the wall to keep the light as long as possible. Turning back around, he blinked at a movement. A roach scurried from the hole he'd just checked. He leapt and crushed it. If the island itself was offering filthy roaches and hideous bats as its own idea of companionship, he'd just shown what he thought of the offer.

The torch sputtered, so he lay down and closed his eyes, trying to clear his thoughts. For sure, Terry would find a way to rescue him, but he could be stuck on the island for a very long time unless another ship happened by. Dice had said more pirates were a real threat, but what if they offered a rescue? If Dice and Sara could survive a crew of pirates and manage an escape, why couldn't he? He turned the thought over, then grunted. In place of escaping, he could very well suffer an ugly death by torture … or even by a government's rope.

How could he entertain such idiocy about pirates?

But what if pirates were the *only* way off the island—ever?

CHAPTER 6

Was it day or night? Time had crept by since Terry had been dumped into the ship's brig next to the forward hold. The lantern outside the small grill opening in the door was flickering, about to go out, so it had to be around sunset. He forced himself to get up and drag the heavy chain as he paced the three-by-seven-foot pathway between supplies stacked against the walls. Had they put the extra ship lines there on purpose, enabling prisoners to hang themselves and so eliminate troublemakers? Mate Talbot and Captain Madison had better realize they wouldn't get rid of him so easily. He would rescue Tom—somehow.

The chain pulled against his ankle too much to keep walking. Lying flat, then pushing up on his elbows and toes, he began counting the modified pushups, keeping his handcuffed wrists under his chest. If he didn't exercise, he couldn't speak for himself at a trial or escape if the chance came. At the thirtieth pushup, he stopped, his stomach growling for food. With the punishment of fasting for two days, he had no hope of satisfying it. Or would he now be forced to go without food for six days or more?

He lay still, thinking of his brother, remembering their treks through the woods, fishing behind their house, and Tom's disagreements with their father—neither understood the other. Their father wanted Tom, a whiz at debating, to become a lawyer. But Tom wanted to be free to explore, not sit at a desk or argue in a musty courtroom. Well, hopefully he was alive and exploring.

Forcing his depressing thoughts away from Tom, he pictured the sky and the constellations until the stars lulled him into his longed-for oblivion.

He woke with a start as the brig's metal door scraped open. Sitting up, he peered into the grayness. Bick, with a lantern, shoved another sailor into the room, plunked down a bucket of water, then pointed to Terry. "Follow me. Don't want you fouling our supplies."

Catching sight of his new inmate's features, Terry's steps faltered. What could the quiet fifteen-year-old Jim have done to deserve a lockup?

"Get a move on, Turd," the newly empowered guard snarled while shaking the club he carried.

Terry followed his jailer to a hole that opened above the bilge. While relieving himself, he held his breath as long as possible, unwilling to show weakness by covering his nose against the powerful reek of rotting fish. When he stumbled away from the hole, the man shook his club again. "Get going, scurvy dog."

After the door closed and the guard's footsteps faded, the shadowy form of Jim drew two bowls from under his shirt. He transferred part of one bowl's contents into the other one and held it out to Terry.

Terry almost smiled in his relief. "Thanks. Breakfast, I

guess?" He settled against the spare timbers next to Jim and picked up one of the dry biscuits, ready to savor each bite.

"Yes, sorry it's not much." The boy's reply held something like a gulp. "Cook Salty slipped it into my hand real fast."

"Why are you in here, Jim? Are they rounding up everyone with a spark of goodness in them?"

"I asked where you was." The boy hugged his knees to his chest. "The first mate's face puffed up like a prodded toad. So I asked him what was wrong. He said, 'Nothing's wrong, and the scalawag's in the brig.' Then I asked what you done so bad. He said, 'You can ask him yourself.' And here I am." A couple of sobs choked the boy's last sentence, and he dropped part of a biscuit.

Terry felt his face heat. "Guess it's a crime to be my friend. And that's sure what you are." He took a final bite. "They've got nothing on you if you just asked questions. You'll get out soon. I'm stuck here 'til Nagasaki."

The door banged open. "Come here, you two," Bick ordered. "Captain don't allows you lolling all day. Orders you to holystone the decks—*all* the decks—then slush the mainmast *and* foremast."

"Him too?" Terry asked, hiding his empty bowl. The boy had worked in the kitchen and never climbed the ropes. After holystoning all day, how could he survive slushing?

"Keep your mouth shut and move! Ain't you learned nothing yet?" Seconds after Jim had rushed out and Terry had dragged his chained foot into the passageway, Bick slammed the door.

The fiend grabbed Terry's wrists and inserted the handcuff key with a hard jerk. "Chain comes off too." He dropped the key next to Terry's heel. "You get these back tonight, but reckon Captain wants you workin' double time, like a monkey with its butt bein' chased."

Up on the deck, sailors smirked at them and continued pulling roped sandstone over the washed deck. Bick pointed to a pile of small soft stones. "Get to work with those. Better not be a spot o' dirt in the cracks on all three decks if'n you aim to avoid the lash. Got till next watch, four bells, to finish this'n." He jerked his head toward Jim. "You boy, starboard side. Ballard's here. Not one word out either'n you."

Terry ignored the scornful looks and took in the fresh air. The sun was shooting gold streaks across the eastern sky. This wasn't how he'd choose to get exercise, but it seemed like anything would beat his prison. He took fistfuls of stones and headed for the stern.

Three hours later, Second Mate Garban slowly nodded his approval for the glistening first deck. After the mate walked away and the other sailors on duty were piped amidship to clean up the rowboats, the cook's new young assistant, who'd signed on in Guam, scurried over to Terry and slipped him a handful of salt pork. "Jim's already got some," he whispered. "Cook Salty's looking out for Jim, and you too, so you're in luck."

Not resting his aching knees and arms for a minute, Terry finished his side of the second deck, then did all its connecting corridors by himself, compensating for Jim's slower pace. That deck was finished one bell ahead of the deadline. But halfway through the quarterdeck, Terry fought to drag himself another foot, as if lead, not blood, slogged through his body. *You can't give up. They'll crucify you and Jim—innocent Jim,* he lectured himself as he moved along the planks, inch by inch. Right as the bell announced the deadline's arrival, he and Jim cleaned off the last bit of grit.

Slushing the mast loomed next. Terry ran his eyes up to the

crow's nest. If he could be back in the brig instead, it'd be worth his full sailor's pay. He never had liked the towering heights. But mopping the mast while dead tired would make it diabolical. Even more, he feared for Jim.

As soon as Terry and Jim climbed down to the main deck, Bick brought two buckets of grease and set them next to Terry. "Since Captain accepted the boy's apology, you'll take his place and do the foremast too." He laughed at Terry's grimace. "Better get to the top fast. Hard to slush in the dark."

Terry cried out silently to any heavenly power for help. Tom said it was stupidity to believe in God, but his parents and a lot of other people said all those Bible stories were true. Now if those words meant anything, God needed to show up.

He situated himself on the slush board that would hoist him sixty feet up, hoping the sailors managing the ropes weren't in cahoots with his and Tom's diehard enemies, like Bick seemed to be. His body already had the shakes. But he'd do the jobs. He didn't have a choice.

Twenty feet up, his stomach began objecting. By the time he reached the topgallant yard, he was doubled over from dry heaves, the height magnifying the ship's roll in the rough sea. He took hold of the bucket that had been hoisted on a parallel line while struggling to control his body.

"Get goin'!" the sailor in charge of the ropes yelled through his bullhorn. "Ain't got all day."

Shooting up another call for help, Terry balanced the best he could. He dipped his brush into the bucket, letting a few drops splatter below.

"Cut it out!" came the bellow. "You'll follow that grease down next time."

"How'd you like the whole bucket on your head?" Terry growled under his breath, slapping the grease onto the mast as if it were his adversary.

The jerky descent from each of the mast's horizontal yards to the next one down kept his stomach churning, but eventually the lower height lessened the rocking motion. At last, he found himself back on the deck, still in one piece. He stood for a minute, hoping his legs would stop quivering, yearning to get prone, if only for five minutes.

Mate Talbot's mouth was moving, and although the words sounded like they came from underwater, Terry understood enough. He readied himself for the next pull up.

The sun hadn't set yet. No storm threatened, but a gray fog, interrupted by bright flashes, afflicted his eyes while he rose higher and higher. Reaching the fore topgallant mast, he clung to the yard, fighting renewed dizziness. Refusing to look down, he mechanically brushed on the grease and began the trip toward the deck. His hands moved like marionettes on strings. Over and over and over, he dipped the brush into the bucket, then dragged the brush down and around the mast. At length, hoping he must be halfway down, he risked a look around.

His head jerked back and his body swayed. Terror shot through him as he slipped off the plank. Wildly, he thrust out his legs and arms. One foot hit a yard and his arm struck the descending board. He grabbed the edge of the plank and grasped a line with his other hand, then pushed up and yanked himself back onto the board. The wind hit the sweat that poured down his back, giving him chills. During his panic, the grayness had left his head, but it was back, denser than ever. Despite the dimness, he located his brush in the bucket and renewed his slushing.

Still in a fog, he sighed as his feet touched the solid deck again. Only one thing was left to do, and that was to deposit the empty bucket out of the way. But where was it? Everything had blurred. He took a step and stopped, unable to get his footing. Then his legs crumpled, and he collapsed.

Voices rose above him. Fingers pressed on his neck and wrist. "Alive," someone pronounced right before hands lifted his feet and shoulders. "Back to the brig, right?" the same voice asked as Terry swung like a hammock. Apparently, the answer had been *yes* because he was carried feet first down the hatch, then into the brig.

Handcuffs clicking onto his wrists was the last he remembered before the darkness became complete.

CHAPTER 7

Tom stood in the drizzle at the other cave's entrance and called *konnichiwa,* like Dice had called to him the two previous days. He was ready to get in a dryer spot, but at least the drizzle was providing relief from the steamy heat, a little less wretchedness to endure. He noticed the pair's buckets gathering the drops, the same as his.

He had continued to eat lunch and supper with them in return for the time he spent watching for sails. Dice had declared no interest in performing hours of surveillance himself, saying he and his sister had no intention of boarding Western ships. Tom had argued in return that not all Western ships were bad and that keeping a lookout was wise in order to observe an enemy's approach, if nothing else. However, he was finished with the hope of a quick rescue—a pipe dream, as his father would say.

Dice came to the entrance. "*Ohayo.* You are early." He held his hand up to block Tom. "You are too wet. Cannot come in."

"It's not like a few drops will hurt the dirty floor. And why are you saying *Ohio*? Ohio is a place in America."

"*Ohayo* means early good morning."

"Well, that's a corker." Tom took a step forward,

maneuvering to get where the moisture wouldn't trickle under his shirt. "Anyway, it's time for me to help with the food supply." For breakfast, he'd eaten pine nuts, slimy seaweed, and the crunchy leftover of a dried fish the two had let him take to his cave the night before. Sara's warm meals were much to be desired, no matter how odd or bland, and he couldn't hope for continued handouts if he hadn't done much to earn them.

Dice blocked him again. "You must wash your very dirty clothes and very dirty body in the sea and rain. Then come back."

"So do I run around naked?" Dice was treating him like his family treated Tuffy when the dog confronted a skunk.

Dice shook his head. "This is very simple. After you wash, put on clothes. They become dry when the sun shines."

"All right. All right. I've got plenty of practice wearing wet clothes, but after my watches on the ship, I got on dry clothes. Now these clothes could stay waterlogged all day and night."

"My sensei used to say, 'Fact of life.' To help for food, you need to get bat guano in the jungle."

"That revolting stuff?"

"Stuff maybe same dirty like you. But it helps plants grow."

Tom huffed. "Any more ideas to cheer me up besides bat poop?" As Dice turned away, Tom grumbled, "Wait a minute, will you? I get what you're saying. Poop it is, and I won't offend your nose any longer. But I'm thinking of slaughtering one of those huge birds—albatross, I reckon—for its meat. Thought you might go with me and show me their nests."

"Six, seven weeks after we came, hundreds left the island. Maybe five still here. Do not know if they are sick. Bat guano helps more. I give you empty gourds for guano. Later I show you where is good water. It is in hidden lake where ridge rises. After we fill our buckets, we can hunt duck. Also, I show you sweet potato plants."

"Sweet potatoes? Here?" He almost laughed at his anticipation. He never would have guessed he'd be overjoyed about potatoes.

"We saved six from Okinawa before Bolt can eat them. I cut them up and planted them. Forty plants growing now."

"That's great. When can we eat some?" The mellow taste would be perfect with duck meat. Duck and sweet potatoes alone were a far cry from the outlays he routinely had at home, but a whole lot better than the ship's hardtack or the island's gourd-and-fish or seaweed-and-clam soups.

"We each can eat four soon. I will give Bolt four too, so he does not get sick. Plant others."

"But they take months to grow. Why don't we eat twice that—except Bolt. Plant the sprouts from say … the remaining twelve. That way we'd get our teeth into them."

"That not smart. Some maybe not grow. Guano helps make a new place ready. You can get your teeth into four." He crossed his arms with an expression like a bulldog.

Tom shrugged. This stiff-necked fellow might drive him crazy eventually, but they weren't his potatoes. Taking the two gourd rinds Dice brought out from the cave, he headed for the lagoon where he'd landed on the island five days earlier.

Standing at the hilltop, he surveyed the beach and then the ocean beyond the barrier rocks, hoping against hope for the sign of a ship. Seeing none, he half-slid, half-raced down to the beach on impulse. Panting at the bottom, he clasped his arms up in a victory sign to his imaginary audience, as though he set another record, like the year he won a Fourth of July race.

The heedless waves swept in and out. The beach stretched to

a rocky outcrop, void of any visible life except a scurrying crab. He dropped his arms. There was nothing to connect to. Just emptiness.

He stripped, then put his boots back on for protection from the sharp coral. After inspecting the rippling waves for lurking jellyfish or a shark's fin, he waded into the clear water. Shivering in the deeper water's chill, he dunked his body and made a quick exit. Back on the shore, the stronger drizzle finished the bathing job.

After scrubbing his clothes in the waves, he laid them on rocks. Then he hunted the shoreline for anything useful. He had swum without clothes before, but he hadn't searched a beach stark naked down to his boots. But then, what did it matter at a truly empty spot?

The tallest palms bore large clusters of coconuts, but only shriveled, rotten ones littered the gritty ground. Shinnying up a towering trunk had no appeal whatsoever, so he turned his search back to the edge of the sea for driftwood.

A fragment of brown wood lay half-buried in the sandy pebbles, looking for all the world like the wood trophy he'd received for that Fourth of July race—as though his memory had transported the prize from his home. His father had put the trophy on their mantle between a candlestick and a blue-and-white pitcher, claiming it reminded him of how Tom never quit when he had a goal.

He dug the knotted piece out. As to be expected, it turned out to be a broken-off stick. Swallowing the annoying lump in his throat, he pitched the fake trophy into the water, saw it float for a minute, then disappear under a wave.

Deciding the drizzle had helped rinse his clothes enough, he started wringing them out.

"Hello, clean man" met his ears. Dice and his sister were descending the hillside!

Tom tossed his clothes onto the rocks and dashed for the sea. He got far enough out so only his head showed. "Go away!" he shouted. Dice would be all right, but how could Sara dare view him? So much for the *shy-Christian-girl* charade.

Dice and Sara didn't stop. "What is problem?" the brother called.

"What's the problem?" Tom yelled. "Any fool can see the problem. Tell your sister to turn around and not look back."

Sara twisted and headed up the hill without a word from her brother.

Tom waited until she disappeared around the curve of the rim before he came onto the beach again. "That wasn't funny," he fumed as Dice stood watching him.

"You not bathe with strangers?" Dice sounded genuinely puzzled, but a gleam glinted in his eyes.

"We don't go around naked in front of females, strangers or not." He scowled at Dice, then rubbed his arms and legs to get off any salt from his unwanted second dip.

"Maybe you worry too much about your skin." The boy took off his dark blue robe and waded into the water, displaying his backside.

"Do men and women bathe together in your country? Without clothes?" That couldn't be true.

Dice turned. "All time." He splashed water onto his chest.

"Truly?"

"*Hai*—Yes."

"Well, it's a problem for me. A big one."

Dice brushed away a water bug. "You scared Sara. She not see you in no clothes again." He ducked into the water and paddled around.

"Good th—" An object struck Tom's shoulder. "Wha—" he squealed just as another missile hit his boot. He spotted a brown, hairy creature in the tallest palm tree, reaching for a coconut.

He jumped aside, managing to avoid the monkey's third missile. Quickly grabbing up the three coconuts, he backed away. The coconuts were prizes although he'd also found an enemy.

Dice clambered out of the water and shook his fist at the beast. It responded with two more coconuts, and the boy, after dodging them, picked them up. "This monkey not like males," he said. "He likes Sara. She helped him after Bolt tried to kill him."

Keeping an eye out lest the monkey resume launching projectiles or go on a ground attack, Tom gathered his wet clothes and started putting them back on. "Is it the animal you mentioned?"

Dice nodded and dunked his robe in the water. "He belonged to Bolt. Monkey took turtle eggs from Bolt's bucket, so Bolt threw him on a rock in the ocean. Hard. He almost drowned. But Sara rescued him, helped him onto cliff's ledge. She gave him food and rainwater for one week. Then monkey disappeared. After we escaped, we saw him in coconut palms. He not throw coconuts at Sara. But he throw them at me and make face."

"I guess that's good if the beast supplies you with coconuts."

"We each got ripe ones today. Very lucky. I can keep yours while you get guano."

"All right." He handed over the coconuts. He'd have to get Dice to show him how to open the shells later anyway. He picked up the gourds, pulled his clinging, wet shirt away from his chest, and exhaled through tight lips. "Next stop, bat waste."

At the forest's edge, the damp, earthy smell brought him to a standstill. He peered into the thick undergrowth, paying attention to the tangle itself since no path lay before him. The fan palms, pines, and other trees pushed upward as though anxious to break out of the gloom. Brambles and vines choked their hosts' trunks. The island's nightmare forest wasn't anything like the New York woods he loved. This one stood as a foe, ready to tackle him.

But alien or not, he had to get the guano if he wanted to keep eating the decent supply of food Dice and Sara managed to get. He straightened his shoulders and tramped into the woods, daring the undergrowth to ensnare him.

The nearest colony of bats turned out to be in a thick clump of trees with less brush beneath. Slipping under the sleeping colony, determined not to attract attention, he scooped up the guano as fast as he could. The worst part was the musty scent, like his grandfather's pair of mildewing boots in the corner of the barn.

Retreating to the edge of the forest, he broke off a batch of leaves to protect his harvest from getting washed out of the rinds. Suddenly, the branches above trembled. A flash of brown fur swung from one tree to the next. Tom covered his head and prepared to skedaddle, but the monkey moved into a tree farther away. Then it stopped and chattered, as though telling him to approach.

"So there you are, adding to the marvels of this disagreeable forest. Want to do more target practice?" Tom glowered at it.

The monkey halfway turned, looked back at Tom over its shoulder, and chattered more, as though asking why he didn't follow.

Not seeing anything in the trees that could be lobbed at him other than cones, he walked toward the monkey, watching his step below and his opponent above.

The monkey swung through several more trees, then gazed back at Tom.

He followed, weaving around the largest obstacles, thankful the monkey avoided areas with low-hanging bats. The animal was obviously leading him, but to what? And why?

After they both came out of the trees unscathed, the monkey led him down the rocky hillside and into the valley's high grass. If he lagged behind, it waited until he got within a few feet, then took off again.

Could the monkey actually want a diversion from its own monotonous life? Previously an enemy and now a friend—wanting to play "follow the leader" or something akin to that in animal society? On the other hand, was it plotting to show him a poisonous swimming hole in the undrinkable ponds?

Tom stopped, studying the monkey's new shenanigans.

It practically danced in front of him. Leaping, then traipsing back and forth in the grass. Grimacing. Fussing. Crooking its long tail as though saying to come on.

Tom rotated on his heel. Enough of this game. He was hungry, wet, and Dice was waiting. He took a step, only to have the soil slide from under his back foot. Throwing himself forward while somehow holding onto the gourds, he lay still. When nothing else moved beneath him, he carefully scooted around and sat up. A black hole, barely visible through the grass, lay two feet in front of him. Shivering, he tested the ground around him, then inched forward, and stared into the gaping cavity. The dank smell signaled a cavern deep in the bowels of the earth.

The monkey was doing little hops as though enjoying its prank. But this prank wasn't harmless. It could have killed him.

"You louse! You filthy louse!" Tom scrambled back and jumped up.

The monkey grimaced in what had to be a grin.

"Think it's funny? I bet you won't grin at this." He threw one of the gourds with its guano straight into the monkey's face. The second one hit the fleeing monkey's back.

What had he done to deserve being stuck with a crazed monkey, let alone a murderous pirate, a despot who thought he knew everything there was to know, and a pretty nobody—who had stared at him naked?

CHAPTER 8

"He *is* a barbarian," Sara lamented in Japanese. She stood a step behind her brother, watching the sailor from the hillside. Gone were the hopeful prospects Tamo had brought to the island—an eventual friendship once her brother trusted him and the amazing chance to learn about far-off America. But expecting reliable facts from a truly barbaric Westerner would be like trusting a crook to sell excellent products.

"I told you that." Daisuke waved a bee away from them and turned toward her. "You stay here. I'm going to see what happened down there."

"Please allow me to come too. Waiting on this island day after day after day is hard." Forbidden tears threatened.

"Come then, but stiffen your spine, and stay back from Tamo."

"Thank you for your good instruction." She moved aside as he took a step down the hill. "How unkind the barbarian is," she said, following as close behind as she dared. "The poor monkey was only trying to play. And Tamo's odor this morning—disgusting." She couldn't bring herself to mention her shame at being yelled at when all she'd wanted to do was bathe. Her only truly pleasant times in the long days were feeling the warm sand between her toes and the waves lapping over her, washing the sweat off her skin. Now because of Tamo, her twice-a-day relief would be mixed with a humiliating memory.

"Yes." Daisuke paused to look back at her. "The barbarian reminds me of a pig wallowing in mud. However, I can't blame him for throwing things at your beastly monkey, whatever his reason."

Sara bowed to accept the contradiction, while thinking that with just a little effort on Daisuke's part, he and the animal could get along, even help each other willingly. Not so with the sailor, obviously. The monkey had wisely chosen against Tamo when she'd still thought him interesting, even possibly God's provision of a companion for Daisuke and her. She'd almost liked his yellowish hair and blue eyes—eyes that had seemed intelligent, observant, and at times, welcoming. How wrong she'd been!

Tamo faced them as they approached. "It's an underground cavern." He waved his arm toward the monkey, chattering a safe distance away. "The dratted animal led me here. Looked like he wanted me to fall in. Can't tell how far down the floor is, but plenty deep."

A chill ran up Sara's spine as her brother and Tamo knelt near the hole. Maybe the barbarian had a good reason to be aggravated, but still, he was totally lacking in self-control.

"We must find out." Daisuke crawled a little closer to the hole's edge. "If trouble comes, cavern is very good." He glanced at her. "It can protect."

Always, always, her brother was expecting trouble. And if they needed a hidden, underground cavern, the trouble wasn't likely a typhoon or earthquake. Did he truly expect more pirates?

Why couldn't he confide in her?

"Couldn't the pirates find us down there? Trap us like rats?" Tamo asked.

Daisuke slapped the ground. "I told you not talk about that."

"Oh, right. Sorry." Tamo rolled his eyes at her and didn't look the least bit sorry.

"Maybe our Lord Jesus helps us if pirates come," Sara said in English. Daisuke looked at her over his shoulder, narrowing his eyes. "I will bring stones from the hillside if you wish," she offered before he could scold her in Japanese for speaking up in English. "You can listen for plunks."

"Your sister's smart and pretty." Tamo clapped Daisuke's shoulder. "Her English is good. I'm starting to see why you didn't want her to talk to a no-good *barbarian* like me."

Not caring for the conversation, Sara stalked away. When she returned with her hands full of small rocks, her brother lay flat and put his ear at the opening. He dropped a stone into the hole.

She held her breath. Was he leaning out too far, perhaps over a bottomless chasm? Would the surface give way? She wanted to warn him to move back, but that would only irritate him.

"Deep, but maybe the ladder can touch bottom. No splash," Daisuke pronounced after having dropped in three more stones.

"If you lend me your ladder and ship's lines, I'll investigate." Tamo moved back and stood. "After all, I *am* a sailor, used to rigging, and I'm wearing the right kind of clothes—not a woman's robe." He quirked a smile, or was it a sneer? "I trust you even if you don't trust me."

She took a step closer to Daisuke, who also stood. "Since you rescued him first," she said in Japanese, "the barbarian has a good reason to trust us, doesn't he? On the other hand, maybe we have less reason."

"It's not for you—a girl—to judge, is it?" he answered, also in Japanese. "He is willing to take a risk. That's something to appreciate even if he is lacking in most other ways. Besides, nothing can happen if we are up here and he is down there."

Sara held her tongue and bowed. Of course, her brother, trained to fight, appreciated bravery, but in her estimation, honoring one's word and kindness were much more important. This barbarian already said he didn't keep *deals*, and his kindness was highly questionable if not entirely wanting.

Tamo squinted his eyes at the pit's darkness. "A torch with a short line to lower it would be helpful."

Daisuke nodded. "Right. Samurai code says, 'Not make certain beforehand will bring shame.' We will lower torch in hole first. See if problem for ladder. Now too much rain. Before we leave, we shall mark place with rocks. Come back when the sun shines."

When the rocks were high enough to show above the grass, Daisuke brushed off his hands and motioned to Tamo. "Come, I give more gourds for guano. The monkey bad."

"We agree about the monkey," Tamo muttered.

A screech stopped Sara as she followed the two. The monkey landed on her shoulder a minute later. "Poor thing," she soothed in English, loud enough for Tamo to hear. She allowed it to stay on her while she walked despite its dirty coat and musty odor. It was nearly her pet, after all, although the strong-willed animal wasn't a bit like what she'd wanted years earlier.

Her childhood with its naïve yearnings seemed a long-ago dream. She had begged for a kitten, but overshadowing that wish had been her desire for adventure. Although she hadn't despised her destiny to marry for her family's good, she'd envied her brother, especially his chances to explore new places and pursue greater learning. Then her inevitable lot in life had been entirely obliterated by *adventure*.

Coming to know the true God was the one shining spot in the recent ordeals. Often when loneliness gripped her, God comforted her through the Bible's words. Just a few days earlier, she'd read again of God's presence with her. But her eyes had also lit on the command to be hospitable to strangers. The promise of God's care was wonderful. But must she be hospitable to a stranger who proved himself to be a barbarian?

The Bible also said the merciful would be blessed. Hadn't she led Tamo to his cave? Filled his buckets? Mercifully provided bamboo and meal after meal? Yet she was far, far, far from feeling blessed. So, if these teachings related to Tamo, they had to be a kind of riddle, and riddles weren't much good if they couldn't be solved.

When they reached their cave, Tamo scowled at the monkey after it jumped onto the calcite pillar at the center of the chamber.

The monkey bared its teeth at him in return and made scolding noises.

Tamo jerked back, then laughed. "That animal better watch out," he said as Daisuke shooed it out of the cave with a bamboo stick, "or it could end up in the pit itself."

She flinched. Did he intend a threat? Or just a kind of joke? Should she be upset or entertained? Only Tamo could tell her, and she couldn't ask. And would she really want to know anyway?

He sought her eyes and nodded to her before he left for the forest and the bat waste he hated. His expression—a resolve to endure—reminded her of Daisuke's each time he had faced their father's discipline. To be honest, despite Tamo's big flaws, she still pitied him. He was not only marooned but even more alone than she. And his planned descent into the cavern made her nervous. What if his tall, lithe body disappeared into the pit's darkness and never came back out? Would she be happy? No, she'd want to go in after him. Help rescue him, odd as that seemed.

So, maybe it wouldn't be too hard to continue showing mercy and hospitality, as her Liege required, even to a disagreeable barbarian.

CHAPTER 9

After two days of drizzle and squalls, the sun shone, bright and warm. The wind that had whipped across the island at times like a half-crazed lioness had changed into a purring kitten, soothing the back of Tom's neck. He kept his eyes on the hillside while waiting by the underground cavern for Dice and Sara to gather supplies after finishing their baths. The two were totally obsessed with cleanliness, bathing in the sea every morning and evening. It was surprising they hadn't scrubbed off all their skin.

A flock of terns flew overhead and turned toward the bamboo grove beyond the ponds. A bee buzzed by. Everything looked peaceful. But he wouldn't fall for that deception. How easily he could have pitched into the hole and broken his neck or slowly starved to death because his calls wouldn't carry from the depth.

What else could be lying in wait for him besides hidden pits? Or a vicious monkey? Or crushing earthquakes? Or vindictive pirates? Always before, he'd gotten help in a tight spot from his parents or a neighbor or somebody, anybody, who cared. Dice and Sara didn't. They only tolerated him. In fact, Sara's once pleasant face often looked like stone, as if she'd been visited by the snake-haired Medusa in the Greek fable he'd read in school.

Why, oh why, hadn't he kept the deals with his father? His father was inflexible, old-school, but his harping on Tom's behavior must have come from caring, even affection. His mother all the more so, and he'd surely broken her heart. He'd never known his sister, who died minutes after her birth. But he knew his mother still mourned when she saw other little girls in their frilly dresses. Now she must be weeping for him and Terry. To top it off, he'd led his brother into years of slave-like work, with no access to higher learning. How could he have been so pigheaded? So blind?

Maybe he had deserved to die in the pit. Maybe he still did deserve to die one way or another. If there was a god, that might be his punishment.

He shook his head. Enough gloomy thoughts. He was still alive. He hadn't fallen into the pit. He would survive if doing so almost—but not quite—killed him.

Tom rose as Dice briskly approached, carrying the ship's line curled from one shoulder and the bobbing ladder on the other. Meek Sara, following behind like always, came with a bucket, shorter spans of line, and several cattail stalks.

"We can lower the torch and look." Dice tied a short piece of the hemp line around one of the bamboo stems, then lit the cattail head with the coals in the bucket. "Duck fat helps torch burn," he explained.

Tom lay next to Dice and watched the torch descending— three feet, six, nine, ten, eleven, twelve feet. The cave's dim floor appeared, so about thirteen feet below them. Since the ladder was eleven feet long, it would rest against the side of the pit, two feet below the cavern's rim. Not bad. Clearly workable.

Shadows bordered the torch's circle of light, and beyond

that, pitch-black darkness. Impenetrable darkness.

The blackness made Tom's stomach queasy. But descending thirteen feet into a pit on a ladder with a line around you couldn't possibly be as rough as the time he had clung to the ship's royal yard, watching slabs of ice collide with giant waves as the merchantman rounded Cape Horn. The wind had driven sleet into his face, and he'd hung on for his life, just a speck on a pole far above the deck. Nothing about the cavern could be as bad as what he'd survived then.

After Dice pulled up and extinguished the torch, Tom reached for the long ship's line and tied one end into a harness around his chest. "Even though we're using this so I don't get lost, it could be a backup in case the ladder gives way or something." Dice gave him a puzzled frown. "Like if what looks solid down there is close-grown stalagmites. I don't know if those things are strong or how high they grow. I'm going to secure the line to that tree there." He pointed to the closest, scraggly pine. "But you both need to hold onto the line too, as if my life depends on it."

Dice nodded. "Come. We can push heavy rocks on the line too."

Once all was in place, Dice picked up another of the cattail torches. "When you are on bottom, I will send a new torch."

"All right. Wish me luck." Tom jiggled the ladder, testing its firmness. He took a deep breath, then scooted around on his stomach and slid his legs into the hole, feeling for the second rung. His chest rubbed against the pit's side, and he briefly wondered how long it'd take to wash his shirt, already raggedy, so the pair wouldn't stick up their noses.

Climbing down the ladder proved easy, but a faint noise like singing or chirping came from deep in the cavern, giving him goose bumps. Stepping onto the hard floor, he shouted for the torch.

The torch flickered, but didn't go out. He found himself at the wall of a cavern extending away from him as far as the light shone. Holding the torch in front of him, he edged toward a gentle slope. Suddenly his feet shot out from under him, and he was sliding on his backside.

"Yahh! Help! Help!" he cried, terrified. Was he heading into a bottomless pit? Bending his knees, he tried to plant the bottom of his boots on the slope, but they didn't hold. While grasping for any handhold with his free hand, he dropped the wavering torch. Just then, a cloud of hundreds of bats—seeming to be in an endless formation—flapped over him and up the hole.

He slid over an edge, fell through emptiness, and abruptly plopped down on a flat surface. Sitting where he'd landed, he tentatively moved each arm and leg. Although he'd no doubt picked up more scrapes and bruises, as far as he could tell, no bones were broken.

The flapping noise of the bats grew fainter. He leaned his head back on the crag behind him, waiting for his pounding heart to slow. At least, with any luck, the departing army of bats meant there weren't more massing deeper in the cavern for another onslaught.

After checking his harness, he got to his feet, thankful for the line. He gave it a tentative tug. The pair had better make sure it held. He began pulling himself up the steepest part of the incline—practically a short cliff. Unable to get any traction with his boots on the slick surface of the cliff's face, he relied on his arm's strength as he moved up the line, hand over fist. After going up three or four feet, he readied himself to squirm over the steeper part's rim and onto the gentler slope, still gripping the line.

All at once, the whole forward part of the line came flying against him, instantly dropping him back down. He landed on his feet with a thud.

"Hey! Hey! What are you doing?" Had the two plotted against him? He jumped, arms raised, and clawed the smooth rock, but couldn't get a grip. "You gotta get me out of here!" he yelled at the top of his voice.

The little halo of daylight was far above. The dark shadows under the opening prevented his seeing if the ladder was still in place.

Daisuke picked himself up. Bats—hundreds, maybe a thousand—had whooshed out of the hole, knocking him back into Sara. Then the line had zipped down the hole. He stared at the snapped pine tree. Why had Tamo put so much weight on the line? Its primary function should have been to keep him from getting lost, not to use for climbing down deeper into the cavern.

His sister was acting like she'd lost her mind—hopping and squeaking as she gulped breaths.

"Be quiet. I have to hear." He darted an angry glance at her.

"Help him! Help him!" She closed her eyes and shook her head. "Please get him."

"Do you think I'd leave him down there? Now shut up, will you." She quieted, and he lay next to the hole. "Tamo! What happened?" he called.

Tamo's cries for help sounded far off.

"What is problem?" he shouted louder.

"Not hurt. Stuck."

"I can get him, Sara. He'll be all right." Even while he

soothed her, he asked himself why he should care even one mouse dropping about the barbarian. Wouldn't they be better off without him? Where he was, Tamo couldn't team up with the pirate if he ever thought doing so would get him off the island. Nevertheless, care he did, maybe because Sara felt so sorry for the fellow after all. Or could his unaccountable concern arise from their mysterious and—did he dare think it—troublesome liege, Jesus?

Sara had knelt next to him, listening too. "Do you have to go down there?" Her voice shook.

"Yes, unless you want to go down—you're so eager to rescue him."

Her face paled. "I can. I will if you wish."

He grunted. "How could a girl do a man's job? Just get hold of yourself. That's a big enough order for now. I know there's danger at the bottom. I won't step off the ladder until I see what happened. You light another torch and lower it when I get down."

Ashamed of his racing pulse, he followed Tamo's moves. At the bottom of the ladder, he shouted up, "The torch, now, Sara."

"Watch out for that slope!" Tamo shouted. "It gets slick and steep. Takes your feet out from under you, and it has a drop-off, almost like a short cliff, halfway down."

Gripping the torch, Daisuke lay flat and extended his arm so the light showed the slope and the edge of the drop-off. "How long are slope and cliff?"

"Maybe nineteen feet—more than two-and-a-half-times my height."

"Ladder is too short. We make a second, longer one. Slope and cliff, which longer?"

"Cliff a foot longer."

"I come back tomorrow or next day."

"What! You can't leave me here!"

"You not a baby." Daisuke pictured Tamo's angry face. "Bats do not like torch's fire. Maybe they not come back. But they not danger if they come. To build ladder takes time. Cut bamboo. Tie vines. Very bad if ladder breaks."

"Wait, wait! I can make it with the short ladder. Move it down the slope."

"If we lose ladder, both you and I are stuck. Sara cannot chop bamboo, make ladders. We cannot take such big risk."

"I tell you, I can make it!"

Daisuke crawled back to the ladder and stuck the torch in a large crack in the wall. "Stay where you are. If you leave your place, maybe you get lost. Maybe you die. I will come back with food, water today, then with new ladder soon. Promise."

"Nooo! Nooo! Nooo!" followed Daisuke up the ladder.

CHAPTER 10

"Drink this, son." Feeling an arm under his neck and a cup at his lips, Terry's heart leapt. He was home! Home! Sweet home! He cracked open an eye.

Doc Murdoch was leaning over him. His hopes plummeted. He was still on the hellish ship, sailing endlessly.

"Drink this. You came close to ending up in Davy Jones' locker. Got you moved here just in time."

Terry stiffened and drank the brew of strong-smelling herbs, then dropped his head back. He should have pretended not to hear. Even a few more hours in the doctor's care would have been worth a king's ransom.

"I'm keeping you here for another two or three days, s'long as you don't do anything rash, like try to swim to another ship. Whatever possessed you?"

"Tom!" The word had come out as a gurgle, and he swallowed. "Got to find my brother. But please, please don't let them take me back to the brig. Got to survive to help Tom." He sensed darkness closing in on him.

"Sleep, son, and hope God Almighty has an angel assigned to you and to your brother, too, if he lives."

Angry voices intruded into Terry's dream of searching for Tom, first on one barren island, then on another shrouded in fog.

"That boy is not leaving the sickbay until *I* say he leaves." The doctor's voice rose a notch louder. "Captain Madison put me in charge here, not you two or Mate Talbot."

"He's shirkin'. His brother was a no-good liar and landlubber. Always messin' up. This boy's just like him. Tryin' to desert ship in a mutiny 'gainst the captain. Tryin' to break his contract—signed voluntar'ly." A chain rattled.

Terry kept his breaths steady, his body still. The spokesman's voice was Zeke's, and the one with the chain had to be Bick.

"Did you hear me? You men almost killed this boy. He's under my care. Guess *you* might value my expertise if either of *you* gets the shakes, or finds a nail in your foot, or you take a fall down the hatch."

"Come on, Zeke. The doc's spoke." Bick's tone bordered on disrespect. "We'll be more careful with the turd ... er, terrapin when he's back in our care. Got to keep him in tip-top shape for his Nagasaki floggings, or hanging, whichever it is."

Dread froze Terry even after the men's footsteps faded.

"All clear," the doctor said. "You can open your eyes in case you didn't sleep through all that guff." Terry rolled onto his back and squinted at the doc. "Seems your reputation isn't the shiniest these days, but we'll let the Nagasaki consul sort that out. Hear he's thorough and just."

How could even a good judge help with the whole crew, except Jim, bearing witness against him? What would it be like to stand in court, hear the charges, be thought of as a criminal? He recoiled, imagining the grim scowls of those believing him guilty.

The ever-present grayness crept over him. As he sank into its chill, his body swayed. He jerked. He was falling! He grabbed for a line, a board, anything to stop his plunge to the deck.

"Easy there." A hand disengaged his grip from what turned out to be the doctor's jacket. "Just rousing you to drink the broth, but we'll attempt it later. Try to put your mind on something pleasant. You'll heal faster." The doctor patted his shoulder and turned away.

The smells of ointment and herbs, not grease, were reassuring. A cot supported him. The sickbay was far better than swaying back and forth sixty feet up in the air, but nothing about the ship could be called pleasant. Good thoughts had to come from his home in Albany.

He pictured when he'd been sick in bed as a child, doctored for a bad cold. His mother had poked a spoonful of cod liver oil into his mouth and forced him to swallow—a fishy, putrid grease yet comforting at the same time. Her cool hand had checked him for fever. His father had ventured into the room to bring him a report of the town's happenings. Tom had teased him for being a softy. Tuffy had lain on the rug beneath him in everyone's way, but ever loyal.

The dark shroud binding Terry eased slightly, and he drifted into sleep.

CHAPTER 11

The torch Dice left sputtered out after twenty minutes or so. At least its light had let Tom determine the floor was safe for several feet. Who knew beyond that? There could be a thousand-foot drop-off. Nests of slimy critters. Teetering rocks. Or other equally horrible possibilities.

Moving out a little so he could see the entrance's circle of light better, he rocked back and forth on his heels, waiting for Dice to come with the promised food. What were probably minutes seemed like hours while the dread of being forsaken grew like a monstrous kraken, threatening to swallow him up as it supposedly had so many ships.

A groan deep from within the earth sent shivers up his spine. What if an earthquake buried him? Or the floor beneath him cracked open? He moved back to his original spot, eager for its measly protection of his backside.

At long last, a new torch was lowered through the entrance on a line. After that, sandals came through the hole. Then all of Dice materialized, balancing a bamboo pole on his shoulders with attached items, as if dangling prizes in a county fair. He replaced the old torch with the burning one, then called, "Tamo, are you there?"

"Of course, I'm here. You left me in a dungeon."

"Here is food. Break open coconuts. Careful. Don't lose coconut water in green one. Eat fish tonight. Eat berries, coconut meat in brown one, and kudzu leaves tomorrow."

Tom reached up for the bamboo pole that appeared over his head and pulled it diagonally so he could untie the items. The bamboo slid farther, then stopped. "Got it … thanks," he mumbled. Maybe Dice should have been stuck in this awful pit instead of him. For sure, Dice could have risked losing the ladder, which wouldn't have happened anyway, and gotten him out, but right now wasn't the time to seem ungrateful.

Dice didn't stay around to chat. He vamoosed through the circle of light at the top of the ladder.

Tom picked up the green coconut—actually gray in the torchlight's dimness—and knocked it against the wall. The fool shell wouldn't crack. He hit it again and again, keeping alert between strikes for the sound of any aroused adversary. Finally at wit's end, he whacked the shell so hard it fell into pieces, letting the precious water pour out. He licked the little bit pooled in his palm and gulped down the mackerel before something could happen to the fish too. Then he felt around for the coconut fragments and secured the packet of berries and kudzu in the largest piece.

Having completed this one little task, he slipped under the bamboo pole. Of course, it didn't provide any protection, not like a tent would, but in a fight for his life, he could wield it against whatever might glide around in the inky darkness.

For hours and hours, he listened for the roar of wings or chirps or another of the earth's groans. The only noise, however, was the murmuring of what was probably a deep, underground stream.

Sometime later a legion of flapping bats woke him from

fitful sleep. Faced with overwhelming numbers, he hunkered down with his head under his body. Once the creatures had flown into the cavern's interior, the distant chirping started. He didn't sleep any more that night. He didn't dare.

After another day of the dim halo of light, the breakfast-lunch-dinner of the remaining food, and a second miserable night of darkness so deep Tom couldn't see his hand, the indistinct faces of Dice and Sara appeared once more at the top of the hole.

"I will lower long ladder," Dice shouted. "It folds in two parts. Then I come. Sara comes too. She can help hold ladder so it not moves."

The new ladder bumped against the old ladder's rungs as it descended. Then Dice climbed down with a torch, followed by graceful Sara. The girl had more courage than Tom had assumed. When the ladder slid over the drop-off, he scrambled up the lower section, then crawled along the top section lying against the incline.

"Thank you! Thank you to your sister too," he gushed, following them up the shorter ladder to the blessed daylight. Who was at fault no longer mattered. He was out!

"Later we will explore." Dice joined Tom as he squatted, catching his breath, fighting the urge to laugh or cry. "To go deep in this cave, people must have two ladders. It is good place for hiding."

"Sure. Sure," Tom replied. Actually, as far as he was concerned, reentering the black hole would happen only in a year of blue moons and talking pigs. "Do you have water?" He'd managed to suck a little liquid out of the second coconut when he'd cracked its shell, but a good draught of water would be blissful. He looked at Sara for a nod.

She looked at her brother.

"So, Sara can't even nod at me?" Tom jerked his arms out in

frustration. "Seems strange not communicating with someone I'm standing right next to, as if your sister's a non-person, a ghost, or something."

Sara's cheeks grew red.

"All right." Dice stepped around his sister to face Tom more directly. "You can talk to Sara, but only when with me. You must not touch her. Never."

"All right. It's a deal." A much better deal. And he had no plan to touch the girl. Peg was the girl he'd ridden horses with in the pastures, flirted with at the country dances, debated with for practice before competitions. "We three can be a real team," he added as Dice stepped back. "You saved me. Then I saved you. And just now, we worked together. We need each other in this godforsaken place. Now I'd like water … if you please." His voice cracked.

Dice wagged his head. "Come to my cave. I give you water. We must make plans for hiding if pirates come."

Tom followed Dice and Sara, entranced by the blue sky, lemon-green marsh grass, the good-smelling breeze, the circling, squawking birds, even a cricket. The world was amazing. It had seemed deceptively peaceful, but maybe he hadn't given it enough credit. Of course, God's existence didn't necessarily follow as a logical conclusion. But given that nature might point to a god who was there … was he good?

His elation at escaping the cavern evaporated. Nature was nice at times, but what about life-threatening earthquakes? And steamy days that sucked out your sweat and strength, but invigorated the roaches, gnats, flies, and war-like jungle. How about the poisonous ponds? Being stuck two pitch-black nights deep underground could hardly be called a good gift from a kind god.

To sum things up, marooned on the blasted island was the opposite of good.

CHAPTER 12

Handcuffed and weak, Terry stumbled next to his guard Bick, who was conveying him from Nagasaki Harbor to the American consulate. Ignoring the dozens of gawking stares, he watched his next step on the cobblestone road. The rat Zeke followed close behind, along with two other so-called witnesses, Joey and Billy. Mate Talbot walked ahead of them, distancing himself from the spectacle. The first mate had been authorized to testify on Captain Madison's behalf and bore the captain's letter charging Terry with insubordination and an enticement to mutiny. In addition, it included a demand for a civil judgment against Terry for attempting to break his contract.

At the gate of the consulate, they caught up with Talbot, who had already pulled the bell. Zeke turned to his cronies and muttered, "Looks more like a New England home than a gov'ment building. This fellow better be a reg'lar official, not some kind o' dandy."

Talbot glared at the sailors. "Keep it down, you hear. Impress the man by whatever manners you can dredge up for a couple of hours. Manners matter to a man like this."

Terry's spirits perked up for a second. A kind-hearted,

merciful dandy would suit him just fine.

After a gatekeeper admitted the group, they followed a stone pathway leading through an attractive garden. Purple and gold chrysanthemum blooms, moss as smooth as velvet, manicured shrubs surrounded Terry—so different from the brig and ocean. Were all yards in Japan really gardens? He'd spend hours sketching the layout if he only had the chance. But chances like that had come to a screeching halt the day he signed on to the *William Parton*. A hard prod from Bick's club forced him to move ahead.

At the consulate's vestibule, a servant spoke in Japanese and pointed to slippers for their use.

"Sorry. No speak Japan," the first mate said, rolling his eyes. Yet he sat on the low bench and started replacing his boots with slippers. He motioned for the rest of them to do the same.

Terry sat at the bench's far end. By using his manacled hands together with one foot to pin down the other foot's boot, he managed to pull both boots off only a couple of minutes later than the other men. He would have been pleased with the little accomplishment if the whole situation wasn't so horrible.

The servant unlocked a compartment in a cabinet next to the door and signaled for Bick to leave his pistol in it. The fool shook his head, waggling his finger toward Terry as if the consulate were faced with imminent danger even with the accused in handcuffs. The servant glanced at the handcuffs, then motioned for Terry and the four others to enter, but blocked Bick with a defensive stance.

Backing away with a huff, Bick deposited himself on the front step. "Not too cooperative," he grumbled.

A pretty Japanese lady appeared in the hallway. "Please wait here a minute," she said in lilting, perfect English. "I will call

Consul Cardiff."

The consul, a strikingly tall, bearded man in his thirties, strode up a couple of minutes later. Terry stiffened as the diplomat ran his gray eyes over the group, holding his gaze on Terry's face for a second longer before turning to the others. "Welcome to Japan and to the consulate, a little patch of America. John Cardiff here." Smiling, he shook hands with Mate Talbot and then Zeke, Joey, and Billy as they gave their names.

The introductions over, the consul turned toward Talbot. "When Captain Madison reported the *William Parton's* arrival yesterday, he indicated my services were needed due to a serious incident on board." He flicked his eyes toward Terry, then to the others. "It's unfortunate the ship leaves so soon—on tomorrow's tide, I was told. Because of that, I've made room in my schedule today for a hearing—just a hearing." He swept his arm out. "This way please. The reception room, doing double duty as the consulate's courtroom, is set up."

"Thank you, sir. We appreciate the accommodation," Talbot said as though he were civilized.

At the door of the converted room, Consul Cardiff paused. "The defendant will be seated at the table to our right." He pointed to a long walnut table with four chairs lined up behind it. "You men representing the captain will be at the table to the left. We won't stand on formality. You may take your seats."

Terry crossed the Turkish carpet, certain he resembled an ogre in his faded red shirt, dirty duck trousers, and handcuffs. His accusers had washed up, and the consul looked the part of a competent judge with a high collar, ribbon tie, waistcoat, and immaculate, dark suit. Yet, at the same time, the man appeared good-natured, without pretense. Terry winced, thinking how far he'd fallen in society. In his former life in Albany, people like the consul were often guests in his family's home.

Once everyone was situated, the consul asked for the document detailing the charges. Talbot stepped forward, and with the airs of an envoy, handed him the captain's letter. Sitting behind the large central, teakwood table, the consul leaned back in his wingchair and slit open the sealed envelope. While scanning the two pages, he glanced up at Terry and frowned.

Terry's hopes for a kind-hearted judge turned to ashes.

The consul set the letter down. "A trial is certainly in order, but the *William Parton* will not return from Shanghai until several weeks from now. Correct, First Mate?"

"That's right, Your Honor. Captain Madison requests a speedy judgment. A decision today would help everyone concerned, even the culprit." Talbot cast a mournful eye at Terry.

"Why, may I ask, would a speedy judgment be good for the defendant?" The momentary expression in Cardiff's eyes reminded Terry of a cat toying with a mouse.

"Oh, I didn't mean to speak out of turn." Talbot gave a self-deprecating smile. "It's just there isn't any question about what happened on the ship, and it seems good to get this sad occurrence over with. Get on with our lives, and let this seaman know what consequences he faces without delay."

"I see." Consul Cardiff nodded. "We can conclude the hearing today, but not the trial, unfortunately. I will work it in the day after tomorrow. We will hold Mr. Terrence Ballard securely for whatever course of action or punishment is deemed necessary by the trial."

Terry shivered. Had he already been assumed guilty of insubordination? Or worse, much worse, acting to inspire a mutiny? Was there no hope? How could a rash moment deserve such treatment?

The consulate's secretary, Fredrick Ball, conducted the swearing in of the three sailors, Mate Talbot, and Terry.

Consul Cardiff faced Terry. "As this is only a discovery hearing, you may remain seated while the charges in this letter are read aloud and discussed. Secretary Ball will record all remarks for later reference."

As the consul read Captain Madison's letter, Zeke aimed a smug smile at his two companions, no doubt relishing Terry's agony. The letter accurately detailed all of Terry's actions, but didn't include the too-prompt departure of the jolly-boat.

Terry raised a hand to object.

"I will hear from you at the right time," the consul said, no flicker of compassion evident. He turned to the letter's second page. "Here we find, if I may continue, the captain's conclusions: *In my humble view,* he writes, *justice for the insubordination and mutinous action of Terrence Ballard requires a minimum of ten years of hard labor in a United States penitentiary.*"

Terry felt the blood leave his face.

The consul paused, then went on reading. "*Furthermore, the damage to the ship's owners caused by Terrence Ballard's disregard for his signed contract should require the miscreant to be fined an amount double the broken contract's wage.*" The consul slid the letter aside and pulled out his fob watch. "Our time is limited. Do any of you witnesses wish to state an additional observation to Captain Madison's account, or do you agree with it as written?"

"I agree with it," Talbot said, and the three others added murmurs of approval.

"I have several questions at this time, Mr. Ballard, which I want you to answer as briefly as possible with no digression. The first: Did you intend to jump ship and swim to the whaleship, which if carried out would have encroached upon your signed contract? Yes or no." Consul Cardiff tapped his chin.

"Yes, but—"

"To be clear, you admit, then, to attempting an action, which if carried out, would have encroached on your contract. My next question: Was this attempt to jump ship an act of disagreement with the captain's decision concerning contact with the whaler, thus insubordination to the captain's command of the ship?"

"Yes, but—except for this one time—I have accepted the captain's command without fail. This is the only time I, uh, fell short." He flinched at his obvious understatement.

"Mr. Ball, you will record that Mr. Ballard agrees to having attempted to jump ship and to limited insubordination. Now for my third question. Have you already experienced consequences of this attempt to jump ship?"

"Yes, Your Honor, I have." Terry swallowed, longing to say more.

"Describe those consequences."

"I was sent to the brig in irons. The next day I was ordered to holystone all the decks with one other sailor and slush two masts from the topgallant yard down. When I collapsed from the effort of completing the commands within the time set to avoid a flogging, I was returned to the brig. But because I had lost consciousness, the ship's doctor had me moved to the sickbay. Hardly alive at first, I was laid low in the sickbay until the ship docked here on the fifth day."

"Is this account correct, Mr. Talbot?"

The first mate licked his lips. "Um …"

Billy nodded his head in agreement. Zeke and Joey stared at Talbot.

"I suppose the orders given on deck are not in question, but if you're not sure about the damage to Mr. Ballard's health, I can interview the doctor this evening before you sail."

"That won't be necessary," Talbot blurted. "As far as I know, it's correct ... or mostly correct. Mr. Ballard overexerted himself." The first mate scowled at Billy.

"My fourth question: Do you agree, Mr. Ballard, that your continued employment on the *William Parton* has been irreversibly damaged by your actions and its consequences? And as a result, both you and the ship would be better served by the termination of your contract, no matter the outcome of the other charges?"

Terry gasped. Was that possible? Could he escape the viciousness that would surely have been the death of him if he'd been found not guilty of the most serious charges and returned to the ship?

"Wait a minute, Your Honor!" Talbot had half-risen.

"I am addressing Mr. Ballard, and I expect everyone present to maintain a courtroom's decorum."

Talbot, his eyes slits, sat back down and folded his arms.

"Your answer, Mr. Ballard?"

"I do agree, Your Honor."

"Now Mr. Talbot, as a representative of Captain Madison, do you find terminating the contract to be advantageous to the ship?"

Terry held his breath, sure his accusers wouldn't yield their prey without a fight.

"I understand your hesitation," the consul said just as Talbot cleared his throat to speak. "But don't you find there can be a fine line between 'overexertion' and a type of torture that threatens a victim's very survival? Accepted maritime procedure forbids extreme punishment without a hearing before an impartial judge or requires a *review* of such punishment if administered far from port. I understand there is a movement in Congress, for example, to outlaw flogging since it can result in a sailor's death."

Talbot grimaced. "I-I have no idea if Captain Madison would agree to the contract's termination. It seems a ... an unusual outcome. But from his letter, I'm sure-fired certain he'd want the fine carried out just like he stated, *if* the contract is ended. And, of course, he'd want the other charges kept in place." He pursed his lips in a scholarly manner. "I ask, Your Honor, that you send a document about a termination to Captain Madison for his approval or disapproval."

"Yes, that is a necessary step to finalize such an action, and it shall be done. In fact, I will deliver it myself. Now, assuming the contract's termination and considering the desire for speedy decisions, I will assess a conditional civil fine for not finishing the voyage and occasioning an unfilled position in the crew."

The consul turned back to Terry. "Terrence Ballard, if the termination is approved, you will forfeit the pay you have already earned, as is customary, and will be required to pay the ship's purser a fine equal to one-half of your contractual pay without delay."

The first mate scowled at the much lower fine, but held his tongue.

The relief buoying Terry for a second gave way to despair. "I-I don't have any money, except one gold doubloon."

"One doubloon, is it?" The consul stared at Terry for a minute, as though looking into his soul. "In that case, if the termination is approved, the consulate will provide the funds, and the payment will be sent to the purser for you. This action will require you to reimburse the consulate by your labor in Nagasaki while awaiting any transport deemed necessary by the trial's outcome. Do you agree to such a repayment?"

Terry nodded, his mouth dry, his mind wheeling.

"I asked a question that requires more than a nod."

"Yes, I agree, s-sir, Your Honor," Terry answered, his voice hoarse.

"Then with this confirmation, the hearing is concluded." Consul Cardiff stood and extended his arm toward Terry's accusers. "Thank you all for your concern for justice. A tribunal will duly consider the more serious accusations the day after tomorrow. After I have a concluding interview with Mr. Ballard, my servant Hada will escort him to the International Settlement's holding enclosure, commonly called a jail."

Consul Cardiff pointed to Zeke. "I heard the guard for the defendant is at the entrance. Kindly ask him to send the key to unlock the handcuffs. Have no fear of an escape. Hada is well-trained in skills of defense and offense. There will be no difficulty with the prisoner."

"All right, Your Honor. I'll see to the key." Zeke rose. "And I'm plenty relieved to hear about them safeguards." He leered at Terry as he left the room.

The secretary escorted the remaining three accusers out, none of whom glanced at Terry.

While the manservant removed the irons, Terry stood in a daze. Possibly he would escape the horrors of the ship, but if he were still convicted of a crime or stuck in Nagasaki for months, what good would that do Tom?

Hada signaled for Terry to retake his seat, bowed to the consul, and resumed his stance by the door.

Consul Cardiff remained standing and pulled out two more pages from among his papers. "The world has not ended, Terrence Ballard. You have two defenders, and their views of what happened are most enlightening. Early this morning, a boy named Jim Mankin delivered confidential letters from Doctor Murdoch and from another member of the crew, whose name and position I will not divulge."

Terry jerked up in his seat, tears springing to his eyes.

"I understand your deep feelings for your brother—Tom, is it not?"

Terry started to nod, but quickly said, "Yes, Your Honor."

"I had a brother rumored to be a prisoner of the South's army in our American war. The rumor proved false, thank God, but I would have done anything to save him, including an attempt to swim to another ship."

Terry was struck dumb at the reversal of all he'd been thinking. Could the consul be hinting at a merciful decision after all? A sliver of hope pierced his dread.

Consul Cardiff left the central table and took a seat across from Terry. He signaled for the secretary to join them. "The doctor's letter states you were in danger of dying when he took you from the brig, thus confirming the severity of the injury to your health. He also mentions that he had previous opportunities to observe you in other situations, in which you demonstrated a good character. The other message here informed me that the skiff left the island at the exact departure time, meaning no search was made for your brother at that time or thereafter. Do you affirm this to be true?"

Terry met the consul's steady gaze. "Yes, sir. That's what happened despite my pleas."

"Truly unconscionable." He shook his head. "Secretary Hall will add the information from these messages to the record. I have no more questions for today. In the trial, the extenuating circumstances and the punishment you already experienced will be taken into account. You can be certain of that."

"Thank you, Your Honor. I-I'm very grateful."

Secretary Ball asked Terry to sign the record, then left the room as the manservant strode forward.

"Hada will escort you to the jail. I would like to trust you to be cooperative. Do I have your word?"

"Yes, Your Honor. And may I ask a question?"

"If it's about your brother's situation or repayment of the pending loan, you'll need to hold it until after the trial, which—in case you don't know—will be open to the public. And although you have my deep sympathy, as you have discerned, I cannot guarantee what the tribunal will decide. I can guarantee fairness."

Terry rose and followed the manservant, a dark shadow incasing him again. So, the coming trial would be open to outsiders and its outcome unknown. More humiliation before his countrymen, who might not be so inclined toward mercy. If found guilty of even part of the charges, he could be publicly caned, definitely a legal punishment, providing vulgar entertainment for a crowd of curious onlookers. Or, might the tribunal actually sentence him to the penitentiary? His heart fell to his toes. Even a short stint of a year would ruin his life and condemn Tom to the island indefinitely—if he still lived.

CHAPTER 13

Daisuke stared at the pirate. The fiend held the monkey by a rope tied around its neck. It had probably tried to steal from Bolt again and deserved its fate. Yet Sara would be devastated to lose her bleak life's only source of enjoyment.

The pirate cackled. "Might ye be ready to bargain?"

"Why I care about the monkey?" Daisuke called down from the top of the bluff.

"Yer sister's mighty attached to it. That's why."

Daisuke turned away. Any bargain would at least involve a supply of bamboo, leading to a ladder, or a far worse demand—untenable favors from Sara. He'd have to rescue the monkey by stealth and teach the smug pirate a lesson.

"If yer thinkin' o' sneaking up on ol' Ben Bolt, better think again. Leg's lame. Ears ain't. Knife's sharp! Snake's ready!"

Daisuke strode away like he didn't care, but found himself praying for the monkey to get away on its own. Then he snorted. Why would God in far-off heaven care about the monkey's predicament? Monkeys' lives ended all the time in the wild. So, what could he do? Telling Tamo about the problem was out of the question. He'd argue to kill the enemy and be done with it.

"Better tell yer sister," Bolt shouted with a curse. "Rope'll get tighter an' tighter."

"So says you," Daisuke muttered. After all, a dead monkey would be no good for bargaining. Equally important, as a samurai, he could hold his own against the pirate. He'd already bested Bolt once, having put his training to good use. And he had a knife to match threat with threat.

To start with, he would use the rest of the day to make another ladder. He could take the shorter one out of the underground cavern, but it was wiser to have it always in place. If chased by pirates—another bad thought—having to carry and position a ladder could be fatal.

Without divulging the real reason for making another ladder, he recruited Tamo to work with him in the bamboo grove, cutting stalks, and then in the forest, gathering vine branches to make the ties. Tamo stayed for the early supper as usual.

Daisuke rose when they finished the meal. "All right. Now we put ladder together. I can show you how to cut stalks." He chopped a stalk the right length for a rung.

"How about we do it in the morning?" Tamo glanced out the cave. "I don't like those giant bats buzzing me."

"I and Sara can do it. You can go." Daisuke waved his hand in dismissal. How could a barbarian with a muscular body and weather-toughened skin act like such a baby about bats? His size alone could intimidate a bear, or something close to it.

"What's the rush? I mean, we already got ladders for our hiding place. Bolt is corralled in his cove. Is there something you're not telling the team here?" Tamo looked at Sara as though expecting her to side with him.

"Maybe I am crazy, huh? Go!" He didn't care his tone was sharp.

Tamo jumped up. "See you tomorrow then." He bowed with a smirk. "Glad I could help with your strange little project."

Sara's brow furrowed. "Is there a problem?" she asked once Tamo strolled out.

"An elder brother doesn't have to explain everything. It's time to finish the ladder." He had enough worries without Sara making his life harder.

In the middle of the night, when he was sure Sara was asleep, he took his knife and crept out of the cave. After picking up the new ladder resting behind bushes, he headed up the hill. Meeting bats was the least of his concerns, but while weaving through the trees, he kept a wary eye out although he'd never caught a glimpse of any nasty, nocturnal wildlife.

Reaching the cliff, he slid the ladder into place, thankful for the sea mist that had rolled in and for the clouds hiding the moon and stars. He lowered himself rung by rung to the ledge the barbarian had fallen onto eleven days earlier. He couldn't scale cliffs, but he could move without a whisper of noise. Crouching on the ledge, he studied the strand below for any sign of the pirate.

The pirate's shack protruded over rocks in front of a shallow cave on the cove's right side. All was in deep shadows except for a small glow from dying embers in a bucket inside the shack. He guessed the monkey was tied up within the cave, making it trickier to reach. He'd have to do his best to keep the beast from sensing him until he got close enough to disable the pirate.

He climbed down the rest of the hill, careful not to dislodge even a pebble. Creeping behind rocks and scrub bushes at the bottom, he circled until he could reach out and touch the side of the shack.

Everything hung on his next movements. After sliding his knife out of its sheath, he crept toward the shack's front opening until he was almost at the entrance. Then something scurried across his right foot. He held back a howl as fiery pain shot through his left foot. A crab! Hidden in a hole under the pebbles and sand.

He plopped down and tried in vain to extricate three toes from the coconut crab's pincer. He shook his foot, gritting his teeth at the torture. The next second, a rope encircled his arms and chest. Lunging forward, he managed to reach the crab's claw with his knife despite the rope. After he pried open the pincer, the giant crab recoiled and scuttled away.

The rope tightened. A muscle cramp caused him to drop his weapon. Horrified, he searched his mind. Was there no possible trick? Or a jiu-jitsu move? He jerked against the rope again, and then again. When it didn't give a hair, he groaned. He'd been outmaneuvered. His failure was doubly bad, for Sara would risk her life to save him. And he was helpless to stop her.

The monkey had started shrieking and continued for several more minutes, either from anger or entreaty. It didn't matter. They were both caught, and that was what mattered. Immensely!

The pirate lit a wick jutting from a clam shell of fish-oil and grinned at him. "Enjoy my little surprise?" He chuckled as he tugged him farther into the shack, where he finished wrapping him in rope and fastened a dirty kerchief over his mouth. "Wouldn't want you to give away any secrets when yer two rescuers shows up, now would I? Nope, ol' Ben Bolt been fightin', robbin', an' survivin' too long to allow anythin' like that on *his* watch. So now, we wait. Heh, heh."

CHAPTER 14

Terry steeled himself for the worst, swallowing hard, as Hada ushered him into the "courtroom" for the trial. Listening to drunk sailors for a day and two nights in the settlement's small holding building, which was like a hut with six tiny cells, had further driven home his foolishness. He ran his eyes around the room, amazed to see so few people. The tribunal of three men were seated at the back of the consul's table—the consul in the center, a navy ship's captain in uniform on his left, and an elderly gentleman to his right, dressed as a New Englander minus a top hat. Secretary Ball stood between the tribunal's table and Terry's assigned place. The pretty Japanese lady he'd seen in the hallway comprised the "spectators."

Consul Cardiff rapped his gavel as though quieting a large assembly. After Secretary Ball informed Terry of the procedures, he had him swear to tell the truth on a large, brown Bible.

Terry stood at attention, his face burning, while Consul Cardiff read Captain Madison's prosecutorial letter aloud for the other two in the tribunal and the one spectator.

Finished with the letter, the consul paused and looked at Mr. Ball, who had moved to a desk at the side. When the secretary held his pen up, Cardiff resumed speaking. "During the preliminary hearing, the witnesses for the prosecution affirmed the details of the incident as did the defendant. Because of the animosity displayed in the aftermath of Mr. Ballard's actions, the court proposed a termination of his employment on the *William Parton.* Both parties have now agreed to the termination and to the fine levied on Mr. Ballard." The consul raised his eyebrows at Terry.

Freed from the ship! Terry closed his eyes, absorbing the news. Part of the weight threatening to crush him, like a boulder teetering above him, crumbled.

"When affixing his signature," the consul continued, "Captain Madison confirmed that the contract signed by the defendant specified all pay would be forfeited if the sailor was culpable in not completing the voyage."

The elderly gentleman lowered his head, revealing a small bald spot in the midst of his gray hair, and sighed.

The navy captain stared at Terry, seeming to watch for defiance.

Terry looked down at the carpet. Relief and worry battled in his heart until the consul's words regained his attention.

"The verdicts concerning the criminal charges are to be decided today. Mr. Ballard, you have sworn to tell the truth. God help you. We wait to hear your defense."

Terry blinked. Was the consul not going to reveal any of the confidential testimony? He was likely doomed without it. But even so, he would not play the part of a criminal.

Still standing, as required, he looked directly at the men. "Your Honors, my words and action—foolish ones, I admit—were because I was desperate to get help for my brother, unjustly marooned by my ship on an uninhabited island. It was not my intention to desert my duties or instigate any kind of mutiny."

"Explain why you say the *William Parton* was responsible for your brother's situation," the captain ordered, his sharp eyes glinting in his weathered face.

"Uh, not the whole of the good ship, sir. Those responsible were the sailors in the jolly-boat, who initially left Tom, and the first mate and the captain, who didn't authorize a search party."

"Let it be noted that factual details, not a generalization as in your first statement, are necessary in a trial like this." The captain frowned.

"I'll be more careful, sir."

The captain motioned for Terry to continue.

"You see, the jolly-boat left the island at the exact time set for its departure, not delaying when Tom was missing." Terry clasped his hands so they wouldn't shake. "And everyone on the ship knows no boat was sent back to search for Tom, although the accepted rules—"

"Yes," the captain interrupted, clearly irritated, "all here know the rules of sailing ships. Was any reason given for this negligence?"

Terry warned himself to watch every word. "The five in the jolly-boat claimed they had conducted a search before the departure time because Tom had wandered off. They said they had been worried about him. One of the five—Zeke, who was a witness at the hearing—even declared he set out before the others to try to locate Tom in spite of the risk of unknown dangers."

"So, it is your supposition this was untrue? That these men were actually hardhearted fiends?" The captain couldn't have sounded more skeptical.

"Even if a quick search was made, sir, Tom had to be somewhere on that small island, maybe with a broke leg or knocked out from a fall." Terry rubbed his cheek, struggling to find adequate words. "No one would choose to stay by himself in such a place, especially not my brother."

The elderly New Englander looked over his square-rimmed spectacles at Tom. "Then what do you suggest as the true reason no one on the ship, except you, apparently cared enough to speak up on your brother's behalf?"

"Tom and I ... were not well liked. Tom ..."

"Yes?" the tribunal said in unison.

It was too late to offer a better explanation. "The most recent reason," he said after a moment's hesitation, "was that most of the crew believed my brother had stolen the navigator's missing bottle of wine. However, when the captain conducted an inspection the same evening, Tom had no alcohol on his breath, but another sailor did, who had gotten wine from a different source. That man was punished. If the bottle hadn't been taken, the other man's disobedience of the rules wouldn't have been discovered. Tom never told me he took it, but the navigator had treated Tom unfairly, so I suspect he did. The crew blamed me, too, because I didn't report my brother."

"I see." The old gentleman stroked his gray beard with a faraway expression.

"Any more questions about a search or lack thereof?" The consul gestured with his hand to the other two.

Both answered with a sharp *no*—as if their minds were made up.

After telling Terry to be seated, the consul pulled out additional papers. Terry leaned forward. Surely these were the confidential messages. But were they in time to change a made-up mind?

The consul tapped the sheets. "I have here two letters from independent observers on the ship, whose names I will not state publicly for obvious reasons. These men corroborate Mr. Ballard's version of the events, particularly the failure to send a search party for his brother. One adds that both brothers, being young and landlubbers, had been mercilessly bullied by the crew throughout the voyage despite their hard work. The other describes the near fatal treatment Mr. Ballard received after the incidents referenced by the captain and adds his testimony to this young man's good character."

The elderly gentleman nodded as the consul refolded the letter. "It appears there are mitigating circumstances. I do have one last question, at least on my part." The gentleman focused on Terry. "If you had reached the whaler and made your plea to that ship's captain, what had you planned to do next?"

Terry clenched his fists as he stood. He didn't have a good answer. "I hadn't thought that far ahead, sir. Since then, I've asked myself over and over why I didn't see that I'd be forcing the two ships to draw side by side to deliver me back to the *William Parton* ... or I would be guilty of jumping ship. Both would have been wrong, the second much worse. Please, believe me. I never planned to jump ship in order to desert."

"Ah, the impulsiveness of youth, never reining in passion," the captain muttered, and the others nodded solemnly.

The consul turned his full attention back to Terry. "Have you anything further to say in your defense, Mr. Ballard?"

"No, Your Honor." He steadied himself by forcing his legs against the table's edge.

"You will wait in the next room during our deliberations." The consul spoke to the manservant Hada in Japanese.

Hada led Terry to a room with straw mats as flooring. The servant—or more accurately, guard—moved aside the four silk cushions surrounding a low table set in front of an alcove, then pointed to a place on the bare mat. Too nervous to ponder the unusual décor, Terry knelt, noticing the mat's slight puff in the silent, empty room. Glancing over his shoulder, he winced. His guard stared at him, one hand holding the handcuffs, seemingly in readiness.

Terry was a bird in a cage—not valued as a parrot or admired as an eagle, but considered a mistreated pigeon by the sympathetic consul, a nuisance of a crow by the captain, and an unfortunate ... he thought for a minute ... an unfortunate turkey by the old gentleman.

CHAPTER 15

Tom stopped, hardly believing his eyes. Sara sat on a rock outside her cave, reading a book. A book! Only it looked dangerously like a Bible, and it probably was because the Okinawa missionary had given them one. For a second, he'd thought a real book was on the island, like a boon from heaven. He sniffed at the irony of his last thought.

Of course, he couldn't expect a library on a deserted island, but it'd sure be nice to have one or two books, or even three or four, to keep from always thinking about being stuck in the middle of an ocean, maybe facing pirates, and worrying about Terry. For sure, once he got off the isle, he wouldn't take books for granted any longer.

The girl looked fully entranced by whatever fairy tale she was reading. He scuffed his boot on a pebble.

She startled and looked up. He thought he caught the trace of a smile before she put her hand over her mouth, but he could have imagined it.

She picked up a stick, and wrote in the dirt: "Have you ~~saw~~ seen my brother?"

Tom grimaced. Did he have to write his answer because Dice

wasn't with them? Still, he'd better take this new team setup step by step with the submissive sister. He shook his head.

"Not at cavern? Not hunting? Not at fresh water pool?" she wrote.

He shook his head again. He'd already walked around most of the ridge, watching for a ship. But occasionally he'd cut through the forest where it was less dense in order to keep an eye out for anything unusual in the valley and to have a break from the relentless wind and noise of the surf.

"Maybe something wrong?" she wrote. "He left early. New ladder not here."

Tom straightened after reading her message. The missing ladder didn't bode well. The ladders had been connected solely with the cavern and the pirate's cove. The only other conceivable use would be to reach coconuts, and the monkey made that unnecessary.

"If your brother needs help," Tom said quickly, hoping she wouldn't repulse him, "we have to communicate better."

She put her hands on her cheeks, shaking her head *no*.

"Just for now. This *one* time."

She dropped her hands and gazed at him.

He took it as agreement. "We should check on the pirate's hangout first. I avoided getting too close this morning. Figured it'd make your brother happier for me not to get Bolt riled up."

Catching a glimmer of fear in her eyes, he added, "Just to check to be sure nothing's going on there. Your brother knows what he's about. Avoids trouble like it's a tiger shark. Don't worry."

Tom headed up the hill. Glancing over his shoulder, he saw Sara hesitate, then turn to follow.

Reaching the area above the pirate's stretch of beach, Tom came to a halt. The top of the new ladder protruded above the cliff. He glanced at Sara, who was slack-jawed. They skirted the tree line until they reached the place where the cliff was closest to the shack.

He motioned for Sara to stay back, then scooted along the ground to the drop-off. He paused before poking up his head. What he wouldn't give for one of the new inventions called periscopes. For that matter, what he wouldn't give to be anywhere but where he was. Taking a breath, he raised his head high enough to get a look.

Dice was half-sitting, half-lying on the driftwood-and-rock floor inside the shack's entrance, with rope wrapped around him like some mummified body excavated in Egypt. The next moment, the pirate stepped out of the cave. Tom scooted backwards, put his finger to his lips, and motioned for Sara to follow as he crept toward the jungle path.

When they came out on the valley side, Tom perched on a boulder, trying to order his thinking. This was trouble. Big trouble. Far bigger than spending nights with the army of bats in the earth's netherworld.

"We have to talk." He motioned for the statue-like girl to sit by him. "Come closer," he said more firmly when she hung back. "Come as close as you're willing. We have to make a plan. Your brother needs us."

Her face paled, and she took a wobbly step. He jumped up to help her, but she managed to sit on a neighboring boulder.

"Dice doesn't look like he's been hurt, but Bolt has tied him up. Tight."

"Where is he tied?" Her voice shook.

"Inside the entrance of the shack. Like he's bait to attract us."

"What can … What can we d-do?" Her eyes beseeched him to come to the rescue, as if he could slay dragons. Problem was—he didn't have the armor and invincible sword.

"Let's think," he said after a minute. "We gotta think logically." He caught her brief nod. "All right. First, we decide what will lead to success. I say it's to knock the pirate plum out before we move to untie Dice. Bolt could have a tripwire that would wake him up if I just snuck into the shack while he slept tonight." Tom gave a puff of air at the ghastly implication. If he got into a fight with Bolt, it would be bloody.

"And next, we must think about what's available to use. Of course, the ladders, my knife, your brother's knife. And what else?"

"Two bows with fifteen arrows and a hatchet." She'd managed to speak without stammering. "Daisuke carries his knife, so we have not that. But … but what does the pirate want? Why he did this?"

"Clearly he still wants you for his wife." An unexpected shudder went through him. "What isn't obvious is the reason your brother visited the beach. Maybe Bolt pretended to need help, then turned on him."

"He is an evil man." She wiped off a lone tear. "Worse than the *tengu,* the goblins children fear. He acts like a demon."

"Anyway, Bolt's not going to get what he's after. Definitely not! We're smarter than him. Can you shoot the arrows? Are you good?"

She lowered her eyes. "Same as Daisuke."

"Same? So, you can hit the winging ducks and pigeons too?

I'd say that's *really* good! Now if I drew the pirate's attention, could you shoot him when he approached the entrance?"

"I could. But I cannot. My brother forbids killing him."

Tom groaned. "Even to save yourself from that fiend's clutches? Or maybe your brother's *life*? Think what you're saying!"

"I cannot kill him."

"Then shoot him in the shoulder or in the leg."

"That is very hard."

"But possible?"

"Only if the pirate does not move. But he also has a knife. And his aim is good. At you."

Tom fell quiet. What a fix! They couldn't let Dice die—after being tortured. At the first slice of an ear, Sara would give herself up, and that was plain wrong.

He rubbed the back of his neck. Taking on the rescue was madness. He sure didn't want to be stuck like a pig and bleed out on the dratted island's beach. But then, it was *two* against one. If he or the girl got in the first blow, he might not get much of a wound, if any. He hadn't died at the top of the ship's rigging in the ice storm, or on the cliff's ledge, or in the earthquake or cavern. If cats had nine lives, maybe people could have five.

"So, you must shoot the arrow before he throws the knife at me." At her shocked look, he added, "And I'll have my knife. I have a good aim too. But just if your arrow misses."

"Excuse me. May I say maybe another way?"

"That's why I'm talking with you, isn't it? To get the best plan—*together*."

Her cheeks reddened, and she looked down.

"Sorry." Tom swiped his hand through his hair. "Our ways

101

are just so different. Say your suggestion, and anything else anytime."

She gripped the boulder as though to borrow its strength. "The cliff above the pirate's shack—the one you looked over— is straight up. And no ledge. But you are a sailor. I forgot to say the ship's lines we have."

"And that would help, how? On a ship, the lines work together with the masts like ladders."

"You could not go down the cliff using the line? A ninja can do that."

"Is a ninja a real person or someone's imagination? I could do it with a nice, fat rope and could even make a soft landing on top of the shack. But the ship lines left from your little boat aren't fat. Real hard to grip."

"We could make the line fat with vines, dried seaweed, and fish gut. You could use it and land on the shack with cat feet."

"Cat feet, huh? That would be good." Even better would be grabbing another of those nine lives if the plan failed. In his mind, he ran through the likely sequence of actions following such a quiet landing. It would avoid a tripwire. He wouldn't have to fight if he knocked the pirate out while he slept. Even if the pirate were awake, he wouldn't expect an attack from above. It *did* have a chance of working.

"If nothing changes before tonight, your idea is pretty good," he admitted. "The element of surprise increases our odds a lot."

"Daisuke said that about *surprise* too."

There was no hint of accusation, but he caught the intended lesson. Their odds would be better still if Tom had kept himself hidden like Dice had wanted. Of course, his sister would side with her brother … as Terry would with him.

"I'll tie a hefty rock into the line's end. Its weight will help keep the line in place, and it'll be waiting for me at the bottom." He jerked a smile. "The pirate won't know what hit him when I slam it on his melon head." Sara's brow furrowed, like she was trying to picture a melon on a body. "You'll still need to go down the ladder and become a distraction in front of the shack if the rock doesn't knock him out. Just don't get close enough for him to grab you and use you as a shield."

"I will do anything."

"Good." In fact, didn't such willingness open the door for her archery skill? "So how about you bringing your bow and arrows with you? Just as backup."

She cocked her head, then gave a quick nod of agreement. His eyes met her dark ones, and he took in their steel gleam. She didn't look like a wilting flower any longer. No, indeed, she didn't.

He could like this pretty girl a lot if he wasn't careful.

CHAPTER 16

The door to the room where Terry waited slid open. Hada spun sideways, then bowed as the trial's attractive "spectator" padded into the room—now with a kind of papoose, no less, on her back. The guard-servant hurried to the table, placed one of the cushions in front of it, gave another deep bow, and exited the room. No doubt he remained vigilant outside the door in case he needed to control the world's fiercest prisoner.

The lady glanced at Terry and knelt down on the cushion, keeping one hand under the papoose, which held a wide-eyed baby, looking right at him. The papoose reminded him of an Indian squaw's he'd seen a few times in Albany, but this one had a loose shawl wrapping up the baby. Also, the tiny child didn't look at all Indian or even fully Japanese, due in part to having hazel eyes and soft, dark curls—darker than his own brown hair but lighter than the mother's. Aside from the customized baby carrier, nothing else about the situation reminded him of anything whatsoever.

Terry started to stand up so he could bow as the servant had done, but she motioned for him to remain as he was. So instead, he slid his feet under him and knelt back on his heels, copying her position and hoping it was polite for him to do so. The momentary curve of the lady's lips reassured him.

"May I introduce myself? I am Sumi Taguchi Cardiff, the consul's wife, as I think you may know." She gave a questioning raise of her eyebrows.

He didn't know, but smiled and mumbled *yes* as though it was quite normal for a high official to marry—marry!—someone of a different race.

"I was moved by your difficulties during the hearing. I understand your heart's turmoil over your missing brother." She ran her eyes over his face again, and his neck grew warm. "However, we both have to wait to learn the verdict. My humble opinion will not affect the trial's outcome. In the meantime, I would like to welcome you to Japan in spite of the circumstances and talk a bit, if you do not mind."

"I-I am thankful for your kindness, ma'am. I don't mind talking. Not at all." How could he? He needed every sympathetic ear he could get.

"I will ask a few things I am curious about. Let us start with your predicament. Clearly, the ship's first mate opposed you, but how about the second mate? Or was there anyone on the ship besides the letter writers who sympathized with you?"

Terry was taken aback. He didn't expect the mild-mannered woman to also interrogate him, but there was nothing for it, but to cooperate. "Jim Mankin, who brought the letters, felt bad about everything, for sure. He even got in trouble for asking about me. Maybe three or four others thought search parties should have thoroughly combed the island, but they didn't make it known. Probably scared."

"How did the ship happen to stop at the island?"

"Captain Madison said we found it because a squall blew us

off course. I wasn't aware of any storm more recent than one we had two weeks earlier, but when I'm asleep, nothing wakes me. My brother used to say God himself couldn't wake me. 'Course, that's not true. The captain sent Tom and the others to get clams and turtles since the ship was right there."

"Would the captain not worry about unfriendly natives protecting their territory? Maybe a fierce warlord guarding the land? Or pirates?"

"The first mate relayed the captain's word that the island was safe. Nothing there to worry about."

"A little peculiar he would know that, don't you think? Having gone off-course and all." The lady flinched just then, the baby having snagged a strand of her hair. She rescued it from the plump hand and inserted the wisp back into her piled-up hairdo, held in place with combs and slender jade cylinders.

"Yes, now that you say that. All I've been thinking about is how to rescue Tom."

"That is understandable." She looked away for a second. "My husband's ship met pirates once. Pirate ships do not have safe havens on Japan's coasts. They use uninhabited islands or Chinese rivers. But we hear occasional reports of the villains attacking in nearby waters, even reports of one or two foreign ships and their crews being lost to pirates. Unfortunately, my country does not have large seagoing ships to fight them." She tapped her fingers on the low table. "The rush of the *William Parton* to leave the island despite a missing sailor also seems strange. This all merits thought."

"Yes, ma'am," Terry said, in full agreement.

"Now a different question," she continued. "I understand you spent two nights in the settlement's holding cell. How did you find it? A foolish query, no doubt." She rescued another strand.

"Terrible, ma'am. I hope to never be in a jail cell again. I hope ..." He gulped. "I hope I'm spared today."

"I hope so too, Mr. Ballard. I was a prisoner once, in a Japanese cell, actually this year at the time of our New Year. It was terrifying although I spent only half a day imprisoned."

"Forgive me, but I can't imagine you could've done anything wrong."

"Nothing wrong in the eyes of God. A relative believed in Jesus on his deathbed. I tried to prevent a Buddhist funeral because I, too, had become a Christian. It is against the law for a Japanese person to be a Christian. Even now. That was my underlying *crime* although I was falsely accused of another too."

"I heard from a sailor once that Christianity's called the Evil Religion here. But it isn't evil." Terry cocked his head. "I don't know a great deal about it, but I know that much."

"My country has a long history of misunderstanding the faith, mixed with ancient political intrigue. You can learn much about Japan if you stay here for a while."

He sure hoped he wouldn't be staying "for a while." But he had to repay the fine, and an added punishment could result from the trial. But then a "half-a-day" sentence? Could he possibly come close to the same luck—a really, really short time imprisoned in Nagasaki and some unimaginable way to repay the consulate's loan *after* he rescued Tom?

"How did you escape a longer sentence?" Was there an approach he hadn't thought of?

"The people in the International Settlement here came to my aid. But I know the real reason. God himself intervened. He had mercy on me, his weak follower."

His hopes plunged yet again. "I'd appreciate that kind of help with the bind I'm in, but it's unlikely." Religious talk was risky, but the nice lady didn't look like she'd fly off the handle. "I don't guess I'm really much of a *follower* of God. My parents took me to church at home, but a lot's gone wrong since then."

"Yes," she said while nodding, "you have had a very trying time while attempting to do good."

"I did ask God, or a heavenly power, for help on the ship one time. Not sure he answered. Anyway, I survived." *But barely.* "I guess I'm not too deserving."

The door slid open, and Hada bowed, then spoke to the consul's wife.

"It is time for you to return to the courtroom," she said as she managed to stand in one fluid motion, even with the baby swaying.

Terry rose quickly too, but jerkily, given that his numb legs weren't cooperating.

"I will be praying for you—for God's mercy, which *none* of us deserves," she said right before she walked toward the door.

Hada spoke sharply to Terry in Japanese. Certain of his meaning, he hurried out of the room, turning at the last minute to bow to the lady and to say thank you. The servant pointed for Terry to walk in front of him.

Before reaching the designated table, Terry took a furtive look at his three judges. The men gazed at him steadily, their faces solemn. He lifted his chin. He had to stay strong despite the sudden terrible longing to be back home in New York. He'd even be happy to be fifteen again, never having left his family. He would sure think for himself and not blindly follow Tom.

"Remain standing, Mr. Ballard, while I read the unanimous verdicts." The consul's tone was firm.

Terry gripped the back of his chair.

"The defendant, Terrence Ballard, is found *not* guilty of

insubordination, other than that already dealt with by disciplinary action on the ship." The consul paused at Terry's guttural utterance. "Further, he is found *not* guilty of an incitement to mutiny." He raised his hand to stop Terry when he opened his mouth to exclaim his thanks. "However, since Mr. Ballard accepted a loan to pay his fine for initiating an action encroaching on his contract, he is required to remain and work in Nagasaki until the loan has been repaid to the United States consulate in full."

"My brother!" Terry exclaimed. "What about him?"

"This judgment is not negotiable, Mr. Ballard, and the court will not take lightly any violation of the terms." Consul Cardiff raised his gavel. "On behalf of the United States of America, the court thanks Captain Harley James and Vice Consul Richard Pendleton for their attention to the case of the *William Parton versus Mr. Terrence Ballard.*" The consul banged his gavel down. "Court dismissed."

Terry's mind clouded. The worst was over, but how could he repay the loan? Tom had to be rescued without any delay. Too late, he realized someone had spoken.

The consul was walking toward him. "Mr. Ballard, I said, 'you may be seated.'"

"Oh yes, Your … Your Honor." Terry sat and looked up at his judge's concerned face.

"Now you need to know of a once-in-a-lifetime opportunity." Consul Cardiff turned and retook his judge's seat. "Mr. Pendleton here"—the consul nodded toward the elderly gentleman still seated next to him—"has offered to hire you for two months, at the end of which, he will pay your wages directly to the consulate's funds to remove your total debt. He has graciously offered to put you up in a servant's room and provide your food."

The consul looked at the elderly man, who said, "Yes, that is so."

"There are several additional provisions for repaying your debt in such an agreeable manner. First: you are not to visit any saloon. Second: you are not to visit any establishment of ill repute. Third: you are neither to use or smuggle opium nor engage in gambling, both of which are illegal in this country.

"You may refuse the offer and the related provisions," the consul continued, "but I would be forced to reveal your situation and threaten a stiff penalty for anyone who would assist you in leaving Nagasaki before the debt was paid. Apart from Mr. Pendleton's offer, paying off the debt would take a half year at least, and that while toiling on the docks or in construction. Then finding a ship willing to hunt for a nameless island after that amount of time would be most unlikely." The consul gathered his notes and gazed at Tom. "You may have a day to consider the offer, if you need it."

"Excuse my asking, but wouldn't it be as unlikely for a ship to hunt for the island at the end of two months?" Terry had dared to think—if he were wondrously released—he might get on a ship right away with a captain willing to stop at an island brimming with turtles and timber. But he didn't know the coordinates, and now that the consul pointed out the poor odds, even that hope looked far-fetched.

"Yes, virtually no chance at all." The consul glanced at Mr. Pendleton. "We will do what we can to help, but I don't know how effective our assistance will be. At any rate, I recommend finishing the repayment as quickly as possible."

Terry took a big breath. "I don't need a day, sir. I will take the offer. Thank you … Mr. Pendleton."

Terry turned his gaze from the elderly man back to the consul. "About helping with the search, sir?"

"We'll discuss the possibilities on another day." The consul picked up his materials from the trial. "But soon. Several issues are involved."

Terry stood up with the others, taking in the fact his awful captivity had transformed into liberty. He'd be jumping for joy if Tom weren't still in a terrible fix. How could anyone survive for long in a wasteland? Or with an angry warlord? Or pirates? Maybe God's mercy—if such existed—wouldn't cover that.

Terry followed Mr. Pendleton down the hill with his one sole possession in his pocket—the gold doubloon Tom had given him as a promise of his safe return from the island. How ironic that gesture seemed, but he had to cling to the coin and to hope. He guessed he'd lost his seaman's chest, still on the ship, but that was a trivial matter compared to what had transpired in the courtroom.

Not guilty. He looked at his wrists. No shameful chains bound him. He faced no prison time. No caning. No return to the hellish ship. And no one on the road had reason to gawk at him. In fact, he could gawk himself.

The cobblestone street was crowded with hawkers of goods, water-carriers, laborers, and kimono-clad women shopping at roadside stalls. Some of the people's clothes looked more like they competed for first place at a costume party rather than carrying out the tasks of daily life. He identified two Russian naval officers in red-and-black uniforms, blue-gowned Chinese, Englishmen dressed like they belonged in Parliament, and probably a few Hollander men in pantaloons and jackets. Were there Americans mixed in, other than the rowdy sailors in front of the three saloons they'd already passed? He hadn't detected any.

The narrow lanes slanting away from the road displayed more walled shops and houses that stair-stepped up the bordering hill, begging for exploration. He kept expecting Mr. Pendleton to turn onto one of the alleyways, but the balding gentleman pressed forward, tapping the stones with his cane, which was topped by a carved parrot. At last, he pushed open a wooden gate and waved for Terry to enter with him. A building resembling a nice, two-story, middle-class home met Terry's eyes, except that it had a garden similar to the consulate's, overhanging eaves, a polished wooden veranda, and, he soon found, a vestibule with an assortment of slippers, which they used right then to replace their footwear.

A man hurried forward to meet them in the hallway.

"This is my manservant, Matsu," Mr. Pendleton explained. "He's one of the people you will take orders from. He'll show you your room. After you take a few minutes to spiff up, meet me on this floor in the parlor. And welcome to my home."

"Thank you, sir." Terry turned to follow the servant while still trying to adapt his thinking to the totally unexpected outcome.

Matsu led Terry to the second floor and to a room beyond his wildest expectation. Although it was small and had the straw mats seemingly all the rage in Japan, the feather bed sitting over a hooked rug claimed his rapt attention. A feather bed! And amazingly, on top of it were three new pairs of trousers and three shirts. And besides that, he noticed with a sense of awe, the room was spotlessly clean. No thick grime. No suffocating stench. He let out a groan of relief. He had landed in a civilized place.

In the parlor, Mr. Pendleton motioned him toward a chair by

a walnut table next to a wall made of paper panels. "You're looking more presentable now. You can shave those whiskers in the morning."

"Thank you for the clothes, sir. I'll repay you when I can." Terry stood by the chair.

"No need, my boy. Take a seat, read over what I expect of you, and sign if you agree. You can read, can't you?"

"Yes, sir. I had finished my ninth year at the Albany Academy when I left home." Terry removed the cover page, thinking he'd be graduating in less than two years if he hadn't been so foolish. But here he was. Whatever his duties and schedule turned out to be, they would be a world better than the ship or prison.

As he read, he kept himself from grinning.

• Rising at 6 in the morning, retiring by 10—better than what the summer hours on his grandparents' farm had been; rather like a rich man's vacation instead.

• Assisting Mr. Pendleton in fulfilling his vocation— whatever the "vocation" was, it didn't matter.

• Performing without complaint all the tasks assigned by the housekeeper, including aid to the cook, manservant, maid, groundskeeper, and stable boy—far, far better than being a ship's lookout in the crow's nest in freezing cold and burning heat, holystoning the deck, or slushing the towering masts.

• Prohibited from leaving the International Settlement without permission—to be expected.

Of course, he'd agree to these expectations and see what the future brought. As much as possible, he'd keep his word. He wasn't like Tom. But if he ended up breaking his agreement by escaping Nagasaki before the two months were up, it would be the least of his concerns, other than eventually reimbursing his benefactor.

Reaching the final paragraph, his heart skipped a beat. In the afternoons, he was to attend to his studies for a minimum of two hours each day except Sundays. And once a week, he was to assist Mrs. Sumi Cardiff's English class. Had he passed on and gone to the Promised Land his grandpa spoke about?

A catch at the back of his throat made him swallow. He couldn't let up his efforts for Tom's rescue. His "sentence" and this agreement could chain him to Nagasaki. Not by suffering—by its tantalizing ease.

CHAPTER 17

Sara approached Tamo's cave after praying for hours that Daisuke would break free on his own and they wouldn't have to carry out their plan. But her prayer hadn't been answered. She switched her bow into her left hand and flexed her right hand's stiff fingers.

Tamo was sitting on a rock next to the cave, watching her. When she drew close, he rose and offered a crooked smile. "Guess I'm ready if you are. Time to get going."

"I want to pray—with you," she blurted out as he checked on his knife in its sheath, then took a step up the hill.

He turned partway toward her. "Aloud?"

"Yes, a short prayer."

"Sure. Go ahead. Why not? It can't hurt anything."

She nodded, her stomach turning over. "Father in heaven, please help us free my brother. Please spare everyone's life. Amen."

"You weren't kidding about short. I wish all prayers were so short and to the point." Tamo chuckled, then sobered. "We do need help … if God exists … and cares."

Her curiosity rose for an instant. How much did Tamo know

about God? Why did he find a belief in his existence so hard? But those questions had to wait for a better time.

They headed up the hill and stole along the row of trees, neither saying a word until they reached the place where they had already tied one end of the enlarged line around a sturdy tree trunk. Earlier in the afternoon, after tying a large rock into the other end of the line, Tamo had lowered it down the cliff and raised it back up. The snapped pine tree leaving Tamo in the cavern had run through her mind. Her heart had thumped the whole time the line was being tested. A failure while Tamo actually descended the cliff—unthinkable!

The scattered clouds in the western sky changed from orange and pink to ash gray. The full moon shone brightly, promising helpful visibility for positioning themselves and unhelpful visibility for revealing their attack prematurely. Her heart was madly thumping again.

Tamo leaned toward her. "You should get ready at the ladder now," he whispered, "but be sure to stay flat until you see me going down. When you reach the beach, remember, keep back. Don't make any noise. Don't do *anything* unless I have trouble inside the shack."

"I understand," she whispered back, resisting the impulse to move away. He really hadn't needed to get right in her face. However, she wouldn't think of objecting. He was risking his *life* to rescue Daisuke, having known him for only a few weeks. Why he would show such kindness was a total mystery—something most civilized people wouldn't do, let alone a barbarian.

"Not a strong wind tonight," Tamo added, glancing at the tree line. "That's good for my descent and your arrow … if needed." He turned to give his attention to the rope.

After lifting a silent prayer again for the help they

desperately needed, she crept toward the ladder.

When he slid over the edge of the cliff, she climbed down the rungs to the ledge. Just then, Bolt dragged her tied-up, wriggling brother, still gagged, farther into the shack. Did the pirate know they were about to attack? Even if he didn't, Bolt might not be where Tamo expected to find him. But she couldn't warn him. He had already disappeared into the cliff's shadows.

The only choice was to go forward. A samurai's daughter had to stand strong. More than that, she was also a Christ follower. She could face death.

But could Tamo?

Using her brother's techniques, she soundlessly crept the rest of the way to the pebbly beach. Tamo's shadowy form hovered above the shack's driftwood roof. Then it dissolved into the rough rooftop. She kept well back and positioned her bow and an arrow, as though targeting a bird.

But the target wasn't a bird. It was a person. Her fingers trembled. If her hands didn't behave, she might miss not only the pirate, but the whole shack. She sent up another prayer for help.

Suddenly a rumbling crash made her jump. The shack's roof must have collapsed! Seconds later, the pirate lit a coconut-oil candle, obviously unscathed by any rock or Tamo's sudden entry.

Sara moved closer, then froze as the pirate yanked out a knife. Tamo, now visible, whipped out his knife, too, and raised it with a harsh cry.

Bolt lashed out with his hook. He knocked Tamo's knife across the room, then spun with his own knife glinting in the air.

"Bolt!" Sara yelled, unable to force the arrow to fly.

He glanced in her direction.

Tamo shoved Bolt's hand away and dove under him. Both rolled on the shack's floor.

She had stopped trembling, but she couldn't get a clear shot.

The pirate, on his knees, swung a piece of the fallen driftwood at Tamo's head.

Tamo ducked, then grabbed the piece and wrenched it away from the pirate as he twisted up.

As quick as a cat on a mouse, the pirate pounced on his knife. He latched his hook under Tamo's armpit, dragging him to his knees.

Sara's chest constricted. She gasped for breath.

Bolt drew back his arm to plunge the knife.

She let the arrow fly, aiming for Bolt's arm. Instead, it hit the knife, which spun away.

Both men scrambled for it.

"Stop, Bolt! I will not miss your chest!" she yelled.

Bolt hesitated, and Tamo grasped the pirate's knife.

"Come out! Sit on a boulder! Then you live!" She had never spoken a command before and wondered at the sudden strength of her voice.

"So the mousy mouse turned into a rat too," Bolt snarled, obeying her by using his crutch to hop over the sand in front of his shack and hobble forward—straight forward, not toward the nearest boulder.

"Go sit, Bolt!" she yelled. Steadying her feet, she pulled the second arrow back, ready to release it. She commanded her shaking body to cooperate.

Bolt stopped, leaned on his crutch, then made an abrupt turn.

She swallowed hard. Had God helped her to hold back for an extra moment?

Bolt propped one leg against the rock and partially sat. "You remember this, lil' rat. Snakes eat mice and ugly rats. And who has the snake?"

She kept her arrow aimed at the pirate, but followed his gaze toward the shack. Instead of going after Bolt to knife him, Tamo had removed her brother's gag and was cutting away the rope binding him. In another glance, she saw the monkey take off through the hole in the roof, so it must have been hiding in the cave.

She began backing away, still with the arrow aimed squarely at Bolt. She could see more of the shack behind him as she got farther back on the beach. Tamo had placed part of the roof's driftwood on the ground in front of the shack and was helping Daisuke across. Her brother had an unsteady shuffle, but finally the two made their way past her. They called to her while climbing to the ledge, and she fled after them. When she looked back, the pirate had walked away from the boulder.

"Wait!" Bolt hollered. "Don't leave me without me knife. I'll starve."

"Good riddance," Tamo said, halfway up the ladder. His hands moved onto Daisuke's waist, helping secure him.

"You murderers! Thieves! Have pity!" The last words ended in a whine.

To Sara's horror, her brother pushed away from Tamo at the top of the ridge and stood dangerously close to the edge, weaving. She rushed up the final rungs and struggled not to scream at him to move back.

"You can have this one." When Daisuke raised his arm, the knife's steel caught the edge of a moonbeam.

"Don't! He tried to kill us!" Tamo grabbed for her brother's arm.

Daisuke threw his knife down to the bottom of the bluff. "You can find knife below," he rasped out. "If you use for evil, evil comes to you."

"You're hopeless," Tamo muttered, as Daisuke backed away from the edge.

A wave of awe surged through Sara. No, it wasn't wise to spare the wicked pirate. But it was merciful.

"See there, sailor," the pirate called. "The Japan boy's more Christian than you."

"Reckon so," Tamo called back. "He is one, and I'm not. And I wouldn't be so reckless."

"Knife is no problem," Daisuke said, facing Tamo, his voice weaker. "He needs it to live. If he escapes cove, he not need knife to kill us at night."

Tamo shook his head in disgust. "Hardly encouraging for a good night's sleep. What happened tonight wasn't child's play, you know. If you'd kept the knife, we could have gotten rid of the villain without you dirtying your samurai hands."

"To keep knife would dirty my hands. Now I need knife from you. You not need two. We are a team, yes?"

Tamo muttered something, but handed the knife over.

Her brother stumbled. "Hard to breathe. Maybe ribs are hurt."

Tamo leapt beside him. "Here, lean on me." He stooped and positioned Daisuke's arm across his shoulders. "I didn't know it was you I was coming down on. Should have expected Bolt to change where you lay."

"Talk later in cave."

Sara moved to the other side of Daisuke, so she could lend support too. As they moved slowly across the ridge and down the hill, more like snails than people, her relief at having defeated the pirate morphed into dread. Her brother couldn't die! Not leave her on the island, squeezed between the two barbarians—although one turned out to be far better than the other.

When they reached the cave and had helped Daisuke lie down, Tamo waited, looking from her to her brother and back at her, until Daisuke told him he wasn't dying, to leave and get some rest. Then he murmured as Tamo turned to go, "Thank you. You have honor. Now I can trust you with my life."

Tamo blinked, like clearing his eyes. "That's good. Your opinion means a lot, especially since we're three peas in a pod—stuck together. And I sure made the right choice in accepting your deal." He gave a wry smile.

Sara handed him a lit torch. He thanked her and stepped out of the cave. Then he turned and gave a deep bow, not to her brother, to her—to honor her! Warmth coursed through her.

After she prepared soup, Daisuke pushed up against the wall, took the bowl she offered and drank it all. Then his jaw tightened. "Do you know the beastly monkey caused all this trouble?" He'd reverted to their usual Japanese. "After Bolt captured it, he tried to bargain with it."

"No, I didn't know." She picked up his empty bowl, then glanced at his face. "I-I'm confused."

"Why's that?"

"I didn't think you cared what happened to the monkey."

"The monkey didn't matter to me, but you cared about the pest. That mattered." He cocked his head, and she responded with a bow, at a loss for words. "You did well with the bow and arrow, Sa-*chan*," he continued. "You are the daughter of a samurai. It is true." He nodded as she clasped her hand over her mouth. Then he slid down and closed his eyes.

After watching him breathe for a few moments, she stepped outside the cave, hardly able to contain the happiness bubbling within. Daisuke was proud of her! He'd never indicated anything so amazing before. Not only that, but he'd tried to rescue the animal he disliked—for her. And he had given his approval to the barbarian, who couldn't be a barbarian deep inside. She smiled to herself, remembering Tamo's bow.

Best of all was how her brother had shown pity. The pirate's death would have been permissible after he drew his knife, even praiseworthy by the samurai code. But the knife had been given back by her brother through mercy. The God in heaven above must have touched Daisuke's heart, and he had obeyed his Liege.

The valley lay quiet before her, the still ponds reflecting the moonlight. The water's silvery sheen gleamed as smooth as her mirror. Beyond the ponds, ethereal light revealed the tall grasses and the sides of the rocky hills. Above the valley, the ridge's dark forest swept in an arc, a majestic sentinel.

How had she missed such beauty before?

She could almost hear her mother recite the poet Sodō's ancient haiku. *Yado no haru. Nani mo naki koso. Nani mo are.* "Within my lodging—In the spring, there is nothing—There is everything."

She gave a contented sigh. She wasn't in her home in the spring with the gorgeous cherry blossoms, but splendor surrounded her, too. And she had her brother's affection, Tamo's friendship, and her Master, Jesus, with her. At least for the moment, she had everything.

CHAPTER 18

Mid-November, 1862

At the consulate's vestibule, Terry pulled his feet out of his leather ankle boots, supplied by Mr. Pendleton so he'd look decent for church services and social gatherings. He never imagined he would live in the house of a man like Mr. Pendleton, a preacher for all intents and purposes. But his employer was nothing like the preacher Tom and he had eagerly spurned when they ran from their grandparents' farm.

After sliding into slippers, he followed the manservant to the room where he had waited during the trial and where Mrs. Cardiff conducted the English class. He stood at the door until *Kadifu-sensei*, as the class called her, noticed him.

"Welcome, Mr. Ballard." She motioned for him to take a cushion at the low table she called a *kotatsu*. "You are right on time."

After the requisite bow, he sat and extended his legs into the pit under the table's quilt, glad he wouldn't have to kneel back on his heels for an hour. Now that the days had turned chilly, the warmth coming through his socks from covered coals at the pit's base were a bonus.

While she gently swayed, rocking her baby to sleep in the papoose, Mrs. Cardiff chatted with her four students, seated in pairs facing one another across the table. Ichi and his sixteen-year-old sister, Mia, were a fisherman's son and daughter, and Mia's two close friends, Aki and Aiya, were daughters of a sweet-potato vendor. They had made good progress, considering they had dived into the language by learning the ABCs only one year earlier. Now they could read and speak in short English sentences.

The day's topic turned out to be the body's five senses. Mrs. Cardiff touched her eyes, asked what they were called, then went on to her ears, nose, cheek's skin, and tongue—amid the girls' giggles. After that, she extended a chart to Terry, which he took, although wary of her expectations.

"Now, Teacher Ballard, please hold up the chart and read each sentence for us," she directed. "Pause at the blank so the students can say the correct word." She tilted her head at him. "Your time of merely observing is over."

Happy for the easy assignment, he read the sentence next to the drawing of an eye: *The eye gives us our ...* The three girls chorused *sight*. The boy Ichi continued his sullen silence Terry had observed the previous week. Since Mrs. Cardiff ignored his bad attitude, he overlooked it, too, although the boy irritated him, like an untreated hangnail. As the girls continued down the chart with him, Terry imagined the delight his mother, who admired teachers, would take in his task. However, when his throat tightened, he rebuffed any more futile thoughts of home.

Next on the agenda was a game to see which student could name the most colors by pointing to different objects and giving their colors. Surprisingly, Ichi won by one point when he came up with "scarlet" for a flower in a scroll hanging in the alcove.

"Very good, Ichi," Mrs. Cardiff said after a second too long, obviously flummoxed. "Here is the prize." She handed him a quill pen.

The boy gave a dismissive shrug and handed it to his sister. "I fish. Maybe she write. Prob'ly she use for scratch my back."

Mrs. Cardiff hesitated, then gave a gracious smile. "You are kind to share. I am sure Mia will use it well."

Terry wanted to opine that even a *disrespectful fisherman* could have occasions to write and that the lady should be thanked for the prize. But he bit back his words when Mrs. Cardiff caught his eye and gave a quick shake of her head. The lady's patience far surpassed that of his New York teachers. Maybe the culture, which seemed to bend over backwards to keep the peace, dictated such tolerance.

"Now we will use some of today's words while we study the sixth chapter in Matthew, verses 22 and 23 today." Mrs. Cardiff passed out papers with the Bible lesson printed in simplified English and in Japanese. "Jesus talked not only about our eyes' seeing or being blind"—she held up a picture card with the word *blind* printed on it—"he also talked about another way we can have sight or be blind." She translated these words even though the girls were already nodding.

While the group slowly read the sentences out loud in English, Terry mulled over what other meanings for sight or blindness might be intended by Jesus' analogy. Maybe having knowledge or lacking it? Or faith? Or if Mrs. Cardiff gave it a Japanese twist, it might be related to the country's obsession with artistry or even politeness. Since he resisted bowing more than once, while others often bobbed up and down multiple times, he'd fit in that mannerism's "blind" category.

He read the sentences again to himself.

22 The light of the body is the eye.
If your eye sees well, all your body will be
full of light.
23 But if your eye is bad, your whole body
will be full of darkness.
If the light in you is darkness, how great is
that darkness!

Mrs. Cardiff praised the group's effort, then pointed to the *blind* picture card. "First, we will talk about our body without having sight. What beautiful or important things does a blind person not see?"

The three girls rattled off flowers, colors, flying birds, and Ichi muttered sharks.

"Now, think about *colors*, which is what you said, Mia," she continued. "Is there a way to describe the colors red or green or blue for a blind person?"

"Maybe … red is hot." Mia offered a sheepish smile.

"That not right," Ichi blustered while Terry still analyzed the possibilities. "Red not burn hand. Blind never understand color."

The sensei dismissed Ichi's rudeness with a shooing wave of her hand. "Sometimes we think red is a hot color and blue is a cold color, so that is a good try, and Mia is right that colors are important things we *cannot* see. Also, Ichi, you are right. A blind person can never really *understand* the idea of colors and many other things as well. It is sad, is it not?"

Terry nodded along with the class, while thinking the lady's husband wasn't the only tactful diplomat in the family.

She extended her hand back toward Ichi. "Ichi said blind persons miss seeing a shark. What other things might hurt a blind person?"

The girls jumped right in again, mentioning a snake, samurai on horses, getting lost in woods.

Remembering the large placards bearing the government's seal posted near the settlement's entrance/exit gates, Terry added the danger of not reading official notices. When his words were translated, Ichi snorted and the girls groaned, but no one offered to expound on their dislike of the notices.

"Now, what do you think could be the other way people can have sight or be blind?" Mrs. Cardiff called on Aki, who was trying not to snicker behind her hand-covered mouth.

Aki managed to control her giggles long enough to speak. "Maybe person blind by not know love of girl."

The girls tittered for what seemed like an eternity. Ichi scowled. Terry felt suddenly older. Did all teachers want to roll their eyes at their students?

Baby Ayako woke up and whimpered. Mrs. Cardiff jiggled the papoose with her hands while she cooed Ayako's name and rocked.

When the baby had dozed off again, Mrs. Cardiff held up her copy of the passage. "Now I will tell you the meaning, *imi,* of what we read. People who are dark inside are wrong in their ideas about truth. They cannot know why they are living." The lady translated her words into Japanese, then continued. "Aki, they do miss the best kind of love. It is a terrible darkness. But when people are right in their thinking and feelings because they are related to their Creator God, they learn their life's purpose, their *mokuteki.* They can know the best love. Do you know how we can get this light for ourselves?"

Terry had no idea. The puzzled expressions on the others' faces as the translation proceeded showed he wasn't alone.

"Jesus said he could give it himself because he was not just a good teacher. He was God's Son, like we talked about before."

Ichi shook his head even before the translation finished.

"What do you want to say, Ichi?" A firm expression replaced Mrs. Cardiff 's smile. "Remember, you may question what I tell you, politely."

"I say people with Jesus *blind*. People like me *see*."

"So, the question is this: how can we know if Jesus spoke truth?" The sensei held up the Bible. "This book has accounts by eyewitnesses of Jesus. An eyewitness"—she pointed to her eye—"saw what happened. When Jesus was alive, the people saw miracles, *kiseki*, with their own eyes. After he died, more than five hundred eyewitnesses saw Jesus alive again. Five hundred men and women."

"Eyewitnesses can lie." Ichi looked like he had won the last alabaster marble in a game for keeps.

She nodded. "That is more to think about. Here is the answer. Many eyewitnesses of Jesus were killed for talking about what they had seen because the government at that time did not like Christians. Like the government here now." She turned to Terry. "At least one of those gate placards you saw offered rewards for turning in suspected Christians, most of whom would lose their homes and be forced to work in the underground mines until their early deaths. You may remember that I told you why I had been imprisoned once."

"Oh, I didn't know that's what was posted." Terry shook his head. "That's really ... severe."

"Yes, it is severe." She addressed Ichi again. "People do not suffer and die for what they *know* is a lie."

Ichi shook his head during the translation and swept a finger under his nose.

She tilted her head toward Terry. "I was not the only one

imprisoned. Mia was too, and Ichi had to step up to help his sister get released. We know firsthand how the government opposes Christianity. The freedom in the International Settlement to host Bible studies, like this one, is the governor's compensation for my unjust arrest and the resulting uproar among the foreign residents."

She looked at Ichi and pointed to the Bible. "We will keep looking for light in this book."

"I not find light there," Ichi scoffed. "I like you. You help sister in prison. I hate Evil Religion."

"It's not evil," Terry burst out. "I don't care what bad thing happened in your country's ancient history. Many good people are Christians in America." A second later he grimaced. What was he doing, taking up for Christians? It was questionable if he was one and might not even desire to be one. And he had definitely not exercised the ever-so-important tact.

Ichi screwed up his mouth as if he wanted to spit in Terry's face. "You barbarian. You know *nothing!*"

The three girls stared at the boy.

"I tell Father," his sister proclaimed.

Ichi's face turned red. "You do, you find shark in darkness."

"Ichi, you know a better way to act." Mrs. Cardiff's sharp tone showed she had at last gotten irritated with the fool. "You should say you are sorry."

Ichi wadded up the paper with the Bible passage, dropped it into Terry's lap, and stood. He bowed to Mrs. Cardiff and mumbled, "Sorry," then stalked out.

Mrs. Cardiff looked at Mia. "Please do not tell your father. Your brother is still recovering from the fright we had at the prison, and he struggles about his close connection with foreigners like me and Teacher Ballard."

The girl stood and bowed low, apparently agreeing not to

tattle. Then retook her position. "He is some darkness," she said softly. "Maybe me too. But here I feel light, not blind."

Mrs. Cardiff's eyes sparkled. "What a perfect thing to say to end our lesson."

She rose, managing not to wake the baby, and rang a bell hanging on the wall twice. "I have a treat for everyone today," she said as a maid appeared with tea cups and slices of cake.

As far as Terry could tell, he hadn't gotten any light during the discussion, probably because of that stupid troublemaker, Ichi or Itchy or Witchy. But the sight of the cake lit up his senses. It had been ages since he'd had any treat like cake or cookies. The ship's second-rate duff pudding—steamed dough with nary a raisin in it—and Mr. Pendleton's custard didn't come close.

While he ate the sponge cake and savored its mild orange flavor, he sifted through the last hour's lesson. Maybe there was more to the Christian faith than he'd realized. He wasn't going to swallow everything hook, line, and sinker. But knowing more about the eyewitnesses could be good, even if it was to put Ichi in his place. He'd quote a few of the verses and politely drive the fool crazy.

CHAPTER 19

Tom stood still, squinting at something on the horizon, refusing to get his hopes up. Three times since being marooned weeks ago, he had imagined a ship's topsails. This time, however, the mirage was becoming larger … and larger.

The ship's white topgallant sails stood out against the sky. His eyes weren't lying.

He ran back along the ridge to the path through the forest and clambered down the hill toward Dice and Sara's cave.

"Hey! Hey! Come see! Come help!" he shouted as he ran. The two had to respond in the next minute, or he'd climb back up and flag down the ship by himself.

Dice stepped onto the rocks outside his cave, put his hand up to shade his eyes, and peered at Tom.

"A ship! Maybe a whaler! For real! Grab torches and something to wave. I'll bring a cattail too."

Within a couple of minutes, Tom was racing back up to the ridge with Dice pounding close by despite his still-healing injuries. Sara trailed behind them, carrying the bucket of coals and a packet of duck fat. When they reached the overlook, the ship's sails were clear although far away.

"Go high in that tree," Dice ordered, pointing to the tallest pine for Tom. "I climb this one. If we need to light torches, Sara shall climb half up with bucket."

There was no time to argue. Tom did as told. This might be the rescue! This very day he could be taking his first step toward home! Home!

He was well into the climb when Dice called over, "We must see if a pirate ship. A whaler can have pirate rulers. That big danger! Also, see if it is Western ship that belongs to America or England—like ones you and our sensei call safe. Don't wave. Don't light a torch till we sure."

Tom yelled back, "All right," not choosing to give away his own intention. He'd finally accepted the near-zero chance Terry could get a ship to hunt for a valueless hunk of rock anytime soon. Turtles wouldn't be much of a draw, and although there might really be pirate treasure on the island, who would count on that?

He looked at the ship again. It was still too far away to tell anything about it. Of course, any country's ship would be great, not just American or English. And if there was no clear sign and an equal chance of it being a pirate ship or not a pirate ship, he would light his torch and wave. Weak fear would not mess up their one-chance-in-a-thousand-days rescue. Missing a true chance—not on his life!

At the treetop, with his hand wrapped around the narrow tip, he scrutinized the ship's progress. Closer now, it had slowed, maybe stopped. Then he saw the reason. A boat, rowed for chasing and harpooning whales, was being hoisted onto the ship's deck. Did a whale get away? It didn't seem the weather could be a big enough problem for the ship to end the hunt although the waves were rough, stirred up by a raincloud in the distance. At any rate, it had to be a whaleship.

"Coals for my torch!" Tom cried to Sara. He started crashing through the branches to meet her halfway. "It's a whaler!"

"No, wait!" Dice yelled.

"Can't wait! After the boats are in, it'll move fast, away from that squall." He looked down through the branches. Sara wasn't climbing up. "Listen! Bring the blasted coals!" he called.

"No, Sara!" Dice yelled.

Tom made it to the ground and headed toward Sara.

She dashed to the edge of the ridge, where she lifted the bucket in the air and raised her other hand. "Stop or I throw this!"

Tom drew up short. The ship would pass by the island in a few minutes. With the rough waves, it wouldn't send in a boat unless there was a reason—like people needing help. He ran back to the pine and shot up through the branches. He didn't need a torch. He'd wave his red shirt. Any minute now, as long as the ship maintained its course, it would be close enough for the shirt to be visible to a lookout with a spyglass in the crow's nest.

Reaching the top, he tore off his shirt and waved it. They had to see him! Another ship might *never* pass again.

Something yanked hard on his right leg. He grabbed for the trunk to keep from falling and almost dropped the shirt. It was Dice! He tried to kick the idiot, but Dice held on and continued yanking. Tom's left leg was on the last branch sturdy enough to hold his weight, so he fought with just the one Dice held, jerking it back and forth. Up and down.

Finally, he pulled loose and stomped on either Dice's hand or head. The boy cried out, then muttered in Japanese. In the moment of reprieve, Tom waved his shirt frantically, then swept his eyes over his whole field of vision.

Another ship, canvas full spread, met his eyes. It was racing forward in the stiffening wind, clearly chasing the first one.

Pirates! No doubt! He hesitated for a minute, his heart hammering. This could be the one chance in years—or in his whole life—to escape the island. Maybe even get treasure. But did he want to become a hoodlum? Or become their slave if the crew rejected him?

Below him, Sara had fallen to her knees, probably praying.

What was he thinking? Blood rushed from his face, and his stomach lurched. It wouldn't just be him who'd be on the pirate ship. Sara would be captured and misused, and Dice too. The brother and sister would be destroyed.

He crumpled his shirt up and rounded to the back side of the tree just as Dice yelled, "Pirates, Tamo! Pirates!"

Tom started down fast and came even with Dice, who glared at him through the branches. "Sorry," he grated out and continued climbing down.

The three of them crawled into the edge of the forest and watched the drama before them.

The second ship, a fast, light schooner, had hoisted the black flag of crossed cutlasses bracketing an hourglass and skull. It was closing in on the whaler. When the schooner came within rifle range, a few pirates were picked off the rigging by the whaler's sharpshooters. But the result didn't prevent the villains from tacking into a broadside position to fire their cannon.

Tom choked back acid. Their hope of rescue would be pounded to the bottom of the ocean or taken by the pirates as a prize. It was horrible! Unfair! Hideous! They had been so close, within mere minutes of a rescue, and it was being destroyed in front of their eyes.

The whaler ran up a white flag of defeat and furled its main sails. So, the ship itself would survive, but only those men worth a ransom would keep their lives, and with small hope of a future release.

All at once the space between the two ships filled with flaming arrows, launched from the whaler. The foresail of the schooner caught fire, then sails on the main mast and the topsails. Pirates scaled the rigging, trying to save sails not yet fully in flames. The schooner began to drift as others of the crew scurried around the deck, intent on quenching the spotty blazes flaring up. The whaler was zipping on now, its riggers apparently having stayed where they could instantly unfurl canvas.

The pirate ship spread its salvaged jibs and spanker sail—all that remained of its canvas after the crew managed to extinguish the flames. The sails caught only enough wind to keep the ship moving slowly forward. Tom could hardly breathe until the crippled ship limped on by, foregoing repairs at the island. Yet the odds were against a permanent reprieve. His red shirt, if seen, had revealed a castaway, useful for ransom demands or as a slave, or both. The crew wouldn't just hunt him down either. When they came across Bolt, they'd hear about Dice and Sara.

Tom dropped his head into his hands. The two from Japan would never forgive him. Dice's words about trusting him with his life would be thrown into his face. And the whale ship was gone, snatched away by the same wind that had brought the ship and taunted him. He was not going home.

Sobs he couldn't stop racked his body.

The raincloud moved over the island. He didn't try to protect himself as the wind whipped sheets of rain onto him and into the undergrowth next to him. Glancing up, he saw Dice and Sara had left. He rose and stepped out from the trees into the deluge.

The ridge was deserted. So was he.

CHAPTER 20

Terry's pulse raced. Zeke and his pal Joey stood less than ten yards from him, gabbing in front of the Dog's Tooth Saloon. He made a beeline for a side alley. He had kept an eye out for the *William Parton*'s return, afraid Captain Madison would somehow manage to overrule the trial's outcome, maybe by fabricating a new charge against him. The ship must have anchored fairly far out, other vessels' sails blocking its Croone and Co. house flag.

"Terrapin! Hold on there," Zeke called.

Terry groaned and wheeled toward the two sailors, trying to keep his facial expression empty of his hatred … and fear.

"Hey, heard you're not rottin' in prison after all. Bet you're chompin' at the bit, though, to rescue that big brother of yours." Zeke sounded almost congenial, in spite of the zero chance he cared.

"You're right. I am." He stayed where he was, hoping Zeke would keep his distance too.

"Been feeling sorta bad 'bout what happened." Zeke and Joey swaggered right up to him. "Might have somethin' fer you."

"Now what would that be?" Terry crossed his arms, ready to

reject any offer. Even if Zeke had the slightest inclination to help, giving real aid was beyond his ability. *Got a bill of sale to supply me a ship?* formed on his tongue, but he held back.

"How about the true coordinates of that island? Heard a third logbook in the Great Cabin is the correct one."

Terry's pulse pounded in his ears. Zeke had to be lying. Only a fool would believe him. Yet he was a relative of the guard assigned to the Great Cabin. He had bragged about his "uncle" letting him look around when the captain was elsewhere. If such a logbook existed, would it be possible for Zeke to reach it? Almost certainly, he was mocking Terry, eager to fillet him like a fisherman would his catch.

But what if he wasn't?

"Interested, eh? Come back in three hours. Two o'clock shore time." Zeke pointed at the saloon. "I'll be at the table farthest back, inside there."

Terry flinched. "Can't we meet right here? Who would notice your handing me a piece of paper?"

"Too public, little man. You don't hafta buy no drink if you're a teeto'ler."

"I was ordered to avoid saloons."

"Well then. Guess if ol' Tomcat's alive, he won't be rescued none too soon."

Pain radiated in Terry's chest. "Oh, tarnation! I'll be at that table." He looked Zeke square in the face. "And if this is on the up and up, I'd do 'bout anything to repay you."

"Now, don't get carried away, but that gold doubloon of your'n would be a nice thank ye gift." Zeke raised his eyebrows with a cunning grin.

"Of course. I'll bring it with me." So, the coin had been Zeke's goal. But the slimmest chance his slippery foe would divulge the coordinates was worth sacrificing the doubloon.

"And don't say nothin' to nobody. Got it?"

Terry nodded, his heart still beating wildly.

Zeke turned toward the harbor, and Terry hurried toward the Pendleton house, hugging the flour and sugar he'd been sent to buy from Jake's General Store.

Matsu met him in the vestibule, took the supplies from him, then gestured for Terry to follow him toward the parlor, where voices could be heard. The servant bowed at the door to the room's occupants and moved aside for Terry to enter.

Mr. Pendleton stood next to Consul Cardiff, who was pointing to a paper on the back table. His sponsor turned and beckoned Terry over. "Ahh, here's the boy, John." He tipped his head toward Terry. "He's doing well. Cooperative. Good at all his tasks. A fine student too."

"Happy to hear it." The consul smiled at Terry. "You will be interested in what I have to report concerning the island where your brother is apparently marooned."

"Yes, sir, I would. I certainly would." A spark of hope rose. Maybe he wouldn't have to meet Zeke, give up the doubloon, which was actually Tom's, and violate the ban on saloons.

"I suppose you've heard the *William Parton* has returned to Nagasaki." Cardiff didn't wait for a reply. "When Captain Madison made the required report at the consulate, I requested the coordinates for the island. He sent a messenger with it in the evening. Happened to be the boy who brought the letters supporting you during the ship's first call here. I asked this boy, Jim Mankin, what he knew about the squall during the night preceding your brother's misfortune."

The consul looked at Mr. Pendleton. "My dear wife was curious about that. She had spoken with Mr. Ballard during the trial and afterward voiced several suspicions worthy of consideration."

"I've had my suspicions too," Mr. Pendleton added.

The consul returned his gaze to Terry. "At any rate, the boy said there was no squall. He remembered seeing the moon half-lit and wondering when it would rain again since it had been about two weeks. Of course, I didn't put too much importance on a discrepancy about a squall's occurrence.

"Jim was anxious to get back to the ship, but I asked him to stay a minute so I could read the message and he could take my reply. While I was writing my response, I told the boy the coordinates given by the captain would be invaluable for finding the missing man.

"Now here's the interesting part. Jim asked me if he could say a word, 'all confidential like,' to quote him. I told him to say ahead, that I knew how to keep a confidence—as I know Mr. Pendleton does, and I trust you do too, Mr. Ballard."

"Yes, sir. I do." His heart warmed momentarily at the thought of Jim. He could never ask for a better friend.

"Jim said Captain Madison kept a third logbook in addition to the one next to the binnacle and the captain's official logbook in the wardroom. He had seen it once in the Great Cabin when making a routine delivery."

Terry drew in a sharp breath. So Zeke was right. There was a third record, a correct one.

"The captain had slammed the logbook closed when he saw that Jim wasn't the person he was expecting," the consul continued. "Highly irate, he bawled Jim out for not making himself known faster."

"So, if the man has something to hide," Mr. Pendleton interjected, "getting the right information about the island may be harder than pulling a tiger's tooth."

"Yes. It turns out the so-called 'official' coordinates he sent fall squarely on an island which has been properly plotted on maps and has recently become a Japanese outpost." The consul swiped his fingers over what Terry saw was a detailed map, lying on the table. "Mr. Ballard, I recall you were informed the island's coordinates were not the same as those found on maps—correct me if I'm wrong."

"Yes, sir. The inaccuracy was part of the reason Captain Madison gave for not telling the whaler about my brother."

"Then it looks like the captain knowingly sent me wrong information. I'd wager the island is more distant from Japan and farther to the southeast, a less verified area. Without the correct coordinates, a ship could look for that speck of an island for months before finding and correctly identifying it as the one to be searched. Maybe never identify it.

"Now here's what I want to know. Is there any way the boy Jim could get the coordinates from the third log for the morning of October eighteenth, also for October sixteenth, seventeenth, nineteenth, and twentieth, allowing a leeway on dates?"

Terry sucked in an agitated breath. "No, sir. There's always a guard posted for the Great Cabin and wardroom. And if he could even sneak into the room without permission, he'd be caught sure as the world, then flogged or keelhauled if he couldn't give a good-enough excuse. Jim wouldn't survive that."

"All right. That's what I feared. I am going to adopt an unusual plan for obtaining the coordinates—one I'm not yet at liberty to reveal. Admittedly, the chance for its success is quite low without help from above. Mr. Pendleton, my wife, and I will pray about the undertaking. Perhaps you will add your own prayers for a good result and also for patience. I can only imagine how hard waiting must be."

"It is very hard, sir." In fact, unbearable with Tom's life hanging in the balance.

Mr. Pendleton nodded at Terry. "Yes, indeed. We fully sympathize. Now, my boy, you will need to attend to your studies so you don't fall behind. Find me later today when you have carefully read the third chapter of *The Wealth of Nations*. Be prepared to explain how the division of labor is dependent upon the market's expansion, according to the author, and how that dependence relates to Japan these days in your opinion. Remember also to study the fourth through seventh chapters of the Book of Acts."

"I will, sir ..." His voice wobbled so much he couldn't continue.

Mr. Pendleton smiled and raised his hand in a dismissal.

Terry hesitated in the hallway before heading to the kitchen to help with the lunch preparation. Should he go back in and tell the men about Zeke's supposed change of heart and the unbelievable offer—an offer making more sense now?

But the two men would certainly proclaim it was a trick and order him not to meet Zeke, especially in a saloon. He couldn't obey such an order. He had to risk looking foolish and being sneered at, the same as when he'd tried to jump ship. Luckily, he had read ahead in *The Wealth of Nations* and the Holy Bible. After meeting Zeke, he could easily make it back to the house in time to meet with Mr. Pendleton.

No matter what it cost him, he couldn't reject any chance to help Tom.

CHAPTER 21

In a small audience room tucked away in the domicile of Nagasaki's Governor Yamasaki, Consul Cardiff bowed to the governor, to Chief Inspector Sato, and to a retainer named Fujino, who all returned equally deep bows. Then he knelt on a dais facing the governor's dais. Because of the confidential conference he'd requested, none of the dozens of samurai normally on guard were present. As required, one enforcement inspector stayed in the room to record the proceedings for the officials in the capital Edo, but this *metsuki* always showed the utmost discretion, according to Governor Yamasaki. Although John was fairly fluent in Japanese, he'd asked his father-in-law, Taguchi Kenshin, to accompany him as interpreter. Mr. Taguchi remained standing to one side. Sato and Fujino took their places on cushions.

As soon as the refreshments of green tea and bean cakes had been consumed and the tobacco pipes had been puffed sufficiently, the governor wiped his fingertips and asked John to present his concern.

"Unfortunately, I must begin with a suspicion of unlawful activities by a merchantman flying the United States of America flag." John spoke slowly for his father-in-law's benefit. "The ship has returned from a trip to Shanghai, where nearly all trading houses deal in the illicit opium trade."

"The curse of opium, is it?" Yamasaki asked after the translation. "Do you have reason to suspect this one ship more than the hundreds trading in our port since your arrival here?"

John sucked in a breath. A natural question, and one without an easy response. "An odd incident aroused my initial concern. The ship's captain provided false coordinates for a certain island. My misgivings were heightened by an unofficial report that he kept a different record in addition to the usual two logbooks."

Yamasaki twiddled his fingers for a minute. "Why did you care about the island's location, if I may ask?"

John steeled himself to be rebuffed if these no-nonsense officials guessed his primary incentive. "Contrary to accepted practices, the sailors assigned to reprovision the ship left an American citizen on the island without conducting a proper search for the missing man. The captain displayed an extraordinary haste to leave the area. His disregard for his crewman's life and his refusal to communicate the island's location naturally raised distrust."

Retainer Fujino motioned to the governor, who gave a curt nod. "If I may be so bold, may we know if this marooned man is an especially important samurai or official in America?"

The governor frowned and instructed Mr. Taguchi to forebear translating their exchange. "Retainer Fujino," he said stiffly in formal Japanese, "there are no samurai in America. Instead, the nation has fighting men lacking in most samurai skills. And the consul's countrymen hold that rank is immaterial in regard to their common law, be he an official, a peasant, a sailor, or even a merchant."

"I apologize for my ignorant question." Fujino's rigid posture showed no sign of embarrassment.

John kept himself from showing any reaction to the governor's indirect criticisms.

Having ordered Interpreter Taguchi to resume translating, the governor asked why this captain would be uncooperative and deceitful, to John's way of thinking.

John nodded. "I'm concerned the captain could be conspiring with pirates using the island in opium trade." A real possibility although outside a consul's normal jurisdiction.

The governor pursed his lips. "What is it you wish from me?"

"If the *William Parton* could be forbidden to further offload cargo until it is searched, your efficient inspectors could confirm the presence or absence of opium. During the inspection in the captain's Great Cabin, before the genuine log could be changed, a demand could be made to see the recent route of the ship before its first call here. My ship's navigator could accompany your men and observe the correct coordinates."

"Ahh, you see, Retainer Fujino and Inspector Sato," the governor responded, "the good American's concern with one marooned sailor has occasioned a greater animosity for opium trade and piracy. Isn't that so, Consul?"

John winced at the droll comment, but gave a slight bow of acknowledgement. "I hope it is a timely concern although originating from a more personal one."

Yamasaki narrowed his eyes. "Searching a ship for opium is reasonable enough and often carried out. Demanding to examine logbooks because of a hunch about piracy would be a highly irregular procedure. Before agreeing to this, perhaps you could consent to return the favor, a *tit for tat* in your language." The governor's eyebrows climbed up his forehead.

"If possible, I would be happy to be of service." John offered a sedate smile while fearing an impossible request.

"Could my country depend on your trading company's sea-going steamer to flush out any pirates commandeering the island if it's not far from our waters?"

John drew in a breath. "I desire to offer my ship, *but* the escort of the *USS Observer*, currently anchored in the harbor here, would be the deciding factor. I sent a courier earlier today to the American Resident Minister in Edo informing him of the possibility of the uncharted Pacific island's misuse by pirates. My ship, the *Retriever,* leaves in two weeks to trade on America's west coast. *If* the minister's approval is given in time and my navigator learns the coordinates, I can assure you the ship will detour to the island with the frigate's escort."

"And so, you may aid your lone citizen." The governor fingered his tobacco pouch during the translation, then gazed out at his shady garden, and finally turned his attention back to John. "I heard from my predecessor you feared the loss of your brother last year in America's war. I hope that turned out to be wrong information."

"Uh, yes, fortunately."

"I gather you would have risked your life for your brother—understandable loyalty. I am surprised at your efforts to aid this marooned sailor—a stranger, it seems. Yet your odd determination appears ... beneficial."

John's spirit gave an unspoken cheer.

"My government also wants piracy eliminated." Yamasaki glanced at the *metsuki*, who began writing more energetically. "Thus, due to your good intention, Inspector Sato will see to the thorough search of the suspected ship and carry out the demand to examine all the logs today. Your company's navigator and our interpreter here"—he inclined his head toward John's father-in-law—"will meet him at the ship?"

"Yes, I will see to it. And I have here the false coordinates the captain gave." Stifling the temptation to beam, lest he be considered childish by samurai standards, he stood and handed the paper to the governor with a bow.

Yamasaki stood to return the bow, then passed the paper to Chief Inspector Sato and gave orders concerning the inspection and the securing of cargo. Once again sitting, he turned to John. "Perhaps you have other tasks to see to also, Consul Cardiff?"

After their usual exchange of pleasantries, the governor held up a hand. "I wish Godspeed," he said in English.

John offered his final bow, covering his astonishment. "Thank you for such a fine wish," he managed to say without any hitch—as though the governor, charged with carrying out the rigid laws against Christianity, hadn't just used a word associated with the "Evil Religion."

While guards escorted John through the labyrinth leading to the front courtyard, his appreciation of the interview's success increased. Undeniably, Terrence Ballard's pleas had gotten under his skin—spurring tenderness for a brother needing help and a compulsion to stand up for a victim of bullies. But what compassionate person wouldn't agree with aiding a desperate individual when feasible? And, of course, these efforts would be all the more worthwhile if the attempted rescue thwarted opium trade or piracy.

More than the governor could have guessed, he genuinely desired *Godspeed.*

CHAPTER 22

No one questioned Terry at the open saloon door. A barmaid winked at him as she flounced by. He peered through the smoke, trying to spot Zeke in the dull glow of the lanterns bracketed to the wall. The sailor waved to him from a back table.

Terry wove through the crowded room, trying to steady his nerves. From the three beer mugs on Zeke's table, the exchange clearly wouldn't be a private one. But whatever happened, he wouldn't act the coward. If he didn't learn the island's coordinates, the bullies might drop useful information unintentionally, like if the island had caves, or signs of inhabitants, or how much food there was besides turtles, clams, and crabs.

Terry took a seat opposite Zeke. "Sure appreciate your helping out." He forced a smile.

Zeke returned a smile closer to a smirk. "Wanna get you some water or juice, whatever young guys like you drink? Guess you didn't take a sup of that stolen wine, eh?" Zeke's flat eyes took on the menacing look of a shark's before he masked his expression.

"Didn't see or touch it, and I'll pass on a drink today. Did you manage to get the coordinates for the island?" The sooner he could leave, the better. He pushed the mug in front of him to the side.

"You got the doubloon?"

"Yes, it's on me." He'd hand it over even if Zeke was pulling his leg. The last thing he needed was to cause a brawl in a saloon.

"Hey, Turd. You jes got yourself in deep cow dung. Shouldn't be a thief, or help one." Zeke ogled him.

"What're you saying?" A shiver slithered up his spine.

Zeke pointed at something behind Terry.

Following Zeke's gaze, Terry strangled a groan. Joey and Billy were motioning to him, but they weren't the problem. A Japanese policeman next to them was also peering into the room.

"Better go peacefully." Zeke shook his finger at Terry and sniggered. "That consul's not gonna be pleased, and arguin' will jes make it worse."

Terry stared at him, his mind whirling. "I haven't stolen anything. You know that!"

"Maybe so, but I'm dang sure you knew my friend George shouldn't got a whippin'. You'll hear the charge any minute. Paid a fisher boy fer writin' out the Japanese." He scraped his chair back and stood. "Better not tarry, Terrapin. The policeman may make a scene."

Terry jumped up to meet the officer while he was still at the entrance. Hurrying through the room, passing drunks and raucous card games, he thought of choice words for Ichi, undoubtedly the only fisher boy knowing English in the settlement, or in the whole country, for that matter. Then he searched his mind for a way to communicate, his mouth dry. How could he have been such a fool?

The policeman grasped Terry's arm and pulled him out the door.

"Please get Mr. Pendleton." The policeman's grim expression worried him more than any disappointment he would cause his kind sponsor.

"Pendutan-*sama?*" The policeman relaxed his grip a little but still held Terry's arm as if he might flee down an alley.

"Not Pendleton," Joey said, shaking his head. "Consul Cardiff."

Oh grief, Terry moaned. The policeman had no right to hold him. He hadn't broken any laws. But what if the consul came and charged him with being in contempt of the court? He'd only been in the saloon for a few minutes, but his former judge might not care about the short time.

If only he could really escape … and end up at home in New York, out of all the craziness.

A second policeman pushed through the small group of spectators who gawked at the show. After the first policeman said something about *Pendutan* and *Kadifu*, the second officer set out.

It was the consul who showed up in no time at all. He nodded to the policeman still holding Terry's arm. "What is the matter here?" he asked, eyeing Terry and the accusers.

Before Terry could formulate his answer, Zeke stepped forward. "Terrence pocketed my gold doubloon when I walked o'er to the bar. I been showing it to these two friends."

His friends nodded their confirmation.

"No, no! That's a lie!" The accusation was so farfetched, Terry couldn't think how to start disproving it.

"I told 'em how I'd found it on the beach at Honolulu," Zeke continued unfazed. "Figured it to be a pirate's. Don't have much to show fer my time at sea. Means a lot to me."

"You *know* I didn't take your doubloon." Terry spoke louder than he intended. The spectators murmured, and the policeman restored his tight grip. "The one in my pocket's mine." He faced the consul. "I remember telling you at the end of my trial that I had one doubloon."

"Seems Terrence wants to start a doubloon collection." Zeke rubbed his hands together. "But when you search him, it's mine you'll find."

"Unusual for pirates to land at Honolulu these days," Cardiff said with a hint of disbelief.

"It's an old doubloon, sir." Zeke glanced at his friends, who nodded again.

The word *old* struck Terry. He pulled his coin out with his free hand and stretched out his arm, keeping the doubloon in his closed fist. "I know the year of this coin. You can ask Zeke if he knows this one's year. And you won't find another one if you search me."

Cardiff folded his arms. "What's its year, Zeke? You're from the *William Parton*, if my memory serves me right."

"Uh, yes ... Hey, don't leave," Zeke called to Joey and Billy who were edging away. "My doubloon dis'peared while Terrence sat at my table—I swear that's the truth—but, but it mighta fallen onto the floor. The boys here thought Terrence filched it, but it's awful dark inside."

"You don't know the date then?" The consul gave him a hard look.

"Guess not since, uh, Terrence is sure o' the one he has. I'll jes go back in an' make a better search." He clapped Terry's shoulder. "And here we was jes gettin' to know Terrence better. Seems he likes this here saloon best. Knows his way 'round some of the best places fer lonesome sailors too."

The consul narrowed his eyes at Zeke. "So, no charge. Just a very unfortunate mistake that's taken up several people's valuable time?"

"Right, seeing as how I jes jumped to conclusions, so upset I was, but you might warn Terrence of the dangers of the flower girls. Contagion and all that." Zeke jerked his head to Joey and Billy, who had moved to the far edge of the spectators, and the three vanished into the saloon, like snakes slithering into a hole.

At that moment, Mr. Pendleton arrived. The second policeman was close behind.

Terry's embarrassment ratcheted higher.

"I'm glad you've come, Richard," the consul said. "Your wisdom will be much appreciated, but first I'll let these officers know I have our American lad well in hand."

After the consul spoke briefly in Japanese to the two policemen, they bowed and ordered the spectators to move on. Then they also strolled away.

The consul inclined his head at Terry's sponsor. "Our model worker and excellent student stirred up a hornet's nest here. A false charge of thievery has been dropped for good reason, but our young man has violated at least one of the provisions connected with your generous offer."

Terry's neck heated. "Sir, if I may speak, Zeke was lying about the places of ill repute. I wouldn't go near that section of town."

"I'll take your word for that, Mr. Ballard. Innuendoes are not a basis for an accusation. But do you deny you were inside the saloon just now? Sufficient witnesses appear to be available other than the three scoundrels."

"I don't deny it, but I can explain. You see—"

"Why, Terrence." Mr. Pendleton tapped his cane for their attention. "Is it possible you have mistaken the place to buy a bottle of brandy for our household?"

"I'm … er, to be honest, sir, I don't understand."

"You see, Jake's General Store carries brandy too. You might not have noticed the bottles on the store's back shelf this morning. Nothing to be ashamed of."

The consul tilted his head, a suspicious glint in his eye. "You're saying you or a servant asked him to buy a bottle of brandy? I didn't think you imbibed the strong drink."

"Not much. Just take a few drops of spirits for my stomach, as the apostle advised Timothy to do, and a nip on special occasions. My last bottle ran dry after being in my pantry for months. Perhaps our boy here noticed." He smiled at the consul and then at Terry. "Seems those ruffians from the ship may have taken advantage of your confusion."

"I'm … But …"

"We're all learning our way around in this foreign place," Mr. Pendleton continued. "Gets us in tight spots sometimes. Now, you need to get back to your studies. That third chapter is one of Adam Smith's best. I'll send for you when I get home."

The consul raised a hand. "Before our lad leaves, I just want to make sure I understand, Richard. You're telling me he should not be held accountable for entering the saloon? This was all a misunderstanding?"

"Yes, that's precisely what I'm saying. Haven't I made myself clear?"

"Not nearly as clear as you usually are. But I'll take your explanation as the gospel truth. You've always inspired me with your integrity."

Terry held his breath. His release had seemed within his grasp, but trouble just reared its head.

Pendleton grimaced. "I've never pretended to be perfect, have I? Have you heard of a massive work called *Les Misérables*?"

"Afraid not." The consul took out his fob watch and glanced at it.

"A couple of weeks ago, Jake had the book, recently translated into English, mixed in with a crate of new arrivals. I rescued it and found the story to be daunting, yet fascinating and inspiring. A former criminal was about to be returned to prison for stealing the bishop's silver, but the bishop rescued him from the police by scolding him for not taking his silver candlesticks too. Perhaps the novel impressed me too deeply, but I find *gospel* to be an apt term."

"I see. So mercy over law. Since you will no doubt make sure our wayward—or confused—young man learns a lesson or two, I'll leave him in your oversight."

"Thank you. A kind decision. Now how about joining me over there?" Pendleton pointed to a teahouse. "I'm eager to hear how things are going with our plan before I head to Jake's store for the brandy myself."

The consul shook his head. "No, I can't now. Before being intercepted, I was on the way to verify that my navigator and my father-in-law connected with Chief Inspector Sato. Stargazer Hunt knew to watch for Sato and his men at the dock, so everyone should be in place. Perhaps *after* Mr. Ballard thoughtfully completes any additional assignments you contemplate, you could inform him of what is being carried out at this very moment on his behalf."

Terry burned with desire for an explanation. Was an effort underway to solve the coordinates' dilemma? He could hardly stand not knowing. But if the consul was intentionally giving him a kick in the pants, there was no use asking questions.

"So far, so good, then." Mr. Pendleton turned to Terry. "Now off with you, my boy."

"Then I'll take my leave."

As he headed to the house, his longing for the news warred with relief and an ache in his heart. When he'd been seven, his mother caught him taking a coin off her bureau, and the disappointment she'd expressed still bothered him. It seemed after ten years, he hadn't become much better by some people's standards. Of course, he hadn't stolen this time, but he'd disappointed two well-meaning men.

After reaching the house, he opened *The Wealth of Nations* to reread the third chapter, but his mind kept straying, rehearsing and refining his excuse. Time crept by so slowly it practically stood still, or even went backwards. At last Matsu summoned him downstairs.

"My boy, how are the studies?" Mr. Pendleton waved him toward his usual chair at the walnut table and sat opposite him. "Perchance, is your concentration suffering today?"

"I guess I didn't use good sense, just like on the ship."

"What had you hoped to accomplish by being in the saloon with those scoundrels? Must have had to do with rescuing your brother."

After listening to Terry's account, Mr. Pendleton retrieved a blank piece of paper from his desk and gave it to Terry, then took his place again. "You might not realize you were on the brink of disaster. John Cardiff is a kind man, but he is not one to overlook a violation of an agreement."

Terry looked down. "I'm sorry I caused you to mislead him at first, sir, for my benefit." Yet should anyone really find fault with his trying to save his brother?

"I knew your motive had to be admirable. Now, before we put this unfortunate incident to bed for good, what do you think you can learn from it?"

Looking up, Terry gave a slight smile. "One thing for sure is to watch for traps."

"Yes, that's one lesson." Pendleton clicked his tongue. "I'd like for you to further analyze this indiscretion. Don't rush. Stay here and think of four more lessons to add to this first one. Then write the five down to show me." He placed a steel-nib pen by the other two items.

"Yes, sir." Terry once again avoided looking at his sponsor, who was acting more like his headmaster. Now in addition to the kick in his pants, his knuckles were being rapped—gently, but nevertheless rapped. No doubt, before Mr. Pendleton had retired from teaching in the boys' prep school, he'd become adept at keeping students in line.

Back in the ninth grade, the pretty-much-unjustified comeuppance would have incensed him, but since then, he'd sustained much harder knocks. And perhaps there would be great news as soon as he completed the assignment.

Within ten minutes, he had come up with four more "lessons." Dipping his pen in the ink, he quickly wrote to watch for traps, not let desires cloud his thinking, never take an agreement's provision lightly, ask for advice from people he trusted, and exercise patience. Then he clasped his hands to keep them still and waited for the elderly man to reappear.

"You've come up with excellent strategies," Mr. Pendleton said a good while later. "I'll add a couple more. First, remember the brink you stood on. Picture yourself on a work crew, pinching every penny of your wage to pay back your debt, living in a shack. No more studies or a quick snooze." Pendleton gave him a knowing look. "Then last but not least, ask God to help you choose the right path, especially when the way ahead is fogged in."

"Yes, sir. I'll try to remember." He hoped his voice sounded contrite. *And now about the news* was on the tip of his tongue.

Mr. Pendleton smiled when Terry stayed quiet. "I see you're applying that final lesson you penned." He walked to the parlor's panel door, looked into the hallway, and slid the door shut.

If Terry had been with Tom, they would have eyed each other over the silly idea that closing a panel made of *paper* would make any difference. But that was the trouble. He wasn't with Tom and wouldn't ever be without decisive actions. *All right. I've been patient. Let's hear it.*

"I'm happy to report," Pendleton said, lowering his voice, "Consul Cardiff has put in motion a way to learn the island's coordinates we are so eager to know."

Terry gripped the table, hope surging through him.

"Nagasaki's chief inspector, a very powerful man, and his officers have already been dispatched to the *William Parton* to carry out a search for secreted opium. During the search in the captain's cabin, the men will also look for the private logbook. When it's uncovered, Inspector Sato will demand access to it as well as to the official logbook because of suspected collaboration with piracy—a genuine concern. That, my boy, is the plan. We mustn't get our hopes up too high. Much could go wrong."

Terry's face flushed. "You and Consul Cardiff were working hard for me, beyond anything I could imagine, and I … I wasn't smart."

"It was a small misdeed, and you have learned from it." Pendleton pointed to Terry's list of lessons. "So as to take our minds off this arduous time of waiting, explain how Adam Smith's theory of expanding trade relates to the opening of Japan by the Western powers."

Terry blinked. Tackling Smith's third chapter, when everything hinged on what he'd hear in the next hour or so, was beyond the pale. But he had to try to apply all the patience he didn't have.

The consul's muffled voice came from downstairs. Terry plunked down the heavy volume of *Les Misérables* he borrowed from the house's library when his studies ended. After skimming through page after page of introduction, pious philosophy, and the recitation of the bishop's countless good deeds, he'd just gotten to the part where the ex-convict was about to steal the silver, moonlight casting a halo-like glow above the sleeping bishop's head. This part had grabbed his full attention. But he didn't have to wait any longer for the news. He took the stairs two at a time.

His eagerness plunged into despair when he glimpsed Cardiff's solemn expression and the slow shaking of Mr. Pendleton's head. "What's to be done?" his benefactor asked as Terry waited at the door. A stranger stood next to the two men, looking from one to the other.

"Ah, I was about to send for you." Mr. Pendleton gestured for Terry to join them.

"Stargazer Hunt, my ship's navigator, is a messenger bringing us very bad news," the consul said. "I'll let Mr. Hunt elaborate on the encounter." He motioned for everyone to take a chair.

Stargazer Hunt, still standing, transferred his cap from one hand to the other. "You see, Captain Madison claimed the information we wanted in his private log had been changed because he had *corrected* it to match the ach'al coordinates.

When he wouldn't budge, Chief Inspector Sato stated the island with the so-called ach'al coordinates was a new Japanese outpost with a day beacon visible far offshore. During Mr. Taguchi's translation, Captain Madison appeared startled, but then alleged—cool as a cucumber, mind you—that the first mate must have misunderstood his order and had changed the *wrong* log. The chief inspector acted like the explanation was good-nuff and gave the captain permission to continue his offloading. Then he spun on his heel and ordered his officers to leave the ship, which had already been declared clean of opium."

"A huge disappointment!" Mr. Pendleton sighed. "But let's not give up. A new strategy and more prayers are certainly called for."

Terry fought back anger and tears. The prayers of the consul, his wife, and Mr. Pendleton clearly hadn't been answered. If the Almighty existed, he wasn't kind or merciful like these people thought. If they really wanted to help, they would have to come up with a better plan by themselves and let go of their wishful thinking about prayers, prayers, prayers. Having an almighty god on your side was an appealing idea, but Tom was right—just a fantasy.

However, the Japanese officials believed the danger from pirates on Tom's island was real enough to justify searching the ship. He choked back a howl from deep within. If true, how could Tom outlast the infernal delays to his rescue?

CHAPTER 23

Tom poked his head out of his cave, heartened by the sunshine after the two days of dismal rain, culminating in a heavy downpour the previous night. He'd caught two measly fish the first day, then had chosen to avoid more drenching of his already soaked clothes. The new bamboo screen kept most of the rain from splashing in at his cave's entrance, but resulted in an even darker interior, lit spookily by the red coals glowing in the bucket. A couple of random tremors, stronger than usual, hadn't helped.

During those forty-eight hours, he'd moped enough for a year. The first day, he ranted to himself, and to a cricket he tolerated, about how he'd fought Bolt to save the pair's lives. He imagined Sara expressing appreciation after listening to him and Dice arguing that Tom had entered the fray, knowing Sara would outmaneuver the pirate. Not true, but Dice was a stubborn mule about his opinions. Dice would also say the fight against one pirate meant nothing compared to tipping off the boatload of pirates to their presence. That did have a little truth to it.

The second day, when the fear of pirates laid hold on him like a loathsome giant, Tom decided an apology would be his best bet to avoid facing the danger alone.

He tossed the fish bones and pinecones, which had yielded mostly rotten pine nuts, into vines farther down the hill, where roaches and other scavengers wouldn't be tempted to share his lodging. Wiping his hands on his still-damp clothes, he headed for Dice and Sara's cave. Didn't their beliefs require forgiveness? That's what he'd always heard. "Forgive one's enemies. Turn the other cheek." On and on. But those impractical commands could be helpful now.

At the cave's entrance, he called out, "*Ohayo*! Good morning!"

No answer.

"Good morning." This time he adopted a sad tone. A cheerful one hadn't been wise.

Dice came to the entrance, his glower announcing Tom was as welcome as the plague.

"I came to apologize. Could we please talk? After that, I won't bother you if that's what you want." He looked down and scuffed his boots on a rock to remove the mud.

"We can talk." Dice stepped out. "There." He pointed to a couple of boulders on the side of the hill.

Tom followed Dice and sat near him, determined to eat as much humble pie as necessary. He needed Dice and Sara.

"I made a big mistake about the ships. I should have listened to you. You were right to wait until we were sure the first one was safe to signal."

"If only made mistake, not evil. But now hard to trust you." Dice's jaw tightened. "You not listen to me. You ready to go with *any* ship to get off island."

Tom wiped the sweat gathering on his forehead from the warming sun. What could he say? Dice had seen it all with his own eyes. After a weighty pause, he nodded. "At first, I just wanted off—you're right, but after I saw the pirate ship and thought about what would happen, especially to you and Sara, I came to my senses. I climbed down fast, on the back side of the tree. You saw me."

"Stupid to wave your shirt." Dice's eyes flashed with anger.

"Yes, I was stupid." *Humble pie.* "I'm sorry."

"Maybe pirates saw you. If saw, they will come. Very hard to escape. Very hard. If we not escape, they will kill us or make us slaves all our lifes. They do awful thing to Sara. Even they receive ransom, they never let us go."

"I understand." Tom stared at their shadows on the ground. Dice made terrible sense. "We're in a huge danger. I agree." He looked up. "And whether or not the pirates saw my shirt, they couldn't have missed the island, where they could hunt for turtles, birds, fresh water, whatever. Besides that, you already said Bolt's lie about hidden treasure could bring angry pirates here. My red shirt may have sped things up and made it worse, a lot worse if they saw it. But doesn't this mean we need each other all the more?"

Dice still scowled, but the look in his eyes was less certain.

"Can we be a team again?" Tom ventured. "Will you give me another chance? I'm really sorry. Very sorry!" Although he meant it, the sincerity in his voice surprised even himself.

Dice glanced toward the cave. The scowl morphed into his usual detached mask. "You cannot talk with Sara alone. Maybe you lose self-control again. But all right, we work in team. You can help get food for underground cavern."

"Sure. I'll help do that." Tom gave a puff of relief. At least, this was a first step back. Dice could call all the shots for the time being. The fellow had a mountain more of experience with survival anyway. "What do you want me to get?" Sweet potatoes would be real nice.

"Many cattails—all plant and root. We eat some parts raw. We cook other parts."

"All right. By the ponds. I already got a few of their heads that were still there. A little stinky from the rotten weeds, but usable."

"Sara will get plants too. You not go together."

"Are you sure? I saw what looked like quicksand. Several places. And it's been wet."

"Do not go together. Stay away from her. She takes a long stick to test the ground. She is not stupid."

Tom felt his ears redden, but kept back a response.

Dice's face softened. "It is done, Tamo. You sorry. Maybe God will help. Sara says that, too many times." Dice stood up. "I go get coconuts and fish. We work to dry fish and also duck meat before pirates come."

Tom stood too. "How long do you think the pirates would stay … if they come?" It sounded like Dice was preparing for a siege.

"One week. One month. Cannot know. They find Bolt. They learn we three are here. If fifty men, they look everywhere."

"They could make ladders too, or just use ropes off their ship to get into the cavern if they spot it."

Dice nodded. "While in the cavern, we cannot take down a pirate ladder. If take down, they know we there for sure. Then they make new ladder or use rope and drop rocks so we not take away again. We must leave their things alone. We must look deep in the cavern for a place to hide. If they not know we in the cavern, they not hunt there much."

Tom started to object to the *we*, but caught himself. Not

much could be worse than being underground in complete darkness with foul, chirping bats and the gurgle of unknown water. But captivity by pirates would far surpass the cavern's torment, not just for Dice and Sara. For himself, too.

And maybe Dice's own terror was making him work with Tom, not all that Christian stuff.

"Daisuke!" Sara's scream rent the air, panic in her voice.

Tom jumped out of the soggy ground by the pond, grabbed his bamboo walking stick and basket, and sprinted toward the sound of Sara's yells, not slowing down until the earth beneath his feet squished like a damp sponge. Then he felt his way so he wouldn't get stuck in a quagmire and need to yell for help himself.

He finally pushed through the tall marsh reeds and stopped, dread chilling him. Sara, with her back to him, was already mired in quicksand above her knees. Her body was jerking with her efforts to escape, making her sink deeper.

"Be still!" he shouted. "Don't move anymore!" He prodded the ground between them as fast as he could. The soil became impassable about five feet from her.

"I can help you. Don't panic. You won't die, but you must trust me. Do what I say!"

She got still instantly. The dirty quicksand was up to her thighs.

"This will scare you, but trust me. Sit back on the mud, and very, very slowly wiggle your feet."

Amazingly she sat and didn't sink any deeper.

"Are you wiggling your feet real slowly?'

"*Hai.* Yes."

"Continue like a snail might do, but don't move anything else."

Her basket was suspended next to her. He poled it to himself and dumped both of their baskets' contents. Then he lay down at the edge of the quicksand.

"I'm pushing your basket, upside-down, toward you with my basket right behind. My pole's threaded through them. When they're in place, I'll tell you to lie back on them and then grab the pole behind your head."

She didn't say anything or move, as if she'd turned into the oft-quoted pillar of salt while seated on a submerged stool.

He wanted to scoot forward and grab her, but then they'd both be stuck. Positioning the pole the best he could, he squelched a desire to call on the nonexistent God for help.

"Now, Sara, lie back," he instructed in the calmest voice he could manage.

She lay back and took hold of the pole.

His heart pounded. The girl was trusting him. The technique he'd only heard about from a woodsman had to work.

"My feet," she choked out. "They coming up."

"Whew! That's good. Really good. That's what we want. Hold the pole tight and only move your toes." He checked to see if she had a good hold. "Keep wiggling your toes. Your feet will keep rising."

"Now I'm going to pull you toward me very slowly," he said after her lower limbs became visible. "Don't let go."

He pulled, and she inched closer. The powerful vacuum still gripped her, so he tugged the pole harder and harder, grunting each time. At last, she came within his reach. He gripped her underarms and hauled her out.

Both of them collapsed onto their backs, mud splattering him as her body grazed his and slid to the side.

Tom sat up first. "That was awful! Gave me a lesson I didn't want on quicksand's power."

Not saying anything, she pushed herself up too. From her hair to her toes, her backside and half of her frontside were covered with thick, sandy mud. A rotten-egg smell clung to her. She dropped her head into her hands, and her shoulders shook with silent sobs.

"It's all right. You're safe." He longed to hug and comfort her despite the smell, but that would scare her as much as the quicksand. Besides her brother would have an apoplectic fit if he touched her.

By the time he had drawn the pole and ruined baskets out from the mud, she had composed herself. "Thank you," she murmured. "I go to wash." She started to stand, but her legs gave way.

"You're still shaky. Do you have another pair of sandals? It's not safe to walk barefoot. I can bring you a robe too."

"Yes, I have. You are kind. You can find sandals and a robe in my part of the cave. I am sorry, but later, we still work apart and cannot talk alone." She offered him a sad smile.

Tom took off. Being discarded like some worn-out jacket didn't sit right. Hadn't he earned more than "thank you" and "I'm sorry"? His acquaintances back home would have called his actions heroic or gallant, or both, even if they weren't good friends.

Reaching the cave, he called out for Dice. As expected, he wasn't there. He hesitated to enter, but the girl needed sandals immediately and a clean robe for the beach. He picked up her items and a basket to replace his crushed one, not looking in any places that might have feminine articles, all the while worrying that Dice might walk in on him. Then he trotted back to the pond.

She stood when he approached, steadier on her feet. "Again, thank you. I will tell Daisuke you rescued me."

"It was nothing," Tom lied. He handed her the items and busied himself in collecting the pile of cattail plants from their previous efforts.

After putting on the sandals, she headed away from the pond, carrying the clean robe at arm's length. She glanced back over her muddy shoulder, turned and gave a quick bow to him, then continued on.

Fighting the ache in his chest, Tom returned to where he'd been digging under roots. Squatting down, he rubbed his forehead. What was wrong with him? Wasn't it enough the three of them were becoming a team again? Sara obviously had been thankful. Why expect more from her—just because he'd saved her? That's what team members were supposed to do in a crisis. Being cut off from civilization must be eating at him. But at least, he was smart enough to stay out of quicksand himself.

He brushed a leech off his left boot, then stomped it as it squirmed on the ground, ending any misery it might entertain. He plunged his left hand under a cattail and yanked the plant out with his right hand. For all he knew, creatures like leeches could get hurt feelings. But plants didn't ... they didn't cause them either.

Daisuke's back was toward Sara as she came down the hill. One net lay next to him, where he sat on a rock cleaning a fish. Another net was probably anchored in the water. Her muscles tensed as she drew closer. After he'd trumpeted her smartness, she'd made a colossal mess of herself.

When she reached him, he jumped up and wheeled to face her, his knife in his hand.

"*Aah, anata.*" He set his knife down. "What happened?" he asked, continuing to speak in Japanese.

When she told him, his face clouded. "Tamo must be very proud of himself, crowing like a rooster."

She lowered her eyes. "I am grateful he heard my shouts."

Daisuke sniffed. "People don't drown in quicksand, but they may starve. I'd have searched and found you before that."

"Tamo told me to sit back in the quicksand. That made my feet come loose and come up."

He folded his arms. "So, you think I should be more thankful to the barbarian for his method? I would have gotten you out." He ran his eyes over her muddy robe. "You were stupid, Sa-*chan*, to get into such a predicament."

"Yes, that is true." She looked down again.

"But you think working with Tamo again proved helpful, don't you?"

"You are wise."

"And with that answer, I cannot argue." The barest twinkle in his eyes contradicted his gruffness.

She bowed, then moved down the beach, away from the second net.

Daisuke sat and started cleaning fish again.

She disrobed and stepped into the water with the dirty yukata in her hands. Lying back and swishing her hair in the ripples, she relished the water's cleansing power. Her shame seemed to flow off her like the smelly mud dissolving off her skin. However, when she scrubbed her robe, the muddy stains clung stubbornly to the cotton material. The robe would be dingier.

But what did its stains matter? Although she'd been foolish, she was alive, and it was Tamo who'd rescued her. He had truly cared for her. His eyes had spoken as loud as his actions. And once more, Daisuke's mind had been touched.

She turned her face upward and thanked her Liege. Then, feeling Daisuke's gaze on her, she offered him a bow to hide her lack of regret.

CHAPTER 24

Terry stood at the parlor door. "You called me, sir?"

Mr. Pendleton picked up a slip of paper from the table. "The *William Parton* was scheduled to sail on the tide this morning—a fact we all applaud—so I believe it's safe for you to venture out. I've given the cook several days off to visit his parents since he heard they're under the weather. I think we should take this chance to introduce you to some Japanese cuisine. There's a popular noodle shop straight down the road, past eight lanes, near Jake's store."

After handing Terry the paper with Japanese characters written on it and several Japanese coins, he pointed to two large characters at the top. "That's the name of the place, and below it is our order for *soba* noodles. A very popular, albeit casual, dish here. If you leave now, the household can enjoy soba for lunch."

"Yes, sir, and thank you. I'm looking forward to the noodles, and could not be happier for the ship's departure." He pocketed the coins. "I'm on my way, by your leave."

While he changed into his boots in the vestibule, the thought came that ships didn't always leave when scheduled. Meeting up with any of the crew again was about as desirable as falling into a nest of scorpions. Would it be possible to shanghai him in a place like Japan?

But the weather was good. The *William Parton*'s offloading and trading had only been delayed by a few hours four days ago. There wasn't any reason for the ship to stay in port. After all, Captain Madison was a stickler for schedules, wasn't he? Just maroon a sailor if he wasn't in the jolly-boat on time. He tamped down his anger and started counting lanes as he walked along the busy street.

The purchase at the shop went smoothly enough, and in no time, he was striding along the stone path toward the road. The packages gave off a tantalizing smell, urging him to walk faster. A turtledove's gentle serenade in a cedar tree called to him, but he didn't pause to listen even though the cooing spoke of fine summer mornings in New York.

But a minute later, he came to an abrupt stop. Had someone called his name, the voice barely audible?

He glanced around. None of the people coming and going past him looked familiar. Was his mind playing tricks?

"Terry!" A head in a sailor's cap poked from around an azalea bush against the side wall, then jerked back behind it.

Terry nearly dropped his packages. "Jim?" Instantly he regretted speaking the name out loud. The boy had to be in danger. He looked around again. No one seemed to pay him any attention. He strolled to the bush and leaned over it, as though watching a dragonfly that zipped away.

"Help me!" Jim pled, barely above a whisper. "Zeke aimed his dirk at me, but missed. I picked the blade up and ducked in here when a horseman rode by."

"Did Zeke see you enter?" Terry kept his eyes on the bush, scared to survey the area behind him a third time.

"I don't think he knew for sure. Joey, Billy, and Zeke all came in and were walking around, hunting me. A clerk from the shop made them leave when they didn't order anything."

"Whoa! They could be outside the wall watching right now. How long has it been?"

"About three hours, I guess. The cook wanted more flour from the general store."

"Was the ship still on schedule to leave with the tide?" He squatted down and acted as if he were rearranging his packages.

"Yes. I was told to run to the store, double time."

"Well, then, the three rats couldn't just stay around to attack you again. But I'm going to get the consul and Hada, just in case. They'll get you out of here and know what to do. Be right back."

He strolled away from the shop, doing his best to act normal on the slim chance the three sailors were still in the settlement and watching. Keeping a wary eye out for any tall foreigners, he stayed in the center of the street that led toward the better residences and the consulate. Finally, he turned the corner onto the consulate's road.

With no warning, three figures jumped him. His packages flew everywhere. A fist landed on his jaw, jarring his teeth with shooting pain. A second punch knocked him to his knees. He bent over, trying to protect his head and stomach from the hard kicks.

Zeke grabbed him by the hair and raised his head. "You lead us to that eavesdroppin' buddy of yours if you wanna live."

"Who? I don't know … What—oomph!" A fist punched deep into his stomach.

Suddenly the attack stopped, and the three dashed away. A man behind him, jingling something while hitting the cobblestones, was hollering in Japanese.

A policeman met Terry's eyes. Hurting all over, he rose and

bowed to the man, who was scrutinizing him. "*Arigatō*. Thank you," he said, bowing again. "I go to *Kadifu*."

The policeman helped him gather the damaged packages. Then he pointed to himself, to Terry, and toward the consulate. He started off and motioned for Terry to follow.

After hearing Terry's account in English and the policeman's account in Japanese, Consul Cardiff made sure Terry wasn't seriously injured, then called for Hada to accompany them to the shop. At the consulate's gate, he ordered both U.S. Navy sentries to come with them as well, then told Terry to lead the way.

At the shop, Terry examined the bushes and bit back curses. Jim was gone!

The villains had gotten his friend! They'd kill the boy. Jim was barely past childhood—only turning fifteen a few months earlier—never hurting anyone. He worked long hours on the ship day after day, unable to play marbles with boys his age, fish, or hunt. Terry ground his teeth. How could the brute beasts have preyed on someone so innocent?

At that minute, the shopkeeper came out, bringing Jim, still in one piece, by the arm.

Terry nearly collapsed, relief pouring through him.

Hada called to the shopkeeper, who answered gruffly and released Jim.

Terry rushed to his friend and took him by the shoulders. "You scared me to death! I thought for sure they found you." He stepped back to catch his breath, to stop panting.

"I ordered three dishes inside the shop by pointing to what customers got. So the workers let me stay until they saw I couldn't pay." The boy looked close to tears. "That's when you came back."

"Everything's all right now. You're in good hands." Terry pointed toward the consul and Hada, who were still with the man from the shop.

Cardiff waved for Terry and Jim to join him. "I've just ordered and paid for more noodles, so everything's settled here. But what a terrible time you've had." He cast sympathetic looks at both of them. "Hada will deliver one of the orders to Mr. Pendleton's staff and invite him to come eat with us. I want you two to come with me now and stay inside the consulate. Since it's likely the ship stayed in port to collect its sailors, I imagine we'll hear from Captain Madison today when he discovers one sailor is still missing, but don't worry. The thugs will be called to account. Before the day is half over, not only the policeman who witnessed the assault on Mr. Ballard but also every shopkeeper in the area will report all they saw to Chief Inspector Sato's office. A secret in Japan is an oxymoron."

Other than telling Jim briefly about his own encounter with Zeke and his mates, Terry kept quiet on the way to the consulate. Frustration, more painful than his bruised jaw, stomach, and back, ate at him. Zeke and his pals amused themselves by exploiting his efforts to rescue Tom. Attacking his one friend fit right in.

When they stood at the consulate gate, Terry clasped Jim's arm. His friend had to be petrified. "You'll be safe. These people are unbelievably kind, and they'll help you. I hate what happened, but I'm awful glad you're here. It means the world that we're together."

Jim closed his eyes and nodded. "I've been here twice before, you know. I'm not afraid of these people. Just of our ship's crew." A single tear slid down the boy's cheek as the group entered the compound.

Once the two of them had been warmly welcomed into the house, the consul invited them to eat the noodles at the teakwood table in the reception room with his wife, Mr. Pendleton, and himself. Terry guessed the unusual setup was to avoid giving a *servant,* namely himself, special favor at the main dining table. Hada was invited too, but declined when he arrived with Mr. Pendleton.

The room looked much more inviting than it did as a courtroom during the trial. In the center of the table, candles glowed next to a straw basket containing a grapevine's branch arching over chrysanthemums—an unusual centerpiece, but one Terry liked. A velvet sofa, two blue armchairs, and a lamp table further softened the space. He winced, however, as he crossed the Turkish rug, recalling his former grubby appearance—a good deal worse than what his clothes had undergone from the morning's attack.

When everyone was seated, the consul turned his gaze to Jim. "Well, young man," he said, compassion in his voice, "you've had a harrowing experience. I'm sure everyone here would like to reassure you and also discover the attack's cause. If it is what I suppose, I am sorry to have helped prompt it."

Jim shook his head. "It wasn't because of you, sir. The captain might have blamed me a little for telling about the third log, but others knew about it too. There was a lot bigger reason. Last night after Captain Madison had his usual smoke on the quarterdeck, he entered the Great Cabin with Zeke, and they crossed the room to look at a map on the aft table. Their backs were to me. I gathered the dessert plates as quiet as a mouse, not wanting to disturb them. Zeke told the captain that a cave definitely hadn't been in the right place on Turtle Island." Jim paused and eyed the group. "That's what they named the island where they left Tom."

When everyone nodded, he continued. "Zeke said he couldn't understand it. He'd been sure it was the right island 'cuz of the rise on one side of the ridge, and 'cuz its coordinates matched so close to what they could see on the hermit's stained map. The captain asked if pirates could have covered up the cave's entrance after Zeke was there the first time. Just then, I dropped a fork, and they spun around like I'd shouted *Fire!* The captain yelled, 'Out!' and then, 'You'll see what happens to eavesdroppers!'"

"An over-the-top, irrational response," Mr. Pendleton said, stroking his beard. "It reminds me of what we heard during the trial concerning the captain's treatment of both you and Terrence before reaching this port."

"Yes, sir, like a crazy person. Believe me, I stayed close to another sailor during my watch. Didn't want to be food for sharks. Then in the fo'c'sle, I didn't sleep a wink, fearing a knife at my throat. When Cook Salty ordered me on land to pick up a sack of flour, I was happy to be off the ship for even a half hour … until Zeke tried to kill me. I left his dirk behind a bush at the noodle shop. It has his initials carved in the handle: An E and B, for Ezekiel Bonner, Zeke says, and not for Ezekiel Bones, like I heard Mate Talbot once call Zeke."

"Interesting mistake—to bring up a pirate moniker. And I suppose Zeke would deny Beelzebub too." The consul's eyes sparked with ire. "Excuse me a second. I'll send for the weapon. We may need the evidence later today. Come, Master Mankin, and describe its location for Hada while we're waiting to be served." He strode to the door, accompanied by Jim.

After Jim and the consul took their seats again, Terry couldn't help fretting. Jim was safe for the time being, but just for the time being. "Sir," he began, despite being seen by those present as young and a servant, "can't Captain Madison argue that the attacks weren't too serious? Or what if he admits the attack on Jim was criminal, but guarantees his safety and makes him return to the ship? Wouldn't that be possible? And dangerous, like throwing Jim to the lions?"

Terry flinched at the consul's frown. Had he been too presumptuous?

But then Cardiff nodded to Terry and leaned forward toward Jim. "You won't need to meet the captain. As of right now, I'm offering you asylum in the consulate under the *full protection* of the United States of America, if you desire it." His words reverberated with authority.

Jim's face lit up. "I accept your offer, sir, with much thanks. I owe my life to you and Terry. I'm sure of that."

"Let me reiterate that you'll need to stay inside until we know the coast is clear, quite literally."

Mrs. Cardiff smiled at Jim. "We will be glad to have you with us as long as needed. Do you have a home in America? Parents? Relatives?"

"Not really, I guess." Jim's eye twitched. "My parents died of the pox. My spinster aunt didn't want a boy on her hands. I've got an uncle and cousins somewhere near San Francisco, but I never met them. Anyway, my aunt knew the cook on the *William Parton,* and he agreed to take me as his assistant. They both said it would be a good education to see the world. But … but it hasn't been, not the right kind."

Consul Cardiff raised a finger to catch Jim's eye. "I presume with such an arrangement that you didn't have to sign any contract. Right?"

"I didn't sign anything, sir. Captain Madison said I could sail as Cook Salty's charge—his responsibility."

"Then any payment is out of the question if the captain has the gall to demand one after your life was threatened." The consul leaned back in his chair.

Mrs. Cardiff reached over to pat Jim's hand. "I'm sure it has been a perfectly miserable experience from the first day you set sail. Perhaps there is a brighter future for you if you can locate your uncle." She turned toward her husband with an expectant look.

"Would you like to go to San Francisco?" Consul Cardiff asked, obviously in tune with his wife. "My ship will leave for that town in about two weeks. I can arrange for you to have a safe cabin and an assignment suitable for your age."

Stunned by the news, Terry spluttered while drinking the tea the maid had just poured.

"Mr. Ballard, don't get your hopes up, at least, not yet," the consul cautioned. "The island's coordinates are an absolute necessity, and there are other considerations as well."

"Yes, sir." He wiped the drops of tea off his chin. "I'll try to be patient, like you told me." Did the group detect his falsehood? He could no more be patient than he could lasso a tornado.

Jim rubbed his knuckles and glanced from Mrs. Cardiff to her husband. "That's very kind, sir. I-I think I'd like that, but I don't know what would happen in California. Everything's jumbled in my mind."

"It's a big decision, son. We can talk later after you've had enough time to think about it." The consul nodded to the maid, who carried in pottery bowls filled with the soba for the five of them."

After giving thanks for the food and God's protection, the consul invited the others to partake of the noodles in any fashion

177

they wished. Their host himself used what Mr. Pendleton termed "chopsticks" to pick up fat strands of the gray soba while holding the bowl in the air.

Terry had been using a fork and spoon while eating with the servants at Mr. Pendleton's house, but decided to copy the consul. The two long strands he managed to suck up tasted great, but it looked doubtful he'd get half the noodles into his mouth by the end of the meal.

"Now from what Jim has told us," the consul said after making a good-sized dent in his own batch of noodles, "we have to conclude Captain Madison and the sailor Zeke have highly confidential information about a cave on an island matching the one where Tom Ballard is. And from the zeal exhibited, the information does not relate to scholarly research on some rare cave creature, but rather to monetary treasure.

"I recall from your trial's defense, Mr. Ballard, that Zeke claimed to have set out alone, before the others, to search for your brother. That must have been when he checked for the treasure cave, don't you think?"

"That seems right, sir." Terry pictured the rat. "I never overheard anything like Jim did, but I always thought the captain favored Zeke."

"And the first mate favored him too," Jim added.

"Why would the captain be in such a hurry to leave the island?" Mrs. Cardiff asked. "Not only did they neglect to send in a search party for their missing sailor, but it seems they didn't make a thorough search for the cave they were so eager to locate."

"I've been pondering that myself," Mr. Pendleton put in, pushing his spectacles up higher on his nose. "They might have worried that a pirate ship lurked close by. A ship armed with cannon, manned by pirates also hunting the treasure, would be fearsome indeed. At the same time, I'm guessing Captain Madison was loath to divulge the island's location to the consul or to anyone else in case Zeke had missed the cave. They might plan a future pass at the island."

"Makes sense, my wise professor." The consul picked his bowl back up and with the chopsticks' help, slurped up much of its contents Japanese-style. "When in Rome ..." he said, then finished his soba.

Everyone at the table did the same. Mrs. Cardiff did it most gracefully, Terry thought, while he slurped most wholeheartedly despite his sore stomach and aching jaw.

The consul ran his eyes over the group. "Well, it's not illegal to hunt for treasure, but an assault and attempted murder are felonies. We shall see how the rest of the day unfolds. In the meantime, Hada will show you two young men to a downstairs guest room. I imagine Jim here needs a soft bed after his sleepless ordeal, and Mr. Ballard may need a respite, too, in spite of bravely carrying on."

The consul pulled back the chair for his wife. She expressed her delight in having had the three as guests for the meal, then led the way out of the room. One of the servants met her in the hall and handed the babbling baby into her arms.

Terry and Jim followed Hada to a room which had one single bed. The manservant opened the cupboard and pulled out a futon, sheets, and a cover. He motioned to Terry, and Terry nodded. He wouldn't have wanted the older servant to make up his bed, but he would have liked to have been the one to make it clear. After Hada left, he spread the sheet out and turned to his friend.

Jim was already asleep and snoring.

Terry dropped onto the futon and stretched out. Tom's dire

situation came roaring back into his thoughts. He had to figure out what came next in rescuing Tom. Every day made his brother's survival less likely.

But what came next was learning the coordinates, of course. Nothing else mattered until they were known. And discovering them would take a miracle. He sniffed. It'd be nice if miracles weren't people's delusions.

He rubbed his sore jaw. Maybe Jim's rescue had been a bit of a miracle—or a huge coincidence. Amazing to have been sent to the very noodle shop where Jim was hiding. But if it was a miracle, why did he have to get beat up in the mix?

And why did he keep meeting so many enigmas that had no answers? Philosophers liked those types of puzzles. He didn't. He despised them. The only puzzle he cared about was how to rescue Tom and get home.

Home—to Albany, where the Hudson River was the only big body of water close by. And back to his family and his horse.

He tightened his eyes against their threatening moisture.

CHAPTER 25

Tom approached Dice and Sara's cave, curious whether his next assignment would be dangerous, tedious, or exasperating—the island's only options other than their lookout duties. He had volunteered to keep watches on the ocean in the late mornings and late afternoons. Dice and Sara were taking various other times.

Six days had gone by since the two ships had passed the island. If the repairs for the pirates' ship took one week and their return to the island added a few more days, their threat was approaching all too fast. In another four days, he might yearn for the current days of isolation, like a prisoner perishing on a work crew might envy the ones left back in their solitary cells.

Sara was perched on a small boulder not far from the cave, reading the Bible. A makeshift grill, made from shaved branches, was fitted over coals in a fire pit close to her. The rising wisps of smoke carried the teasing smell of roasting meat. No doubt the slices covering the grill were what remained from the previous day's hunt.

Dice poked his head out the cave's entrance, then turned back to whatever he was doing inside.

"Why are you drying the meat out here?" Tom pointed to the grill when Sara looked up and laid the book aside.

"The sun and wind help dry it fast. After Daisuke and I prepared the meat last night, he wet his sash in seawater and used it to wrap the slices. So he kept them safe until we can smoke them today."

"That makes good sense. You and your brother know an awful lot about surviving." He swallowed back his embarrassment at his meager contribution from the hunt. He had missed all but one of the birds he aimed at with Sara's borrowed bow and arrows. On the other hand, Dice had brought down nine out of the eleven birds he shot at—three ducks and an unbelievable total of six pigeons. The amazing thing was that Dice hadn't rubbed in Tom's dismal showing. Just told him it was a samurai skill that took heaps of training and to hunt for feathers and suitable stones to replace the lost arrows.

Sara ran her eyes over his still damp clothes and unexpectedly offered a warm smile. "To remove the stain, it is hard." She brushed her hand over her robe. "We have reminders of quicksand. Thank you again."

He returned her smile. "I'm glad we didn't lose a team member." *Especially you, since you're the grateful one.*

She rose and used a clam shell to scrape up one of three flat pancakes he hadn't noticed on an edge of the grill. "For the moon god," she said, looking uncomfortable. "I do not think a god is in the moon, but each year, my town celebrates him. My family eats round foods, makes poems, and watches a full moon with old friends. I was too sad to celebrate it in the correct month with only my brother. Now you are here, and almost a full moon shines above. I want to share the festival." She looked for a second like she wanted to cry rather than celebrate.

"How did you make those pancakes?" Tom gestured to the remaining two, aiming to turn her thoughts from home. "You're like a magician with the little we have."

"I ground up cattail roots. This one is for you." She pulled a small bunch of kudzu leaves from her sash and slid her concoction onto them. "Kudzu, so the cake not falls apart." She handed the warm, crumbling pieces to him.

The make-believe pancake gritted like sand in his mouth and had the same zero flavor as the ship's hardtack. "Very good," he said. At least, cattail root had to contain some food value.

"I am happy you say it is good, but your face does not agree." Her grin was visible before she covered it with her hand. "Does anyone celebrate the moon festival in your town?"

"No. Everyone there believes in just one god if they believe in any. But around two weeks ago—if I'm figuring right—some people in my town would have celebrated Halloween. I don't think anyone believes in the tales that go with it, but the children like the sweets."

"What kind of tales?" She actually looked like she was enjoying their conversation.

"Stories about witches' spells, ghosts, black cats. That sort of thing. There's one famous tale about a headless horseman. A schoolteacher named Ichabod Crane was fooled by a Jack-o'-lantern. That's a face carved out of a gourd, like you use for soup. The teacher thought a ghostly horseman had really thrown his head at him. But the live horseman, who was probably a prankster—someone who plays tricks—had thrown the gourd Jack-o'-lantern, not his head. The spooky valley where this took place was supposed to be haunted by ghosts and goblins. Guess that might explain why the teacher was so gullible—so easy to fool."

"You like this story?" Her tone hinted at skepticism as she sat again on the boulder.

"Sure. We didn't read it in school. I don't think my teacher liked the prank." He squatted with his back against a large boulder near hers. "My father read it to my brother and me when we were little. He acted like the headless part was true until my mother fussed at him. She kept insisting the story was meant to be humorous. He was usually very cautious, but he liked to make us shiver a little." Tom battled his own wave of homesickness.

"Is it fun for you to shiver?"

"Yes, when there's nothing really to fear."

"Like bats?"

He jerked, irritated, then saw the twinkle in her eye. "Ouch, Sara. We'd say you gave a low blow—something not allowed in boxing, one of our sports."

"A special day with witches does not sound good. Also not good is a tale that insults teachers."

"You wouldn't have respected that story's miserable teacher. But how about your day, honoring the non-existent moon god?"

She cocked her head. "The two days are a little the same, I think. My father does not care much about the god or pay attention to the god tales, like your parents do not believe the spooky tales. The same as children in your country, Daisuke and I wanted sweets."

"Well, there's another holiday coming soon in America that you'd like better, called Thanksgiving. But by that time, I hope we've escaped the pirates and been rescued." He frowned. Going home—if they did make it off the island alive—meant Sara and Dice would go their separate way. The two were hard to understand, and at times downright odd, but while marooned, at least, they'd become almost like family. In fact, just seconds ago, hadn't Sara observed the moon-god festival because he was with her?

"Maybe you and Dice could come with me to America when we leave here, and not return to your country until it's safer for you." He rubbed his hand on his chin's stubble that he'd neglected to scrape off. "I'd really like that. We have other interesting holidays, such as Christmas."

"We celebrated Christmas in Naha with the sensei's family." She sighed. "To go to America would be—I don't know how to say. Exciting. A wonderful dream. But not possible. You know it is impossible."

"Actually, no. It doesn't sound impossible to me. But everything about the future is uncertain, isn't it?"

"To think about it, I could lose my head and be headless like that horseman." The girl he had always viewed as strait-laced actually indulged in the slightest of chuckles despite the grim topic.

He pointed to the Bible. "Is it really so interesting? Guess there aren't any tales that bring on a shiver."

"There are stories of dangers and evil people, who really lived. Of course, the stories are not scary to read because no one can defeat God. Maybe without the truths in this book, I would want to die. We could be here for years and years. And if pirates come, that is worse. Much worse." She rose, held her hand near the grill, apparently testing its heat, then sat again.

"I don't see why those stories help any." He really did wonder why the Bible had such an attraction for her.

"No matter what, Jesus is my Shepherd. God gives me hope."

"If there's no rescue, what can be hoped for? Heaven?" She had to be really desperate. "There are lots of reasons to live if we're lucky. Right now, we're not lucky. Well, right now *is* good, talking with you. Very good. But overall? Being marooned with pirates prowling close by is the height of unlucky."

"Have you read the Bible?"

"No, but I've heard parts of it. Almost every Sunday at home."

"What have you heard?"

Tom searched his memory. This conversation was getting awkward, but he didn't want it to end. Sara was talking more freely than she had the whole time he'd known her, and they had permission with Dice close by—as ridiculous as that was.

"Something about being swallowed by a whale." More long-ago stories came to mind. "Angels coming at Christmas. Moses crossing a sea on dry land. Daniel and the lions. The star for the wisemen—that one seems more likely, thinking of comets, constellations, and other unknowns. And Adam and Eve, of course, and their big mistake with the snake."

He laughed. "Look at me. I've contributed a poem for your festival. 'Big mistake with the snake' rhymes."

"Oh," she huffed, "you must not joke like that. And the poems must be right style."

"I see. Well, full-blown poems in a 'right style' aren't my … uh, specialty. But I can listen to yours, if you want."

"Mine is secret." Her coy look reminded him of Peg's expression when she wanted him to squeeze a secret out of her.

He was about to take the challenge when Dice stepped outside.

Sara closed her mouth like a clam.

"Sara-san needs to go with me to collect eggs. You can watch this fire," Dice said, pointing to Tom. "Don't let it go out. Don't make it too hot. If the air near the fire burns the hand—too hot. Turn the meat every half hour. You judge time."

Tom swallowed back his grumble at the onslaught of orders. "Whatever you say."

Sara sprang up, leaving the book on the rock. She took one of the two baskets Dice was holding and handed him his pancake-topped kudzu. Then she turned to Tom. "You can read our Bible if you want. Maybe if you only watch the fire, you will get bored. If you read, the New Testament is good for a beginner."

Tom stood and muttered his thanks, frowning at the beginner label. Did she also think that about him when it came to most everything else? Although he clearly wasn't an expert about living on deserted islands, wasn't that to be expected? Last he heard, no teacher in the whole United States gave lessons on survival if marooned on a rock in the middle of an ocean.

After the two were well on their way to the marsh, he held his hand over the fire to feel its proper warmth and then found the supply of wood behind the larger boulder. He watched Dice and Sara until their bobbing heads were barely visible among the distant reeds. Sara was right. This was going to be a tedious job—maybe exasperating too. But the jerky would keep well if they had to stay in the cavern, and the Indian-like stealth of Dice and Sara would help in the egg hunt.

He picked up the Bible. Sara no doubt hoped he would give in and investigate it. The little lady was a sly manipulator despite her submissive mannerisms. Luckily, there was a table of contents. He ran his finger down till the magic heading appeared, then snorted. If she'd just said Matthew instead of New Testament, he could have found it without looking at the front.

After adding a couple of sticks to the fire, he rigorously tested the heat. Dice would raise a stink to high heavens if he failed in this easy job—one that didn't require even a smidgin of samurai skill. Then he moved back from the fire, so the already steamy day wouldn't be more stifling. Taking Sara's place on the boulder, he read through the first seven chapters of Matthew before he needed a break, having paused only to tend the fire and turn the meat.

While he relieved himself and then scooped a drink from the trough-like shelf at the back of the cave, he mulled over what he'd read. It wasn't like the myths he'd expected—not the least bit resembling the superstitious imaginings of Ichabod Crane. The teachings of Jesus were not only interesting, but even rational. He had no idea that the theoretical God counted thoughts as well as actions, but he could sure see the close connection of hatred and murder.

If thoughts counted, he'd be in real hot water, and not just for hatred either. But then, except for maybe hermits, wouldn't every person in the world be in some level of hot water, including grumpy Dice and sweet Sara? So how did these impossible requirements give hope? And did he really want to know? He'd left his grandparents' farm—a very comfortable spot, comparatively speaking—partly to escape a parson's sermons.

Dice and Sara returned, each with ten duck eggs in their baskets. Dice examined the fire and meat, then said, "Looks all right. Continue. I come back soon."

As Dice turned to leave, Sara stepped back out of the cave, just in time to speak in her brother's presence. "Did you read much?" She pointed to the Bible still in Tom's hands.

"Seven chapters."

"Oh, that is much. You read fast."

He smiled at the surprising praise. At least, he wasn't a beginner in reading.

She pivoted and gave a little bow to her brother, her dark hair flowing around her shoulders and glinting in the sunlight. "I will prepare pigeon hearts, but they will not taste same without ginger." She reentered their cave, taking a little brightness—and considerable beauty—with her.

After a few steps, Dice stopped and faced back toward Tom. "This afternoon I will teach you jiu-jitsu moves. To learn well needs many years. But I can teach a little. Maybe you need if you fight bad men in your country. We not use here with pirates. If they come, too many. Too strong. So, we hide from them. After we do jiu-jitsu today, we explore the cavern and take extra ladder. Keep it from pirates."

"Aye, aye, sir," Tom answered reflexively, turning the newest challenges over in his mind. The pigeon hearts would be tiny and cooked, so the organs couldn't be that much worse than chicken livers. Japanese-style wrestling might come in handy, even be a lifesaver somewhere, sometime. Although he would rather have teeth yanked out than enter the cavern again, at least he wouldn't be underground alone with the bats. Besides, he had to get over his squeamishness with bats. *Squeamishness* was different from *fear*, as any simpleton should know, no matter how Sara chose to think.

CHAPTER 26

Daisuke led Tamo to a section of the marsh beyond the cavern's entrance. The ground needed to be soft so the sailor wouldn't react violently. He had to be careful of his own body too.

"We not do much jiu-jitsu today. My ribs still not all healthy. I teach you two joint locks now and how to do locks with throw-down. Every day of no hard rain and no pirates, I can teach you more moves. If we are on the island for long time, we can do the real thing."

Tamo relaxed his defensive stance. "All right. I'm not eager to be tossed around while I'm still learning."

"Jiu-jitsu means *bend body*, not be tight. If you tight, enemy can knock you down easy."

"Right. Staying loose doesn't sound too hard." Tamo flexed an arm muscle.

A desire flared in Daisuke to start the lesson like his samurai master had begun with him. Tamo would benefit from the unforgettable memory of being upright one second and then struggling to breathe the next while lying flat on his back—an excellent lesson in humility. But one didn't increase heat under a pot that could boil over easily.

Tamo mastered the elbow lock quickly, pressing Daisuke's elbow against his thigh much harder than he had demonstrated with Tamo's arm.

"Don't act too strong, Tamo. I am like a fish that let you catch me. I am out of ocean now."

"Oh, sorry. I forgot about your ribs. If I forget again, do what you have to do. I'm sure you're not helpless."

Tamo's memory turned out to be short. When the shoulder lock extended Daisuke's arm to a painful level, he administered a well-placed kick, and the next second, Tamo was looking up from the ground—getting the lesson in humility after all.

"You weren't helpless," he sputtered. "That was impressive."

Daisuke nodded. "I teach the break-falling skill next time. Enough for now, and no tricks. If we have a real match, I watch for feint. No referee is here, so use honor."

Tamo got up slowly. "If I tried a trick, your payback wouldn't be too enjoyable." He offered a weak smile.

"Without doubt." The sailor was showing much more control than the shirt-waving calamity predicted.

At the cavern's entrance, Daisuke waited until Tamo succeeded in carrying the extra ladder down safely. Then he lowered the other equipment. It was risky having both of them exploring, but riskier still doing it alone. Once down, he moved the extra ladder out of the way and used a heavy stone to make the long ladder on the slippery slope more secure.

"You go first without your torch." He reached out his hand for the one Tamo had lit. "I lower it down."

Tamo hesitated, then gave up his torch.

"Try not to shake ladder at drop-off."

"All right. I know what I'm doing," Tamo muttered, not as cheerful as he'd been while learning jiu-jitsu. He climbed down backwards with only a little jiggle despite his size.

Daisuke sent down the glowing cattail head, the bucket of coals, bamboo poles, and lengthened rigging lines, then followed Tamo to the lower level. After tying one end of the line around a stony outcrop and coiling the rest around his shoulder, he lit his own torch. "You want me to go first now?" He looked at the darkness beyond the torches' dim circles of light. He'd never experienced such a well of darkness, without a single discernible shape in it. It was as if the black depths could absorb anything venturing in, as if a body could simply vanish. "I understand dark now." He hoped his voice hadn't betrayed his apprehension.

"I'll go first," Tamo said, his voice gruff. "Glad you understand."

"Use your pole before you step. Before all steps. Maybe another slick incline ahead of us." Daisuke shuddered at the pictures in his mind. "Maybe a cliff goes down, down, down, where you break neck. Water running below, so maybe many holes in cave floor. Maybe hard to see."

"Yes, yes. Maybe I know," Tamo muttered.

Tamo's annoyance tempted Daisuke to quote the Bible's words about pride going before a fall, but he held back. The unbeliever would just get more aggravated. "Tie the end of the line around you," he said instead. He uncoiled part of the line and exchanged it for Tamo's torch.

After securing the line around his upper chest and reclaiming his torch, Tamo moved forward at a snail's pace, either from fear or wisdom.

While they felt their way, Daisuke concentrated on the cavern floor's rough surface. Avoiding the rocks strewn across the chamber wasn't too hard, but stepping across each rope-like fissure demanded all his courage. Cooler air from an unknown depth crept up from the larger cracks. The layer they were tapping across might be uniformly thick and stable. Or, it might be thin in places like an eggshell.

Momentarily glancing forward at Tamo's shadowy figure, he sensed movement from the corner of his eye. Icy fingers pricked the back of his neck at the sight of large shapes gliding along the side wall. Were specters trailing them? Then he grunted as a wall shape duplicated his arm's movement. Of course—the close torches magnified his and Tamo's own shadows. Disgusted at himself, he returned his attention to the real perils at his feet.

The far wall ended abruptly. He joined Tamo in looking through an opening near its base. The passageway they faced narrowed and slanted downward, but looked traversable.

"Would this work?" Tamo extended his arm into the tunnel. "We could hide most of the entrance with rocks."

"Rocks look different. The pirates can move them and look behind."

"Moving ahead then." Tamo crawled through the hole. Then while crouching because of the low ceiling, he stepped forward, forgetting to tap the floor.

"Tap!" Daisuke growled. Strangely he didn't want Tamo to die, not just because he was needed in the crisis, but actually because he liked the barbarian a little … or more than a little.

"Right! I forgot." The tapping began again, mixed with the scraping and thumps of Tamo's boots. A few minutes later, Tamo stopped short. "Look. There's a kind of fork here." He extended his torch through the opening to their left, then peered into the hole. Seconds later, he jumped back, barely missing Daisuke's sandals. "Oh, the bats! Sounds like I bothered them."

Daisuke could clearly hear the augmented chirping too. "Guano bad for a hiding place except for our ladders. Stand back. I look at cave floor."

"No, I'll check. Just be ready to hit the ground if the bats come blasting out."

Tamo leaned inside the opening, then took one step inside. "Smells bad. Really bad," he reported in a loud whisper. "But the floor's level with only a few bumps as far as the light shines."

"Good. We can explore this chamber farther if find no other place." Maybe Tamo was becoming braver about the bats.

Tamo drew back and stood still, as though thinking. "The bats and guano might hold the pirates back too. We might be safer on this chamber's far side."

"So you think to go that way?"

"I don't want to. Just looking in there makes me jittery— more jittery than how I already am—if you have to know. But facing bats is better than facing pirates. I'm sure you agree."

Daisuke brushed past Tamo and poked his head into the opening while keeping his torch outside the chamber. The murky shadows led into black nothingness. A stronger sense of foreboding took hold of him. He withdrew and rubbed his temples, debating. Exploring beyond the bat chamber made good sense even if the pirates could guess their route. The closest chamber might open into another, and the second into a third, all with a confusing number of corridors, extending on and on.

But something was wrong. Unhealthy air? A hollow echo with the chirps? The fissure at the entrance was larger than what they'd seen so far. Was that causing his unease? Common sense said to cautiously explore the possibility. But his spirit resisted. Was he shaming his ancestry by an irrational fear? Or was the cavern warning him?

He turned his back on the chamber. "I want to check the other opening."

Offering no objection, Tamo headed to the untried outlet. "It's a low tunnel, but seems to open up at the end," he reported. "Looks fine. Clear of bats."

"Remember to tap."

Tamo crawled a little too fast. At the far end, he wiggled through the opening and stood. "Come on. It's good here. Lots of icicle-like stalactites way above and columns like a church."

Daisuke put his bucket of coals down and followed. Moist, chillier air coming from the chamber made his nose colder.

"Whoa! Help!" Tamo yelled just as the remaining part of the coil slid off Daisuke's shoulder and flew along the cave floor.

Dread squeezed Daisuke's chest. He tore after the line, extinguishing his torch in his haste.

"I'm on a ledge." Tamo's voice came from somewhere below the cave's damp floor. It's next to water. Give me a second. The wall's slippery, but I can get out."

"Wait! Stay where you are! I go back through tunnel and relight torch. Then I help you not fall in water. Big danger there!" He scraped his elbows in his rush back through the tunnel, but didn't care. Thankful for the bucket's faint glow, he steadied his hands and lit the torch.

Tamo hadn't waited and was coming out of a nearly invisible hole when Daisuke made it into the chamber again.

"Guess I'll never forget to tap. It looked safe. I-I couldn't see the hole at all. The water below seemed to be moving pretty fast."

"That stream could go over big drop-off. Not know how long, how steep. Or it disappears under a big rock and takes person with it." Daisuke stared at Tamo's dim figure, hoping he'd get the picture.

"I had a close call, all right. I knew this cavern could kill you. Give me a minute to pull myself together." He sat and hugged his bent knees. "Reckon we don't have much choice. We can go deeper into the disgusting bat room, hide here, or take a long, dark swim to who knows where."

Daisuke nodded, then held his torch up, amazed by the height of the ceiling that disappeared into gloom above him. Lowering the torch, he examined the walls, checking for any more openings. The room looked fully enclosed except for the exit through the bottom surface. "If only one hole, we can cover it. Take turns to sleep here if need to hide. Air not too unhealthy. Get on the ledge below if pirates come close. The ledge is how wide and long?"

"I don't know exactly, but it felt like room for three to stand arm to arm. I was too shaken up to find out all the dimensions in the dark."

If you waited for the torch, we would know went through Daisuke's mind. But who wouldn't be "shaken," falling into a cavern's hole that might have been bottomless? While he tapped the rest of the room's floor, keeping his distance from the hole, Tamo sat and watched him, apparently still having unsteady sailor's legs.

"No more holes." Daisuke stopped investigating. "We can make a bamboo cover. Put rocks near the far wall. Hide supplies behind rocks and stalag … stalag?"

"Stalagmites," Tamo finished for him.

"The pirates not look this far into the cavern if think we not here."

Tamo pushed himself up. "That's probably the best we can do. And now we can get out of this blasted pit!" He gathered his pole and flameless torch, from where they'd fallen next to the hole. "You lead this time."

Daisuke tapped their way out, nervous the surface could open up just a step or two away from where they had traversed earlier. And if it did, Tamo was just overconfident enough to fall in and not strike a handy ledge the second time.

When they both made it back to the rim of daylight, Daisuke breathed a prayer of thanks. Tamo scrambled up the ladder, like a bear fleeing a forest fire. At the top, the sailor pranced around, jabbering about how blue and open and great the sky was. Daisuke couldn't help chuckling. Luckily, as a samurai, he was able to summon his belly's strength, or else he would be equally overcome by the joy of an open, bright expanse over solid earth. Or at least, earth that seemed solid when there were no tremors.

As soon as they arrived back at the cave, Tamo settled on a rock nearby Sara. Daisuke took one of the mats she had brought out for them and leaned against another boulder.

"Did you find a good place in the cavern?" Sara asked as she closed the Bible. She had never subdued her curiosity enough to refrain from starting a conversation with men. But if they lived on the island the rest of their lives, or they were killed by pirates, or she had to disguise herself as his young brother back in Japan, it wouldn't matter.

Tamo began the account, his coltish eagerness evident. Sara allowed a giggle to escape about the atrocious bat room before she covered her mouth. Daisuke felt the beginning of a smile himself. But then a weariness settled in his bones. What a bleak future his trusting sister faced. If they escaped the island, would she be better off somewhere besides their country? Not with Tamo, of course, but with a Christian semi-barbarian who had basic samurai virtues? Yet how could the daughter of a samurai ever desert their sacred land? He couldn't bear to think about it.

"You know now," he told Sara when Tamo drew his report to a close. "Time to do lookout. Be careful when you climb trees."

She offered him her customary bow and laid the Bible down with a glance at Tamo. "I turned the meat right before you came," she said and walked away.

Tamo watched her for a second, then patted the Bible and turned toward Daisuke. "Do you really believe all this?" He gave a slight roll of his eyes.

Daisuke pulled his mind off the interactions between Sara and Tamo. He'd examine his concern at their growing familiarity later. "I believe what I learned till now. English hard to read. Some parts hard to understand. But I like what it says." He couldn't tell if Tamo was genuinely curious or mocking the faith.

"Well, as for myself, I've got plenty of doubts. But I can read this out loud for you if you want. Some parts are more interesting than I thought."

"No need. We have no time now. And you and us, the way we think is different. While you watch fire, I go to far side of the valley. I get more shikuwasa limes and what you call hog plums."

Daisuke strode away, leaving the Bible by Tamo. The barbarian needed a code to guide his life. Of course, not being a samurai, the timeless Hagakure guide, telling the warrior's duties for living and dying, would mean nothing to him. But if Tamo learned enough of the Bible, he'd see standards as high, or higher, than what the samurai code taught. The Christian code, he had found, surprisingly demanded not only self-control, duty, bravery, and sacrifice, but also unwavering honesty and the strange-and-difficult ones of giving mercy as well as showing love to God and everyone.

Admittedly, he himself still struggled to grasp the last two demands—even a little.

CHAPTER 27

Terry watched the people stand to sing in the church service in Mr. Pendleton's parlor. There were still a few empty chairs, so he wouldn't need to bring in more. He joined the other servants at the back of the room and ran his eyes over the attendees. Consul and Mrs. Cardiff and her baby were there, of course, with Jim sitting on the far side of the consul. An elderly couple sat next to Mrs. Cardiff, most likely her parents. Next to the couple was an ancient lady, who he guessed was a relation. Mia, Aki, and Aiya were there. Ichi was noticeably absent, which was a good thing after his traitorous translation for Zeke. Three samurai sat on the front row. Scattered among the other rows were several American or European couples and a weathered, scruffy man—a sailing master, by the looks of the cocky fur cap he belatedly removed.

Mr. Pendleton's topic was on prayer. Terry knew this because one of his least-liked duties had been to make twenty-five copies of the day's program. He had written the English, and Interpreter Taguchi had later filled in the Japanese translation. As Mr. Pendleton launched into his speech, Terry prepared to endure a totally irrelevant message. Too bad the topic for the day wouldn't offer a little entertainment, like some of the stories about defeating lions and giants.

Just as he started to daydream about showing Jim around the settlement, Mr. Pendleton mentioned how God had answered the apostle Paul's prayer to go to Rome in a way no one would voluntarily choose. God's answer had begun with the apostle's arrest.

Terry considered that fact while Mr. Pendleton translated his words into Japanese. At first glance, the famous Christian and he had arrests in common, but that was where any similarity ended. If he had devoted his life to *almighty* God like the apostle had and then got arrested, the benefits of following Christ would be all the more questionable. Although Mrs. Cardiff had seen something good come from her few hours in prison, both she and the apostle, from what he'd already gathered in the Book of Acts, hadn't deserved such rough treatment.

Mr. Pendleton proceeded to read parts of the last chapters of Acts aloud, which Terry had flipped through a day earlier with little interest. It looked impossible for Mr. Pendleton to make his message benefit the sincere-looking people in the audience. He'd bet none of them, except Mrs. Cardiff and her student Mia, had ever set one foot in an enclosure with iron bars.

Having finished reading, Mr. Pendleton looked up from the Bible. "God's way isn't always the easy way." His eyes fell on Terry for a second. "Not only was the brave apostle confined on a ship as a prisoner, but he had to endure a tempest and shipwreck on the way to his trial. Yet, islanders heard about Jesus because of the wreck, and the apostle made it safely to Rome."

Terry held back a snort. It would be hunky-dory if an apostle would so conveniently have a shipwreck next to Tom's island, tell any natives there about Jesus, and provide Tom a trip to

Nagasaki. Then the coordinates wouldn't be an issue. But that was simpleminded thinking. Nothing else.

"Although the apostle was kept in Rome under guard in rented lodgings," Mr. Pendleton was saying, "he could tell people about Jesus freely, and he wrote letters that ended up in the Bible, helping people to this very day. We may not always understand what God is about," the elderly man concluded, "but if we have Jesus Christ as our Savior and King, God is working it all for our good and his purposes. And He answers prayer to accomplish it."

How nice it sounds, and how unlikely. Terry shifted his weight, relieved the service was almost over.

At the end of his message, Mr. Pendleton mentioned an ill acquaintance's need for prayer. Then he asked Terry to come forward—with *no* prior warning and *no* word of explanation.

Terry cringed, debating whether to shake his head. If only he could snap his fingers and disappear—this time from the church instead of from the front of a saloon. Maybe he should *pray* for a way of escape.

Mr. Pendleton repeated his request.

Staring straight ahead, Terry made his way to the front. The gentleman put a hand on his shoulder and turned toward the audience. "I want us to petition God for this young man's needs. Shall we pray." Then he held his other hand over Terry's head.

Terry stood there, frozen.

"Our heavenly Father," the man began, "we thank Thee for keeping this young sailor safe throughout his many trials. If his marooned brother is still alive, we ask that he be rescued and both brothers be reunited. If it pleases Thee, we ask Thee to reveal the island's location and provide the needed transportation. In the name of our Lord Jesus Christ. Amen."

Several of the attendees echoed the "Amen."

"You may go back to your duties, my boy," Mr. Pendleton instructed, as the person known as Lady Anne took her place at the pianoforte for the closing hymn.

Terry stood at the back again, unable to leave since he had the job of transforming the room back into the parlor. His face burned at the humiliation of having his private needs prayed for publicly. A totally unnecessary, tactless action. But, of course, his sponsor had meant well. The man was always trying to look out for his wayward charge.

Forcing a smile, Terry thanked the well-wishers who exited by him.

He hadn't been peeling potatoes in the kitchen long when Matsu came and motioned for him to come with him. Drying his hands, he determined to be patient—*longsuffering*, he'd heard Christians say. The manservant led him back to the parlor, where Mr. Pendleton and the weathered newcomer who had been at the service were talking at the back table.

"Come here." Mr. Pendleton waved him over. "I believe we have received a partial answer to our prayers in record time. Mr. Wilkes is the sailing master of a whaler that made port last evening. I'll let him tell you his story."

"My whaler had been closing in on a sperm whale, when we saw two things at once. Someone was waving a red cloth in a tree on an island we were passin'—suppose'ly un'habited—and a pirate ship's topgallant sails 'peared on the horizon. By the time we got our boats in, the pirates were upon us. We pretended surrender, and when the villains moved in close to take their prize, my good archers—five Satsuma offenders, rescued by my ship from starvin' in the Loo-Choo sugarcane fields—sent flamin' arrows into their canvas. A storm was brewin', the wind filled our sails, and off we flew. We daren't stop at the island, but

I been bothered 'bout that marooned soul ever since. If he wasn't your brother, he's somebody needin' help, 'specially since the pirates coulda seen the red flag too."

"He knows the island's correct coordinates, Terrence." Mr. Pendleton pointed to an X with a note on the map. "Depending on the weather, it's an eight-day sail from here. About the right distance, I gather, since your ship had returned to its usual course before you were in the doctor's care for close to five days."

Terry's legs weakened. He gripped the closest chair.

"Is the boy all right?" The whaling master shot out a hand, bronzed by the sun.

"Gave him a shock. He'll be all right." Mr. Pendleton gripped Terry's shoulder. "News too fast can do that." He rang for Matsu and ordered him to bring a small amount of the brandy he'd bought the previous week. "I'll update John Cardiff, and we'll see how the second part of our prayer gets answered. I've no doubt the good Lord will continue the work he's begun."

"I'd help out if I could, but my crew wouldn't stand fer goin' close to this spot again." The sailing master tapped the map's X. "Lightly armed as we are—good archers though we have. Too dangerous with pirates skulkin'."

"Rightly so," Mr. Pendleton said.

Terry wished the whaler didn't have such a ghastly justification as he swallowed the brandy with three gulps. But now that the coordinates were known, at least the first hurdle was over.

Mr. Pendleton studied Terry's face. "Ah, the brandy has helped. You're getting your color back, but I'm excusing you from any remaining tasks for the day. After you fully recover, you may want to introduce your friend Jim to the settlement."

"Thank you, sir." Terry felt a tingling down to his toes. "I was dizzy for a second there, but I guess that sup of strong drink did its job. I've been thinking Jim needs to see where he's at."

An hour later, the consulate's gatekeeper and the two sentries, recognizing Terry, let him in as if he belonged there. The consul was entertaining his wife's parents and her great-aunt, but sent word for Jim to enjoy himself.

"Jumpin' Jehoshaphat!" Jim exclaimed, with a shake of his head, as they started down the cobblestone road. "Who'da thought we'd be roaming free today? No rigging in sight. Soft beds. Good food."

"I sure didn't expect it," Terry said after a moment of taking in Jim's cheerfulness. "Sometimes I wonder if it's a nice dream, but then I think of Tom, and it's more like a nightmare suffocating me." He stepped around horse manure missed by the street sweepers. "But nightmare or dream, you won't believe what happened after you left this morning."

"You mean after the prayer? That was a sight to behold—you thunderstruck. But I did pray along with Mr. Pendleton."

"And you expected an answer?"

"Sure—maybe different in some details, but an answer. You came to the noodle shop when I was prayin' for help. You think that was just an accident?" Jim stopped walking and looked at Terry.

"Not certain what I think. Never questioned much before sailing, cuz everything was easy back home."

"So those hoodlums on the *William Parton* started you doubting? They did the opposite for me. To my way of thinking, not all those jack tars were evil, but every one of 'em looked out for just themselves, 'cept you and Tom."

Terry didn't divulge that a big reason for his initial friendliness had been the need for at least one friend on the ship besides his brother. "Anyway," he said instead, "a part of Mr. Pendleton's prayer was supposedly answered."

As Jim listened to the account about the whaler, his face broke into a huge grin. "There, you see," he said at the end. "That says it's for real—God, Jesus, the Bible. Right?"

"It could be coincidence. Luck. Unusual good luck."

"You really think so?"

"Not saying that for sure." Terry grimaced at Jim's puzzled look. "I guess the scale would tip in God's favor if the transportation shows up and Tom's all right." He swallowed hard. "But if a ship goes and there's no Tom, or just his bones"— he struggled to finish—"then sayin' the prayer got answered wouldn't be sensical, now, would it?"

"Guess not." Jim rubbed the back of his neck. "So maybe that should give us hope."

Not quite getting Jim's point and wanting to change the topic, Terry pointed to the entrance of the Dog's Tooth Saloon as they walked by. "Got in some trouble inside there. Involved Zeke, wouldn't you know?"

"So what happened?"

He recounted the incident, chuckling at Jim's astonishment that a novel had inspired Mr. Pendleton's help. Yet Zeke's deceit still knotted his stomach.

"You'll like this news," Jim fairly chirped, dodging straw brooms poking out from a peddler. "Consul Cardiff put out a warrant for Zeke's arrest. Charges of assault and attempted murder. The notice is in the settlement's newspaper and posted on the gates. Zeke won't dare show his face in this town again."

"You bet I like it." The sun appeared to shine a little brighter. "I reckon Zeke will get his payback someday and the other villains too."

"If not in this life, then in the next," Jim added.

"Well, if you ask me, that's simply wriggling out of explaining injustice." Terry raised his eyebrows at Jim, but gave up the conversation since the already crowded road had gotten harder to navigate. They didn't talk anymore until they came to Jake's General Store.

Terry stood still as soon as they entered the store's large room, breathing in the scent of leather and tobacco. For a moment, he saw his home's stableman spitting tobacco juice before pitching hay into the stalls. He could almost hear his horse's whinny. Admiral had always acted like he missed Terry if he didn't spend time with the stallion for a couple of days. What must Admiral think of his master for neglecting him for over a year?

Sighing, he joined Jim, who was eying the new shipment of fishing poles next to the saddles. "Jake's is the supply store for the whole International Settlement," he explained. "You never know what you'll find crammed in here. Things we took for granted before setting sail, and unusual things too. Really unusual." He managed a feeble laugh. "I heard Jake even had a live tiger for sale once. The Nagasaki bigwigs took charge of it quick as a wink, and no more was heard of the beast."

"Guess I won't be buying a tiger, fishing pole, or anything for myself." Jim ran his hand over a bag of marbles. "Forfeited my pay, you know."

"But if you don't ship out for California, you can drop in here when you're bored. Maybe get some part-time work. Not much to do in the town for a good Christian, or for a servant on a leash either. But I'm not complaining. No sir, things could've been a hundred times worse. It's just the delay in finding Tom that gnaws my bones—and thoughts of home that sometimes come out of nowhere."

After Jake's, they strolled toward the harbor. Terry pointed out Cardiff & Associates' large headquarters and separate warehouse on prime property and then the Customs House. They ambled along the port's retaining wall, taking in the view of the docks, teeming with people and goods. The cries of seagulls mixed with the clanking of machinery, deep-throated boat whistles, and the steady racket of impatient shouts and curses.

Terry pointed to the *Retriever* anchored farther out in the bay. "That beauty belongs to Consul Cardiff's company. He's a part-time, honorary consul and a full-time merchant. So that's the ship that might be waiting to speed you o'er the waves." An ache ate at his heart. If only it would speed *him* to Tom.

"Ships and sailing and docks—the smell of the sea—all that stuff excited me when I was real young." Jim offered a sad smile as they turned to retrace their steps. "Not any longer. No siree."

"Me neither. Can't believe I was stupid enough to follow Tom onto the *William Parton.* Thought it'd be great, sailing to the other side of the world, exploring exotic lands. Hah! Nothing further from the truth."

"You gotta stay here another five weeks to pay off your debt, right? Maybe you can borrow a horse and see how the people really live 'cross the bridge. Explore, after all. If anyone's lookin' for exotic, seems here's the place to find it."

Terry shook his head. "Can't leave the settlement. Contract's order. You might get to, though."

"Hope I do, but it'd be a whale of a lot more fun with you." Jim scrunched up his face.

"Sorry, ol' pal. Even if I could get permission, I wouldn't have time to see much. Mr. Pendleton keeps me busy all day, every day, like a grist wheel always grinding corn. When I'm not doing household work, he's pushing me to catch up on the schooling I missed while on the ship. Anyway, even if I could explore, I'd be worrying about Tom the whole time."

"Wish I could help somehow, but—" The urgent blast from a docking tugboat's horn overpowered Jim's words.

"You're the best," Terry said, raising his voice above the increased noises after Jim uncovered his ears. "Brought the letters that saved my future and, I hope, Tom's too." He pointed down the embankment's stairs, ready to get away from the racket.

"What if we switched?" Jim asked when they reached the road leading back to town. He was beaming. "What if I took your place here, and you took the passage the consul offered me?"

"What? Take my place?" Terry nearly stumbled over a pebble. "Have you thought about being stuck in Nagasaki until the consul's ship made another voyage east? Could be a year, or never. And you'd start out as an unpaid servant, not a guest like now at the consulate."

"No one's waiting for me over there. I like Mr. Pendleton. He's a kind, good man. I wouldn't mind serving him. In fact, when I'm around him, I think I'm real lucky to know him."

Terry clenched his teeth against the hope starting to sprout. The consul hadn't agreed yet to having his ship visit the island. A *big* obstacle. Then even if the *Retriever* was sent there, Consul Cardiff might think Terry shouldn't leave Nagasaki, that he'd be getting off too lightly for his court-ordered repayment, especially after his visit to the saloon. His judge had said "no negotiation." Trading places—it had to be too good to be true. Wishing and hoping and dreaming wouldn't change it.

"Thank you, Jim," he managed to say after a lengthy minute. "No matter what happens, I'll never forget your offer as long as I live."

"You don't think it's possible?"

"Guess it all depends on the consul—*if* he orders his ship by the island and *if* he's willing for us to switch. Guess Mr. Pendleton wouldn't object *if* the consul agreed."

"Then, I'll ask about it tonight." Jim grinned, as if taking Terry's place were the greatest prize in the world.

Terry drew in a breath. For a second, he could almost think that Mr. Pendleton's and the Cardiffs' prayers were making a difference. Maybe the *Retriever* would steam toward the island with him on board. And Tom would race down to the beach, arms wildly waving, shouting Terry's name as the jolly-boat approached. They'd both make it home, and he'd ride Admiral again, his shirt flapping in the wind, while Tom courted Peg Stevenson.

But this dream could too easily behave like a kite that had once escaped his grasp. For a short time, its string had dangled low, just inches beyond his reach. Then an updraft had taken it clear over the rooftops, out of sight.

CHAPTER 28

John Cardiff glanced at his wife, expecting her smile. He wasn't disappointed. She had been bringing up the Ballard brothers' dilemma every day for prayer. Richard Pendleton apparently saw the smile too, and a twinkle lit his eyes.

John turned his attention back to Jim, sitting quietly at the dining table, gazing expectantly at him after presenting his jaw-dropping proposal. "Thank you, Jim. That's a very kind offer. We'll discuss your request and let you know as soon as we reach a decision." He glanced at Jim's plate. "If you've finished your dinner, you may be excused. If you like, you can check with our housekeeper later for a taste of dessert."

The boy bobbed his head and stood. "Whatever you decide about my offer, I know it'll be best." He looked at Richard. "Like Mr. Pendleton said this morning."

John nodded with the others. "Well put, young man."

After the maid followed Jim out and closed the door, John turned to Richard. "Well, what do you say? I don't see a problem with the trade, but you're the one directly affected."

"The switch is fine. But I have a further innovation to add. I've been thinking of doing something, and all this business over the marooned boy has made up my mind. First, before revealing my plan, I'd like to immediately pay off Terrence's debt. I don't intend for that to end the period of service—*Jim's* service with the change—but it would get the fine off the books."

"There's no rush to settle the account, but I suppose the payment may simplify the transfer." John drew a cheroot from his vest pocket and offered it to Richard.

"I'll accept this with thanks and light up at home." He pocketed the cheroot. "Now, I must apologize for the suddenness of my request. Since Margaret passed, I've been wanting to spend time with our children and get reacquainted with the grandchildren. Therefore, I'd like to book passage on the *Retriever* to California."

"Goodness!" John slapped his forehead. "Losing the honorary vice consul is not a result I'd have expected or desired. And it wouldn't be just the consulate's loss. Sumi and I would be losing a great friend, a trusted counselor."

"A tremendous loss," his wife chimed in. "Like losing one of our family."

"You wouldn't get rid of me that easily. I couldn't stay away from both of you, the little one, and the Japanese people for long. I'd be back within two years. But John, if I didn't return in six years, the house would be yours to dispose of."

"And in the meantime, what about that house and your servants, which would now include Jim?"

"Would you mind seeing about engaging a good renter in the next month, one who could afford adequate wages for the staff in exchange for his paying a very low annual rent? If I hadn't dithered about leaving for so long and if the *Retriever* weren't sailing so soon, I'd see to it myself."

"Would I dare mind after all you've done for me and Sumi?

It'd be a privilege to help out. But I'm still trying to get my mind around this sudden revelation."

"Well, here's another thought that just came to mind this minute." Richard looked as if he were about to produce the rabbit from a hat trick. "If Jim is willing, I'd like to take him along as my companion instead of leaving him here to finish his weeks of servitude. You know, losing my helpmate hasn't been easy. Jim is a fine boy. He'd take an edge off the loneliness I sometimes feel in the evening as well as lend a hand on the journey."

"Oh," Sumi breathed out. "I wish we had been more sensitive to you. But how wonderful that would be for Jim, and it appears a gain for you too."

"As long as I'm presenting these impulsive ideas, here's one more, but it may already be crossing your minds as well." Richard rotated his hand as if to produce an even greater magic trick. "Now that Terrence's debt no longer tethers him to Nagasaki, I assume he could take advantage of your original offer to Jim about a working passage to San Francisco. Right?"

"Yes"—John hesitated, hating to pour ice on his friend's eagerness—"but I'm sure you realize there's much to consider. First off, Terrence might not want to leave the area unless he found his brother."

"But if the hope for a rescue works out, using the coordinates we now know, the boys could be reunited at the island. They could go with me all the way to California. Further, if Thomas Ballard isn't anywhere on the island or not found alive—God forbid—I suggest the best option for Terrence would be to head to his New York home. If another ship picked up Thomas, he wouldn't know to look for Terrence here."

"We're assuming a lot. An awful lot, I'm afraid." John looked from Sumi to Richard, saddened at their anxious expressions. "The biggest assumption is that the *Retriever* will actually visit the island. Although the ship's twenty-four-pounder cannon could match a pirate ship's fairly well, I'm not willing to risk the crew's lives. Only if the **USS Observer** turns out to be available, can I send the ship to waters where we are now certain pirates lurk. When we enlisted the governor's help in probing the logbooks, I told him the gunship's protection was required for the *Retriever* to visit the island."

The furrows in Richard's forehead deepened. "Isn't it too late to determine the frigate's availability? Since I hadn't heard otherwise, I assumed any necessary arrangement had been made."

"Partly made." John cocked his head. "I did start the process. Before our setback with the *William Parton*, I spoke with Captain James. Because of piracy, he was eager for the **USS Observer** to accompany the *Retriever* to check out the island if—and I repeat—if Minister Resident Pruyn didn't object. So I immediately sent an urgent message to the minister by a fast courier, requesting the escort. I hope to receive an affirmative answer by the end of this week, but we can't count on Pruyn's approval yet."

"Relieving the world of even one set of pirates would be an admirable cause." Richard looked over the rim of his spectacles. "No telling how many innocents have been sacrificed to their greed. And finding that boy alive would lighten my mind a great deal, and yours too, I'm sure."

"Indeed. So now, we'll have to hope for the best." His lame conclusion stuck in his craw and undoubtedly hurt his friend and Sumi, as their silence testified.

"You're doing your best," Richard said after an awkward pause, "and I'm eager to hear Jim's decision."

John wiped his brow with his handkerchief, glad for the more cheerful topic. "I can't imagine Jim turning down the opportunity to sail as your companion. The boy wouldn't be launched into unknown territory alone. I can give both of you a stateroom to share if that would suit your needs, or you can each have a smaller cabin."

"The stateroom would be preferable. And I plan to cover both our fares."

"That's not necessary. I'm expecting a nice profit from this run." Fairly certain he wouldn't face an argument about the fares, John reached for his glass.

"Well then, if you insist." Richard held up his glass in a salute, matching John's.

"But then, what will you do after you arrive in California?" Sumi asked.

"I'd begin with the most pressing—to help Jim look for his uncle around San Francisco. If that doesn't work out for the boy, I'll extend an offer for him to continue as my companion, with rigorous aid for his schooling."

"Your family is still in Connecticut, right?" Sumi's brow wrinkled. "All the way across the United States?"

"They're still in New England, but they moved a year ago to Boston, following after my oldest grandchild. If the war hasn't ended, I'll have to search out the safest route to cross the continent. If hostilities have ended—as we all dearly hope—I'd like to stop in New Orleans on the way and check out fifteen acres my brother deeded to me."

Sumi's eyes shone with the trace of a tear. "I do hope you will be safe. And Jim and Terrence should know how blessed they are. Your generosity always has amazed me."

"It makes me happy to think that Margaret would be pleased,

as I trust the Lord is also."

"Well, it's not hard to see the earmarks of Providence in how this is coming together for Jim and hopefully for Terrence too." John squeezed Sumi's hand. "With that in mind, I have one last question. If approval is given for the escort, would Terrence be proficient enough in math to train as an apprentice navigator?"

Richard tapped his chin in thought. "He's quick enough in what I've assigned him. I haven't had an occasion to test him in math. Perhaps Stargazer Hunt could examine him."

"A good suggestion." John glanced at his fob watch. "I see we're running behind schedule. Even the maid has left us. But we've practically been turning summersaults in making plans."

"Now if I can tempt either of you at this late hour," Sumi said, displaying a brighter countenance, "I believe the cook has elderberry pudding available as a nightcap."

"Who could resist elderberry pudding at any hour?" Richard answered, with John seconding him.

As the pudding was served by their housekeeper, who had taken the maid's place, John settled into a more comfortable position. What an astonishing evening. How grand it would be if his request for the frigate was honored in time and the Ballard boy was found alive and healthy. How fine, too, if Jim located his uncle and he turned out to be an upright, compassionate man.

But no matter what, they were doing everything they could. And naturally, the outcomes lay in God's hands. The Lord had surprised him in the past, even terrified him at times, but his ways were inevitably good. The key was to be aligned with those ways.

He earnestly hoped they were aligned.

CHAPTER 29

December 1862
Southeast of Japan on the Pacific Ocean

Terry opened the cabin door at Mr. Pendleton's welcoming call, glad for the chance to get away from the *Retriever's* stifling forecastle and continue his education. He dreaded only one part of the two hours, and that was the torture of trigonometry, a result of being Stargazer's apprentice.

The last fifteen days had been a whirlwind, starting with the frigate's approval to take part in the pirate hunt. That triggered his initiation as a sailor on the *Retriever* while still at the port, followed by the sendoff for Mr. Pendleton, far more beloved by Westerners and Japanese citizens than Terry had guessed. While the ship steamed toward Tom's island, the on-going riddles of navigation continued to puzzle him every day. He'd impressed Stargazer by his quick grasp of the constellations—since he'd already known them—but he'd unimpressed the man with his fumbling use of the sextant. Something about overcorrecting for the optical zero error. But he wasn't giving up, and every nautical mile brought him closer to Tom.

Jim jumped up when Terry stepped inside the room. "We've got a treat waiting for us right off the captain's table if we both master our studies today, and I've already finished mine. You'll never believe it." He stretched out both arms as if preparing to catch a small hippo. "Sassafras tea and apple-pear pie, the kind of apples the Japanese have!"

"Hope I don't mess things up." Terry gave a halfhearted laugh and sat down across from Mr. Pendleton. Apple pie was a longed-for treat, but he wasn't a child needing that kind of motivation.

Mr. Pendleton gave him one of his knowing looks. "I'm not worried about your doing your best. You've made excellent progress in your brand-new field of study. How are things with the crew?"

"Still as fine a group of jack tars as you could have on the best of ships, sir. Stargazer Hunt, both mates, and Captain Whitson are first rate too." Terry reached for his stack of assignments, wishing he could move the trigonometry worksheets from off the top. "The sailors here show our troubles on the *William Parton* weren't all due to our being landlubbers. Half of that crew were just mean, crude beasts." He glanced at his elder.

"The pie will help us celebrate how the Almighty provided for both of you young men." Mr. Pendleton slid a copy of Dickens' *David Copperfield* across the table to Terry. "Work on today's trigonometry first. Then you can take a break with a couple of chapters from Dickens."

"Yes, sir, I'll do my best." Terry placed the tantalizing novel to one side.

"Now," Mr. Pendleton said, smiling broadly at Jim, "Captain says you can be at the helm when the ocean is calm. Looks like you've a chance right now. Just don't steer us to Davy Jones' locker."

"That's great, sir!" Jim bounced on the balls of his feet. "Regular sailors on watch for the *William Parton* took turns, too, when nothing hazardous was happening, but I didn't dare ask to do it myself. Captain Madison would've said I was being too presumptuous for my age, like a pup tackling a mountain lion, I guess."

"I'll go with you and make sure whoever is at the helm knows you have permission to assist." Mr. Pendleton pushed back from the table and left with Jim.

Terry started reviewing the differential equations from the previous day, but Tom's pleading face shone in place of the befuddling numerals and signs. Just two more days to the island, and the awful suspense would end—either wonderfully or terribly.

Mr. Pendleton came back before Terry made much progress and looked over his shoulder. "Slow going, I see. Too much to think about, I wager."

"Yes, sir. I've been thinking about what you said a couple of Sundays ago and how things have mostly gone well since I reached Nagasaki. I'm hoping everything continues good—no shipwreck like that apostle's, no pirates … and Tom's all right." He swallowed, but couldn't relieve his throat's tightness.

"Hard times aren't God's only method." Mr. Pendleton took his seat again. "And think how he's answered our prayers so far. I believe we'll find your brother alive and well." Confidence shone in his face.

"I wish I could believe like you do … uh … I mean, I wish I could believe *that*." Terry smacked his chest. How could he have spoken such a mixed-up bunch of words out loud—and to Mr.

Pendleton, of all people?

"If you mean it, I'll tell you a few foundational points—or axioms like in mathematics—underlying a belief like mine." His effort at a calm tone failed to hide the old man's eagerness.

"Well … uh, I guess I do mean it." It was a lie, but what else could he say? Mr. Pendleton was the kindest, most generous man he'd ever met. In return, he'd have to be polite and try not to mislead him any further.

"Well then, the first axiom, or key, is to grant that Jesus and his followers—his disciples and the hundreds of other eyewitnesses—were truthful, not prone to lie, especially about something so consequential as Jesus' character and resurrection. You've read quite a bit of the Bible now. As you think this point over, how do these first-century, historical records strike you?"

Terry pondered the question. It did seem reasonable that if he didn't want to mislead Mr. Pendleton, Jesus and his followers would be far less likely to invent an enormous mass of lies. Then there was Mrs. Cardiff's logic that eyewitnesses testifying to Jesus' resurrection wouldn't die for something they knew was false. "Yes," he answered after a minute, "it seems they wouldn't *purposefully* lie." At least, he could honestly agree with one of Mr. Pendleton's points.

He was rewarded by Mr. Pendleton's enthusiastic nod. "A good start. Then the second axiom is that Jesus' resurrection *proved* he was who he said he was—the Son of God. How about that?"

Terry recoiled inwardly. Had he fallen into a trap, set by the nice gentleman? But if the resurrection wasn't a lie, what other conclusion was there? Of course, it could be a mistake, which is what he'd momentarily considered with the first so-called axiom. But Mr. Pendleton would then ask how such a huge mistake was possible with so many eyewitnesses and their contemporary records.

"It seems to follow logically, doesn't it?" he admitted grudgingly, wanting to avoid the hassle over the possibility of a mistake.

"Indeed. You can see how things fit together."

Terry sucked in a breath. He could see, all right. He was covering up his doubts too well. Trying too hard to be polite.

"Now, the next key is to believe that Jesus is our Savior because he gave his perfect life as God's Son to pay the penalty for our sins." Mr. Pendleton gave him an expectant look.

"How do we know that, sir? Did Jesus say so himself?" Here was a chance to slow things down. Find a loophole that even his opponent would accept.

"Yes, he said he was giving his life as a 'ransom' and that his death would fulfill the Old Testament prophesies of a Savior for all people, written hundreds of years earlier."

"Awfully rough for the son, I'd say. But then, I reckon *if* everything doesn't rest on a lie or a mistake … a person *might* think that point follows the others." He definitely disliked the feeling of getting ensnared.

"Here's the final point. If anyone wants God's forgiveness, it's offered as a gift because of Jesus. But they have to take it. And we take it by realizing we need it, and then asking Jesus to come into our life to forgive us and become our king."

"That's all?" He was sweating. He'd ended up agreeing with pretty much everything, but nevertheless, he could *not* accept it.

"That's it." Mr. Pendleton was studying him. "Accepting Jesus as our Savior begins a close relationship with Almighty God and at the end, gives us a welcome into heaven."

"It seems far too easy, really, for such a … a good deal." He cared for Mr. Pendleton, deeply cared for him. But there was not any way he could take this step.

"Receiving a gift is easy. However, sometimes people aren't fully convinced it *is* a good gift. Or they want to be the sole captain of their ship, even if they sink it."

"I guess it'd be smart to take a gift like that, but … but I'm sorry. I can't. It's too big a package for me to get hold of." A package so cumbersome, he'd fall beneath it.

"No need to apologize. You're still looking for answers. If you look as hard for what's true as you've looked for your brother, you'll find it."

"Yes, sir. Thank you." He picked up one of his worksheets, relieved the conversation was over and uncomfortable at the same time. He'd disappointed Mr. Pendleton—no doubt about it—and he was more confused than ever. Ichi's sister Mia would probably say he was in 'some darkness.' But at least he wasn't going so far as Ichi and calling Christianity *evil*. That should count for something.

A loud thud jarred the table. Terry leapt up as the ship tilted, then righted itself. He rushed to the porthole, alongside Mr. Pendleton, and looked out.

The ocean's slow rolling surface appeared calm enough.

"Can't see anything wrong out there." Mr. Pendleton turned away from the view.

"Surely Jim didn't run into something in the middle of the ocean. A whale? An underwater reef?" Terry headed toward the door.

"All hands ahoy!" boomed from Mate Brewer's bullhorn.

Seconds later, Terry and the ones already on duty were ordered up the rigging to spread canvas. It had been six weeks since he'd climbed up to slush the two masts. His mind skittered away from the black memory as he raced to the royal sails.

Once down on the deck again, he learned from Stargazer that a boiler had malfunctioned and the ship wouldn't be using steam until it got repaired—taking a minimum of a full day after picking up an engineer from the *USS Observer*, steaming a half mile behind them. Obviously, they'd be tacking a lot to use sail in the unfavorable wind. Terry's heart sank at the slowdown, but at least it wasn't a shipwreck and the frigate was handy. In fact, Mr. Pendleton would probably say it was *providential*.

But wouldn't it be more providential if the boiler hadn't broken down in the first place? Another puzzle. Another reason to doubt. And an additional day for his mind to go crazy, seesawing between hope and black despair.

CHAPTER 30

Tom stopped filling his buckets from the water in the volcano's crater atop the ridge's hump. He glared at the fool monkey, fussing its head off in one of the encircling forest trees. The beast should be used to his company. He'd come here every morning during the week's dry spell. The lack of rainfall had helped the three of them in preparing the jerky, preserving the duck eggs in a pot of salt and mud, and gathering more shikuwasa limes, coconuts, cattails, breadnut tree's nuts, seaweed, and a few end-of-season hog plums for their stock of food in the cave. But the dry weather had left his water buckets empty. This morning's early fog had contributed only a few drops.

When the monkey sounded more agitated, Tom set his two buckets down and prepared to defend himself from whatever missiles the beast hurled.

Suddenly his heart skipped a beat. Voices! Angry ones! Four or five men at least. He kicked the buckets far into the undergrowth and swung up into the nearest tree, fortunately a good distance from the tree harboring the monkey.

He peered through the leaves, unable to catch more than a flash of the men who'd tromped to where he'd been standing minutes earlier. The nightmare frequenting his sleep was happening before his eyes.

"Here's the high pond you been yapping about," a man with a black skullcap snarled. "So where's the cave?"

"Right 'bout there. The island's a earthquake magnet." Tom recognized Bolt's voice. "One o' the strong quakes must've covered it."

"It all better be there, Ben. Get at it, boys," Bolt's captor ordered.

The monkey's agitated chattering caught the attention of one of the men, who aimed a rock at its tree. The beast screeched its disapproval, but then stopped its racket. Tom felt a twinge of sympathy for his old opponent as they both faced vicious enemies skulking below them.

Gradually the pirates, accompanied by groans and curses, moved the rocks and dirt enough to reveal a cave on the right-hand side of the hump. Although nearly paralyzed by fear, Tom's mind whirled at the implication. Treasure—oodles of gold and jewels—right under his nose all this time.

"Ain't nothin' here save two Mex'can dollars!" one guy called from the back of the cave.

"Where'd you put it, Ben?" the pirate with the skullcap growled. "Reckon you need that right arm to keep yourself fed?"

"Stop!" Bolt howled. "Didn't touch it, I swear! Those three rats found it 'fore the last quake. Had to. We find 'em. We find the treasure. No time t'lose."

Anger jolted through Tom. He should have killed Bolt when he had the chance.

"Turn him loose," a third voice ordered. "For now, anyway. You say they live in caves, Ben? You better deliver."

"I been stuck in the cove where you left me, Slate, but I got a relate'ship with the three. Here's a fact. You talked 'bout a red cloth wavin' from a tree. When the varmints saw yer ship draw up on the whaler, I reckon they knew you spotted the flag and you'd come, sure as the sun rises. They're not too dumb. So what's the first thing they'd do?"

When no one answered, Bolt continued, obviously talking nonstop to save his good arm or his life. "First thing they'd do— find a safe place to hide, don'cha know? But here's where we gets 'em. They don't know you be here. Right?"

"Aye," a new voice said. "Ship's anchored with its canvas down, and we landed the rowboat on a juttin' point. Fog helped."

"So they're not hidin' yet. I'll call to 'em. Tell 'em I'm off the beach 'cause o' pirates, and they gotta hide quick. We seen hillside caves last time yer here. But I'm bettin' their safe cave's underground. There's bamboo here too, an' the thick forest you sees, but too easy to get flushed out. Underground caverns— that's what's ideal fer hidin'. But if you watch the hillside and valley after I calls to 'em, you'll nab 'em 'fore they settle into one with mazes like a pretzel."

The branch under Tom's right foot abruptly cracked. Too terrified to glance below, he eased his weight to a different branch. Regaining his balance, he hugged the tree even tighter.

"You see somethin' red in the branches there?" the nearest pirate asked.

"You think it's gonna be a red-flag signal to us?" the pirate who had been in the cave jeered, but his voice sounded like he was coming closer.

The monkey chose that moment to launch a pinecone barrage. While the pirates cursed and chunked rocks toward the animal, Tom rolled his shirt up to his armpits, then plastered his face against the trunk, imagining the men turning their sharp eyes back toward his tree. He gripped the trunk harder to stop the trembling in his hands.

"Don't see nothin'," the man from the cave replied a minute later, disgust in his voice.

"Must'a been a bird," the first one said and spit.

"We need t'catch that monkey," Bolt was saying. "If'n by some chance, they's already hidin', that animal can lead us right to 'em."

"All right. Leave off with the rocks," the man named Slate ordered. "Monkeys go fer shiny objects. Razor Jake, you take Red and Billy Bart and git a net and rope from the ship along with somethin' shiny and heavy to trap the pest."

"Aye, aye, Slate," came from the man who had glimpsed Tom's shirt.

Tom was loath to move an inch. Pure evil crouched beneath him, like a cobra ready to strike. But he couldn't stay put—a cowering victim while the stalkers laid their trap.

After the pirate Razor Jake and the other two took off, Tom edged over to where a gap in the leaves gave a better view. One pirate was scooping up water at the pond, and the apparent leader, Slate, was squatting in front of the empty cave, watching Bolt talk while he drew something in the dirt.

Leery of another branch's betrayal, Tom tested each one as he descended lower and lower. At last, he slid down the back side of the trunk and huddled in the undergrowth, listening for footsteps. When none came, he crawled and slithered through the tangling vines and bushes, biting back yelps at the thorns. Reaching the rim, he checked for any lookout, then raced around to the secret path through the trees and scrambled down the hill.

"They're here! Go! Go! Go!" he panted at Dice and Sara's cave's entrance, thankful neither one was out bathing or heading for their lookout duty.

The pair grabbed two baskets and two buckets they'd already positioned and ran after him. Once they were down the cavern's first ladder, Dice lit a torch with a bucket's embers. Tom helped him move both short ladders and hide them behind stalagmites in the bat room. Then while they caught their breath with Sara at the bottom of the incline's drop-off, he told what he'd overheard.

"So Bolt says we have the treasure." Dice's tone could have turned fire to ice. "It is a lie. But if they find us, they torture us. Try to make us tell where is it."

"Bolt does not care a gnat's wing about others." Sara's voice quivered. "He is wicked."

"Yes, pirates are devils." *And you,* Tom yearned to say, *are an angel.*

"If the pirates cut through trees at the hump, maybe they saw us run here." Sara's figure appeared to waver in the flickering light.

"I don't think so." Tom thought back to what he'd seen. "One was busy at the pond. Three of the men had gone to their ship to bring back items for trapping the monkey. The chief pirate was occupied with Bolt while waiting for the men to return."

"They want that dratted beast to expose us," Dice breathed out.

Tom nodded. "Its diversion—a pinecone onslaught—helped keep the men from spying me. I'm glad of that, but the creature could easily lead them here. Maybe you two need to pray about the monkey's behavior. If God really cares about people like Jesus claimed, we could use some higher help."

Sara bit her lip and nodded.

Dice grunted.

"So," Tom said, changing the subject and looking at Dice,

"how many days can we survive down here with what we've gathered?"

"Two, three weeks, maybe longer. We can put bucket and pots under opening if raining. Move them if pirates lower torches, ladder, or rope. Also have coconut waters." Dice leaned over and crammed the torch between a small stalagmite and the wall. "Maybe the pirates decide to sail away. Maybe want to find island with wild goats, hogs. They like meat." He rolled his hand so it cast shadows like ocean waves. "But they might stay here very long time. Eat birds, fish, plants like us. Use our caves. Other caves. Maybe go and come back. Who knows?" He glanced at his sister and shrugged.

Tom sighed. He had left out what the pirates said about spotting the red cloth days earlier. Dice and Sara had descended with him into another level of hell, and at least part of the reason was his fault.

CHAPTER 31

"Who's the leader of Japan?" Tamo spoke in a loud whisper.

Sara hesitated to answer. Was it all right to utter the rarely-spoken words to satisfy a foreigner's curiosity? While leaning against the short cliff next to the long ladder, she was closer to Tamo than proper, but necessary in order to hear. There was just enough light from the distant daylight to see his dark shape. When she first encountered him on the island, she never imagined she'd actually like being this close to him. It helped that he no longer neglected his bathing, and either his rough manners had improved or she'd grown used to them.

Three days of dim light and utterly black nights had crept by. Her own clammy skin and grimy clothing had been an insignificant discomfort compared to the horror of being hunted. She took her turn as a lookout in the shadows under the cavern's entrance—an enormous responsibility. But even while elsewhere, either exercising or eating or briefly reading the Bible in the torchlight, she constantly listened for sounds of the enemy, as though a dragon stalked her, ready to devour her. The only time she relaxed a little was during conversations with Tamo.

Although his ideas were often peculiar, they opened the door to a whole new world. An added benefit, totally unexpected, was learning about his desires, his family, his search for what was really true—seeing into his heart.

"Don't you know your leader's name?" Tamo faced her, but she couldn't make out his expression.

"I know his title. I hardly ever heard it said out loud." She dropped her voice to a true whisper right at Tamo's ear. "Our leader is the highly exalted *Shōgun*. The word makes us nervous because he is so grand, so untouchable."

"Like a god, then?"

"Not that high. Our emperor is more like that. I used to think the emperor was—what is correct word?"

"Deity? Divine?"

"Yes, divine. But now I know the Holy Bible, so I believe just one God."

"I don't think you need to believe *everything* the Bible says, but I agree with you about your emperor." Tamo gave a kind of snuffle as though he was trying not to laugh.

Sara grimaced. They had agreed about a number of subjects in their underground conversations, but their disagreement about God dwarfed everything else. Still, they were remaining friends, able to think about different ideas together. Even in the darkest, scariest place, God had given her a bit of pleasure.

"Who is the leader in America?" she asked after a minute.

"Abraham Lincoln. He's been President for almost two years. He was elected late in 1860—that means chosen by all the men, except slaves."

"All the men chose? Even merchants? Artists? Farmers?"

"Right. My girlfriend Peg thinks women should get to choose too. Maybe so, but most men don't think so."

She managed not to giggle. "Women helping choose the leader is like a tale with shape-changing foxes and maybe headless horsemen, but ... there might be less war. Do you have many girlfriends in America?"

"Uh, no. Peg wouldn't like that. Fellows should have only one girlfriend at a time. At least, that's what all the girls think."

"We cannot be friends?" Her heart skipped a beat.

"Now wait. A friend who is a girl—that's you—is different from a girlfriend."

For once, Sara was glad for the dim light as she felt her cheeks redden. "So maybe a girlfriend is a *geisha* or *flower girl*? Someone to ... pillow?"

Tamo's cough had a strangled sound. "Not that either. A girlfriend is a special friend that the fellow might like to court— spend much time with—and possibly marry later. In my case, a lot later. And a girl's boyfriend is the same way. Did you have any boyfriend before you were kidnapped?"

"I had only three friends. All girls. When I was very young, my parents arranged a man for me to marry. But I never met him. I am sure the arrangement is broken now."

"Whoa! I heard about arranged marriages, but you really had one. Were you angry?"

"Angry? Not at all." A laugh like a snort escaped her lips in spite of her effort to be quiet. She covered her mouth and waited to hear Daisuke's reaction from under the opening. When he didn't make a shushing noise, she continued. "I was thankful to my parents. But I did wish I could have adventures first, like men have. Visit the capital Edo. Shoot arrows in contests. Now I have too much adventure."

"Another thing we agree about. If I make it out—"

She jumped up at the same moment as Tamo. Daisuke was

scrambling down the ladder.

"Quick! A rope ladder coming down!"

Tamo reached for the upper part of the incline's ladder and helped shoulder it with Daisuke. The three of them scurried like mice through the passageway with Daisuke in the lead, holding the torch. After the ladder was deposited in the bat room's hiding place, Daisuke led the way into the large chamber. They had stored their supplies against the far wall as inconspicuously as possible, but a careful inspection with torches would reveal their use of the area. How she hoped and prayed the pirates wouldn't dare penetrate so far into the cavern.

"Are you keeping up, Sa-*chan*?" Daisuke asked in Japanese, his voice low.

"*Hai*," she answered, continuing to crawl after him. None of them had stood up in the large space. Her brother was carrying the torch in one hand and reaching forward on the cave's floor with his other.

"Here is the hole," Daisuke whispered, holding the dying torch above the bamboo cover. "I lay the cover on the far side. You can pull it over again, Tamo."

The torch went out.

Daisuke's fingers touched her knee, then felt for her hand. "Hold my arm, Sa-*chan*. I and Tamo will help you onto the shelf, like usual."

Sara gripped Daisuke's arm and let him draw her forward on her knees. Her heart raced like a pursued rabbit. If only there were a flicker of light. They had practiced escaping onto the ledge every day since the pirates came, but always with a torch.

Daisuke removed her hand from his arm. "Wait until I tell you to come."

She braced her hands on the rock floor. How close was the

edge? What if she stepped down wrong and fell into the stream? She could never escape in the total darkness.

"You're safe," Tamo murmured the next minute. He grasped her under her armpits and moved her half around. "Your brother and I won't let you fall." At Daisuke's word, he slid her feet-first into air.

She sucked in a breath just as Daisuke grabbed hold of her and her feet found the ledge. He grasped her arm again and pulled her against his side. "Now, we move over to make room for Tamo."

A splash sounded and she strangled a gasp. Was Tamo gone?

"The cover," Tamo whispered. "Can't be helped."

Strength returned to her legs. Crammed between Daisuke and Tamo, she stayed still as if turned to stone. The only sound besides their breathing was the stream's gurgle beneath them.

Tamo had pointed out the stream's high-water mark the first time she stood on the ledge before the pirates came on the island. It was about two-arms' length below them. Daisuke had wanted to scoop up water in the bucket and test it on her monkey. She had infuriated him by sobbing in her distress, and to her amazement, Tamo had sided with her. But as a result, they didn't know if the water would poison them if forced to stay in the hole for days.

"Ugh! Bats!" a voice cried out, adding a curse. "Doubt they'd be in there. Dung all over the place."

"Could be a second chamber yonder," another voice piped up. "I'll take a gander."

"Go slow there, mate. Yer temptin' the fates," a third voice warned.

"I'll watch me step. Looks all—Hey! Ya-eeee! Help! Hee … elp!"

Shivers ran up Sara's spine.

"Good thing we left that bat room alone," Tamo whispered in her ear.

"He's gone! Done for!" the first voice pronounced. "I'm bloody ready to get out o' here. If they're in here, they're not gonna show themselves 'til they're starvin' fer food or water."

"We got more sense 'n Billy Bart," the second voice answered. "Jes take it easy. Check each step. Let's see what's through that opening o'er there. Then we'll holler fer someone up 'bove to come down and reel us up o'er that slip'ry cliff."

"Likely to leave us if'n we stay down here too long. They'll figure this place ain't safe."

"They jes might leave us anyways if we don't find signs of them three vermin. Dang monkey seemed mighty interested in the hole."

"One more passage. Then I ain't goin' one step farther."

Sara's heart lurched at the sound of heavy steps drawing closer. Then boots crunched the surface above her, and the space beyond Tamo changed from pitch black to dark gray.

"Well, looky at what's behind these rocks." One pirate stopped walking. "Leafy mats—fer sleepin', ya guess? Not good fer a disguise. And here's baskets and pots, plum full. They're here somewheres close. Keep yer dagger handy."

Daisuke grasped her arm. "We have to move over farther," he whispered. "Turn around. Try to find finger-holds in the wall, and scoot your feet. Quietly. Quietly."

Praying she wouldn't faint or slip, she did as told and sensed Tamo doing the same. Her fingers ached as she inched along, gripping the wall's small protrusions one after another.

One piece of wall broke off under her hand and bounced over the ledge. Terror shot through her while she grabbed for another.

Something alive skittered next to her. She forced back a scream, remembering the hairy spider with orange legs they had spotted during a practice.

Finally, Daisuke stopped moving. She clung to the wall, panting.

"The shelf here is narrower," he whispered, "but you can edge back around and slide down the wall to sit. I will help."

"I will try," she choked out, already dizzy.

"Hey, Hey! Watch out for that hole!" came from above.

She froze, but her mind was in a frenzy. What would happen if one of the pirates saw the ledge and landed on it? Would Tamo use his knife or wrestle him? He might overcome one pirate with the jiu-jitsu moves he had learned from Daisuke. But then what?

Trying to calm herself, she took deep breaths. She must not, absolutely must not faint.

Tamo's hands brushed against her head. Then his hands were on her shoulders, steadying her before he too stiffened.

Only the water kept flowing.

"Hand me the lantern, will ya?" The pirate spat. "There's a stream down there, but could be some space fer hidin'."

A lantern descended through the hole, the circle of light falling just short of Tamo. Sara's muscles constricted, as if preparing to shrink away from the lantern by themselves.

"Might be a shelf. Can't tell fer sure. Not leanin' further in 'til we gets mates with us. Air smells fine, but don't aim to be bashed on me head. Slate'll hep with the hole. But we gotta be sure there ain't no more holes or openings 'fore we bring him here. Don't want *him* riled up cuz of an ambush from another tunnel."

Sara shuddered. The captain called Slate was most likely a fiend as black-hearted as the pirate captain who had kidnapped

Daisuke and her—a man with ice-cold eyes, who smirked while victims died and wielded his whip at trivial irritations. This time these pirates wouldn't think of her as a child. Daisuke would try to protect her, and they'd kill him. Before the pirates were anywhere close, she'd declared her new liege would help. But everything she believed was shaking, like tree branches in a typhoon.

She closed her eyes in the darkness, rebuking herself. Hadn't God helped them during their kidnapping? In the awful storm? On the island? Yes, he'd even brought Tamo in time for them to escape the earthquake's tomb.

But God's help this time could mean an early entrance into heaven. It had happened to a lot of people in the Bible. She took a deep breath. She could accept that, couldn't she? She was a samurai's daughter and a Christian, after all. And heaven was called the "blessed hope."

But how about Tamo? With his defiance? She held back a groan. She should have told him more about God's goodness and mercy before it was too late.

Tom stared into the darkness, its emptiness seeping into him. Even if he and Dice could pick off these pirates and the next batch too, eventually the sheer numbers would overwhelm them. Once he'd have joined their enemies' side—at least temporarily—to escape torture or death. He couldn't imagine doing that now.

However, he could slip into the stream. That wouldn't hurt Dice or Sara. When his parents and Terry realized he wasn't ever coming home, they would be sad. Terribly sad. But they wouldn't know what happened. Dead was dead, whether you were drowned in the cavern or butchered by a pirate.

But first, he'd get things straight with God. He'd been on the wrong path, fighting a stupid battle against the world's creator. All those Bible verses spelled that out as clear as the handwriting on the wall had done for some ancient king. If he was going to lose his life, he'd better not lose his soul too. He'd get right to the point like Sara had with her little prayer.

"God," he mouthed, amazed he was actually whispering a prayer, "I know you don't like what you see about me. I don't either. I want to get onto your path, the narrow one Jesus talked about, the one he died for." He sucked in air. "If you and your Son will have me, I'm yours."

He bit his lip. That was the best he could do. Was it time to slide into the water? It would likely be a swift death when the stream took him away.

Hearing Sara's soft whispers, he hesitated. She and Dice had to be talking to God too.

"And please listen to Sara and Dice," he dared to add. "If you see fit, give them more time on this earth. I shouldn't have waved my shirt."

He drew in another ragged breath at the next thought—its logic indisputable. If the two pirates above were finished off, they couldn't call for more. That might make a difference. Maybe help answer his prayer for the pair. And if he was killed while fighting them, it would be a better way for him to die—a more noble way, hopefully as quick as drowning.

"I'm going up," he whispered to Sara.

Gripping his knife with his teeth, he placed his hands on each side of the hole's rim and pulled himself up to where he could see the chamber. The two men had propped their lanterns between rocks and were checking along the far wall. Heart thumping so loud he feared they could hear it, he pulled himself all the way up.

He rushed the closest one the minute they spotted him.

The pirate raised his dagger.

Tom drove his head into him, then plunged his own knife into the pirate. It stuck under his shoulder.

The man lost his grip on his dagger and stumbled backwards, but didn't fall. He yanked out Tom's knife, raised it, and lunged at Tom.

Tom jumped sideways, then threw himself into his attacker's side and rode him down to the cave's floor. The pirate's forehead smacked against the rock. Tom twisted and slid onto the man's back, grabbed an arm, and did a shoulder lock.

The pirate's screams merged with a sound of scuffling and a yowl that came from behind Tom.

Dice appeared out of the shadows. He struck the prone pirate's right and left shoulders above the collarbones. Both of the man's arms went limp. The next second, Dice's knife blade pricked the pirate's neck.

"Mercy," the pirate whined.

Dice glanced at Sara, who was passing them. Then he looked at Tom. "Kill or not?"

Tom stared at the shaking man. He'd just asked for mercy himself. "Not," Tom ground out. "We ... or you ... can listen to the lies, maybe get a grain of truth. Then decide." He raised his hand toward Sara to take the rope-like vines she'd gathered off their supplies.

The pirate suddenly flipped onto his side, leapt up, and raced for the tunnel, blood dripping from Tom's knife wound.

Dice's knife flew over Tom and found its mark deep into the pirate's upper back. He cursed, stumbled, and collapsed. A spout of blood bubbled onto the rocky floor.

Tom joined Dice at the body. "Looks like he's not breathing. I'll check for a pulse." He felt the man's neck while guarding against a trick.

The pirate's slowing pulse became fainter, then nearly indiscernible before it disappeared with the body's final twitch.

"Gone to his reward," Tom said, quoting the phrase he'd heard repeated at home. The words no longer seemed as irritatingly trite. "What happened to his partner?"

"In a minute, I will say. But he is dead too." Dice pulled out his knife. Then together they dragged the body to the hole and shoved it in past the ledge.

Sara was sobbing her heart out.

After wiping his bloody hands on his robe, Dice squatted next to her and said nothing.

Tom wiped off his own knife, then sat down heavily, wishing he could comfort her. But it wasn't his place.

When she quieted, her brother spoke to her in Japanese. She nodded her head and wiped her eyes.

Dice turned to Tom. "He would have brought the others."

For a minute, Tom couldn't speak. Finally, he said, "It couldn't be helped."

Dice nodded with a sigh.

After another awkward minute, Tom asked again, "What happened to his partner?"

"Sara helped kill him."

Tom's mouth fell open.

Sara let several more sobs escape.

"She acted like the daughter of a samurai." Dice rolled his head at her. "But she not really kill him herself. I told her stay on ledge. I followed you. She pushed herself half up from the hole when pirate jumped me. She grabbed his ankle. He kicked. She not let go. Then he pulled her most way out of the hole. I not move. Afraid he makes her fall. She let go his ankle and got out of hole. Pirate turn toward me, but took wrong step backward. He fell into hole."

"So we don't know for sure that one's dead?" Tom pictured the pirate climbing out as a whirling dervish.

"We heard big splash. He not come out to fight. He is gone. For sure."

Tom walked over to the hole and peered down at the life-ending darkness, where he had planned to go himself. How strange he was still alive—breathing, talking, walking around after all. He glanced back at Dice and Sara. Gruff ol' Dice was earnestly talking to his sister, probably scolding and attempting to comfort her at the same time. Odd as the pair was, he liked them. Really liked them.

Beyond question, since they had fought and survived the first two pirates, he needed to stay around and join the fight again. In fact, drowning didn't make sense any more. He'd been looking for an easy way out, like when he'd thought about jumping off a cliff his second day on the island. Only this time, giving up wouldn't just hurt him and his family. Giving up would be unworthy of the team … and maybe of Jesus too.

Stepping away from the hole, he surveyed the chamber. If they managed to defeat pirates until no more actually entered the cavern, would they still be forced to hide? Would this place be their tomb after days or weeks or months? Might that be how God would answer the prayer to give Dice and Sara more time? Not a pleasant thought, but then, speculating about what God would do probably wasn't wise.

"Two pirates down," Tom said when Dice turned toward him. "Well, actually three. But dozens left. I guess it's a start." He picked up the dagger of the pirate he'd fought and dropped it behind a rock for safekeeping … or for a backup.

"We stay on the shelf until nighttime." Dice had taken up his stoic, outwardly-unfazed attitude again. "Pirates are superstitious. When three do not come out, and it is dark, they will fear spirits. Then safer for us to come off the ledge."

"All right. I'll go down first if you want." Tom forced himself not to think of the two pirates who'd preceded him as he lowered himself onto the ledge and then helped Sara.

Once the three had moved into sitting positions, Tom sat cross-legged. Even though the two pirates' bodies were supposedly long gone, he didn't like the idea of slippery fingers tugging on his dangling feet in the darkness.

Sara began whispering one of the psalms she liked.

Tom picked out *through the valley of the shadow of death … fear no evil … thou art with me.* Was he going to believe it or not? If so, he had no business worrying about disembodied hands. He unbent his legs.

Being in a black hole under the cavern—a hole within a hole—was as close to being in the "shadow of death" as you could get, but they weren't dead. Yet.

CHAPTER 32

"Land ho!" rang out from the crow's nest high above the decks.

Stargazer walked over to Terry on the quarterdeck. "If this here is the right island, we've hit a bull's eye. With a little more coaching, you could get us to America."

"Uh, it's due to you, sir." As if primed for a race's starting pistol, a hundred knots knit Terry's muscles, but he couldn't rush away without permission. "Mind if I take a look from the bow?"

"Go ahead, but make it quick. We've got tricky navigatin' ahead. This part of the island's not promisin'. Captain can't get close enough for the jolly-boat without foundering on them rocks. Reckon there's no channel in the offin'."

"Yes, sir." Terry half-leapt down the ladder and raced to the bow. His speed got him a central position before the off-duty sailors squeezed in next to him on both sides. He studied the distant island, wishing he'd sketched it instead of watching Tom and the five rats row through the surf. It had looked lopsided, best he could remember. One end rose higher than the rest, and that had been on the left side, not on the right, like what confronted him.

When Stargazer heard his vague description minutes later, he clapped him on the shoulder. "Good eyes in that head o' yours. Captain Whitson'll be happy for every thimbleful of information."

As the ship rounded the high end of the island, "Sail ho! Fine off port bow!" rang out.

Terry raced to the port rail alongside Stargazer. A schooner with the black flag of piracy stood off from the island. The ship's twenty-four-pounder cannon spouted out from its gunports. The *Retriever*'s own gunports were rasping open two decks below.

A cannonball from the pirate ship arced across the water. Terry jumped back and gaped as it fell short by a few yards. Balling his fists, he followed Stargazer's finger pointing toward the stern. The smoke from the frigate's funnel—the most beautiful sight imaginable—came into view.

Four boatloads of men, who had shoved off the beach, rowed furiously through the rough surf to the pirate ship. Men on board, looking like dwarfs in the distance, climbed ratlines to spread canvas. With the gunship in plain view, they'd switched to fleeing. Terry sucked in an agitated breath. The pirates' retreat was good for him and the *Retriever*, but what if Tom were already a captive on their ship or tied up in one of the boats? If only he had a long-glass telescope in his hands.

The last boatload of pirates were still jumping onto the starboard ladder when the sails caught the wind, and the schooner tacked to sail away.

The frigate steamed past the *Retriever*, its forward thirty-two-pounder guns pivoted toward the pirates.

Don't shoot! formed in Terry's mouth. Yet even the result of granting that plea would be awful. If the pirate ship escaped with Tom on it, torture by pirates could be worse than his chances on a doomed ship.

The frigate caught the schooner while it was still in view above the horizon. The *Retriever* had dropped anchor, but Captain Whitson ordered that no boat go ashore until seamen from the *Observer* could accompany them. Terry joined the off-duty men gathered at the forward rail to watch the battle. The men were cheering at the top of their voices. Terry was panicked.

"Terrence." Mr. Pendleton spoke in his ear. "Come to my cabin. Now, if you will."

Terry tore his eyes away from the smoke and flashes of fire, and followed the old man.

When he entered the room, Mr. Pendleton knelt by the bunk next to Jim, who was already kneeling. "Join me if you are willing to pray for your brother."

Terry remained standing. "I'd like you to pray, please. God is more likely to listen to you and Jim."

Mr. Pendleton nodded and bowed his head along with Jim.

Terry caught only a few words of the prayer. Sweat poured down his back as his mind replayed the battle's cannon blasts and billowing smoke.

At the amen, Terry offered his hand to Mr. Pendleton, helping him rise. "Thank you, sir. You are far kinder than I deserve. And now, may Jim and I be dismissed?"

"Go, and God be with you. Jim stays with me. Neither of us is the right age for the search party, I'm afraid." Mr. Pendleton motioned Terry toward the door.

He pounded across the deck to the forward rail, where only three men still lingered. The pirate ship had vanished. The frigate was already steaming in his direction. He headed toward the jolly-boat. If only he'd find Tom still on the island, the agony would be over. Was there any chance? Acid ate into his stomach while he paced the deck, waiting for the frigate seamen to take the lead.

After what seemed unending hours, three boatloads of men from the gunship took to the water. The jolly-boat was ordered to follow them in.

A bearded ruffian limped halfway down the hillside to meet the landing parties. "Ain't nobody here but me," he called.

"No!" Terry tore after the men already climbing the hill. "Please, my brother may have been on the pirate ship—as a captive. Were there survivors?"

One of the men stopped to answer. "Aye, we picked up nearly thirty. Twelve had been captives from the *William Parton*— both common sailors and officers. That merchantman was taken and sunk a week ago by those devils."

Terry's head jerked at the news of his former ship's calamity, but pushed past it to the main matter. "I'm seeking my brother." He struggled for control. "He was left on this island accidentally—or so they claim—by the *William Parton.*"

"Could've been with that group, but none of them piped up to say they'd been marooned right here."

A lump choked Terry's throat. To be so close, and maybe to have lost Tom by the frigate's fire.

"Sorry, son, not to be the bearer of good news." The man's blue eyes shone with sympathy. "Best wait and see if your brother's not somewhere on this island since you're already standing here. Then we'll ask on the *Observer*. We'll be combing this wilderness for any remaining pirates, so if your brother's here, we'll find him soon enough."

The leader from the frigate issued orders to his seamen and to the *Retriever*'s sailors for the search, designating two men to stay and guard the ruffian. After that he turned to Terry. "Captain

Whitson didn't send orders for you. Just don't hinder the search."

Standing at a loss, Terry mumbled, "Yes, sir." Then he rebuked himself for neglecting the very man most likely to have answers. He followed the two guards down to where the scruffy man stood, watching them.

"I'm no pirate," the man snarled at his guards and Terry. "What good fer pirates be a lame man with a hook an' jes one good hand, I ask ye?" He squatted down on one of the rocks covering the hillside.

"Doesn't mean you don't have a history of pirating," one of the guards bit out. "Reckon that'll come to light soon enough." He spat tobacco juice. "Doubt you picked up that cheekbone scar in a gentleman's duel."

Receiving permission to talk to the man, Terry sat on a rock a yard from him. Pushing down his angst, he asked the rogue as calmly as possible if he'd been shipwrecked off the island's coast. To encourage the man to open up, he gave him a sad-dog look.

"Sole survivor, I was."

"My brother was marooned here by my old ship."

The man's eyes took on a gleam of interest. "Now, don't that beat all. The sailor was yer brother. Two from Japan was marooned here too—practic'ly the Baltimore station fer maroons."

"Can you tell me what happened to Tom? Is he here? Still alive?" His voice trembled in spite of his efforts.

The man squinted at Terry. "Is the boy so important he's got a merchantman and frigate lookin' fer him? Or, be you taggin' along with the pirate hunt?"

"He's not all *that* important, except to me, of course, and to several men helping me."

The suspected pirate curled his lip and spit.

"But I could put in a good word for you if you help find him or, at least, let me know what happened to him."

"Don't need no good word, I tell you." The man's eyes flashed. "I ain't no pirate, and there's nobody can say a thing different."

"Well, it must be hard to be guarded just 'cause you're on the island." Terry avoided any hint of sarcasm. "Do you think you'll have to defend yourself to the frigate's captain or a judge?"

The self-proclaimed innocent scowled, then forced a grin, his mouth showing yellowed and missing teeth above his red beard. "Not worried. Nobody's got anything on ol' Ben Bolt. Anyway, I think yer brother went with them pirates that fled the island. But how would I know?"

Terry steadied himself at the news he'd dreaded. So, Tom had survived until this day, and now all was in limbo, if not lost. He wanted to shake his fist at the sky. If the ships had come earlier, Tom and he might be slapping each other on the back, telling their stories. *If only ... If only ...*

"O' course, yer brother could still be on the island." The man shrugged, then laughed.

Terry's mind whirled. Was the man touched in the head—maybe the main reason he'd been left on the island? Or was he playing a cat-and-mouse game? If so, two could play at that.

"I guess you wouldn't know, the way the pirates took off. And I'm stuck here for the rest of the search." Terry looked around as though curious. "Was this island the pirates' hideout?"

"Not a hideout. A pile o' coral with no animals? Not good fer hidin' or resupplyin'."

"Well then, were they looking for the treasure?"

The man glowered at him. "What ye know 'bout treasure?"

Clearly, he'd touched a raw spot. "Another sailor on the *William Parton* talked about pirate treasure on an island identical to this one." In case this fellow would escape a pirate's noose, he wouldn't involve Jim.

"What's that sailor's name, boy?"

"Zeke." The perfect one to involve.

"Zeke Bones! That skunk still walkin' the earth?"

"He was a few weeks ago when I saw him." Terry had no idea where the conversation was going, but it was moving fast, already confirming Zeke's pirate connection as well as their mutual loathing of the rat.

"And he sailed on the *William Parton*?"

Terry could see the man's mind spinning. "He was when I knew him, but since that time, the *William Parton* was taken by those pirates that just fled—as you might have heard directly from them. And now the pirates' ship was sunk a couple of hours ago by the frigate."

"No! By Jove, them dogs got what was comin' to 'em!" The man looked like he wanted to dance a jig.

"A lot of them got it, all right, but the frigate rescued some of the pirates as well as some of the captives from the *William Parton*. Maybe Zeke was one of them. He always seemed tough, a survivor to me."

The pirate faced Terry directly and squinted at him. "Now you looks like a honest feller. You wouldn't be lyin' to ol' Ben, would ye?"

"Why would I lie, er, Ben? If you don't believe me, why don't you ask these guards what happened to the pirate ship and the *William Parton*." He pointed to the two men, who frowned at them.

"About that good word." Ben spit out a glob of phlegm close

to Terry's leg. "Who would pay 'tention if almost no one but you gives a cursed half-cent 'bout yer brother?"

"One of them happens to be the American vice consul in Nagasaki, and he's on the merchantman."

"Well now." The pirate straightened. "Reckon you could arrange fer me to speak with him? Private like? Don't reckon he's one o' the searchers."

"I can, but I'll have to wait until a boat crew finishes here. The guards may want to escort you to the frigate before he could come on a return trip."

"If'n you tell them guards about me havin' a interview with the honor'ble Vice Consul of Nagasaki hisself right here on this island, they'll hafta agree. You arrange the interview, and you'll reel in the information you be fishin' fer."

"It's a deal." Still seated, Terry held out his hand, wishing he could choke the information out of the villain instead. After the ruffian roughly shook on it, Terry stood. "I'm gonna look around," he said casually, not wanting to seem overeager, "but you just give a loud halloo when a crew returns. I won't go far."

He cut through the forest, keeping an eye out for snakes in the thick undergrowth. Finally freeing himself from the encumbering vines, thorny bushes, and ferns, he gazed down at the valley, catching sight of two sets of searchers. Were there any straggling pirates, hoping not to be caught and hanged besides the suspect he'd just left? He pictured the boatloads of men that had sped off. An enormous gang of outlaws had roamed the island. Had they been fouling the place long, terrorizing Tom? Or had they killed him? Terry's blood ran cold. How could Tom, and maybe the two from Japan, have found a spot to hide without being discovered by the ship full of bloodthirsty men? It looked impossible.

How miserable this waiting was! He wanted to run all over the island, yelling Tom's name, but the searchers wouldn't put up with his interference.

He saw the first search party returning before the pirate glimpsed them. Hurrying over to the man in front, he asked him to tell Mr. Pendleton on the *Retriever* that he was needed on the island without delay.

The man hesitated, then said, "Still no luck yet with your brother, I take it. All right. I'll pass the word."

Six rowers of the frigate's seamen beached the boat carrying the vice consul. Terry rushed forward to help him onto firm ground.

"Any more news?" Mr. Pendleton looked from Terry to Ben as the rogue limped toward them. "The rowers told me the search for pirates is still ongoing, but they hadn't heard of any maroons being found."

Terry swallowed hard. "No, sir. Not yet, but Ben here may be of help."

"That be my sincere hope, Yer Honor." The rogue oozed politeness. "First, me thinks the brother might want to see the boy's cave. If yer men lend a hand, it'll be my pleasure to lead you there, and we can reach a right good understandin'."

Hobbling with the help of a driftwood crutch, Ben led the way around the rim and finally through the ring of trees. Leaning heavily on his crutch at a sharp angle, he thumped his way down the rim's back side. Two of the rowers, also designated to act as guards, helped Mr. Pendleton down the slope. So they all made it to the indicated cave.

After a coughing spell, Ben cleared his throat and pointed to the make-shift bed and low pile of rocks. "This be a good place fer our conf'rence." He turned to Terry. "I figure this one's yer brother's place. Seems the Japanners took the bigger cave lower down fer themselves."

The two guards assisted Mr. Pendleton in sitting on the pallet although he protested he was quite able to manage. Terry chose one of the larger flat rocks. Ben leaned on his crutch. The rest of the escort took up posts outside the cave.

Relieved not to find signs of a struggle or—heaven help him—a corpse at the destination chosen by the man of questionable sanity, Terry took in the cave's primitive condition. Tom's life must have been horrid, yet the fire pit, pallet, and bamboo screen shoved off to one side showed the cave had provided shelter at least from the elements. No telling what else had threatened him in addition to the pirates.

Mr. Pendleton leaned forward. "Might I learn how to address our island guide?"

"Benjamin Bolt at yer service." He managed a small bow in spite of his crutch.

"Ah yes. Well, Mr. Bolt, it's greatly disturbing not to have located Thomas Ballard yet. But then, you may be of assistance?"

Ben hunched his shoulders. "I have that intention. You can be sure o' that. But first, I'll explain me sitchation. I been stuck in a cove alone fer a year. Pirates left me there when I didn't cooperate none. And with no boat, not even the Jappaners or the sailor boy could bring me out."

No mention of a shipwreck off the coast. Terry kept quiet while wishing he were better at detecting lies.

"But when this batch o' pirates pounced on me four days ago, like a lion on an antelope, they brought me 'round to the rest o' the isle. Tried to force me to tell where this boy's brother"—

he tilted his head toward Terry—"was hidin' with them two from Japan. At first, I didn't know the spot, but while them pirates was busy with their ship, I found it out. When I refused to tell 'em, they threatened to take off me one good arm, but the good Lord saved me by yer arrival with the gunboat."

Terry's heart leapt. Didn't a "hiding place," unrevealed, imply that Tom was alive and still on the island?

"You've had a hard time. It's a wonder you survived those outlaws." Mr. Pendleton gazed full at Ben's face.

The rogue didn't flinch. "Before pointin' out the maroons' hidin' place, I'd like to ask yer help."

"Say on quickly, so I can determine what's possible." Mr. Pendleton's voice reflected irritation for the first time.

"Yes, o' course. See, Yer Honor, one of the unfortunates rescued by the gunboat may be a vill'nous man who use'ta be a pirate. He hates me, and he may accuse *me* o' being a pirate. *Falsely* accuse me."

Zeke. And he might not be the only one to accuse him, Terry figured, trying not to show his agitation at the continued delay.

"What I'm proposin' is a letter, written by Yer Honor, sayin' I'm to be left alone fer any past sins, which none exist, so none can be proved. An' that I'm free to follow me nose to any port I choose."

"My authority isn't quite so grand." Mr. Pendleton glanced at the guards. "I could write a letter stating you were not part of the pirate crew the gunship has captured, *if* that's true, and that I am not *aware* of your having committed any past crimes. Being acquainted with Captain James, I believe he would honor my letter, and it would prevent your being taken on board the *Observer* and held for a trial. As long as you stayed on this island, my testimonial would most likely keep you from being arrested in the future unless you engaged in piracy after today. My letter would not carry weight elsewhere."

Ben clasped his forehead and tightened his lips. He held still for so long, Terry feared he had decided not to cooperate. Then his eyes narrowed with a calculating look. "They says sometimes a li'l sugar sweetens the pot. Well, I ... um, stumbled onto some treasure, mebbe what them pirates was after at the start. I'd be pleased to hep you fer your trouble and also hep the boy here and his brother on their journey home with part o' the treasure if that merchant ship might jes squeeze me in."

"Now wait just a minute." Mr. Pendleton's face turned red. "That sounds like a bribe, and I'll have none of that."

"Oh, never!" Ben rammed his crutch down hard enough to crack it. "Jes thinkin' of a kinda gift to friends. But I sees how that can be taken wrong."

Terry kept his mouth shut although he wanted to yell that his brother's life was at stake, for pity's sake. How could the man stand there and try to finagle a better deal than the generous one already offered?

"The *Retriever* is not available," Mr. Pendleton said sternly. "Captain Whitson would be unwilling to transport a suspect off this island. He would see it as aiding and abetting a possible criminal escape justice and would insist on the frigate transporting you to Japan instead."

Ben couldn't have looked more frustrated.

"Now from what I've heard thus far," Mr. Pendleton continued, "while absolutely rejecting any offer of bribes or gifts, I am still willing to provide the letter I offered so that you can remain here unafraid. Of course, the innocence of your role on this island will be evidenced by revealing the location of Terrence's brother."

"I trust yer word not to change yer mind, Yer Honor."

"Please note that I said from what I have *heard thus far*. May I add that I am known as a fair and compassionate man. Isn't that right, Terrence?"

"Yes, sir. And I benefited." Terry nodded to Ben while the volcano smoldering inside him threatened to erupt.

"Then I'll take that letter if'n you please. 'Course, I can't guarantees the three's alive and well, but prob'ly they are. My ol' monkey shown the ideal hidin' place. His carrying on made me think they's gone in there more'n once 'fore them pirates came. Mebbe found a pathway through the danger."

Terry's stomach clenched as if a fist had slugged it. *No guarantee. Probably. Maybe.* The blackhearted schemer was far from sure.

"Come on, then, boy." Ben straightened and raised his crutch. "The good vice consul can watch from here. Grab six o' them cattails. Guess they'll be better lights than the sticks I had on the shore." He pointed at a bunch of the plants by Tom's pallet. "You needs the six husky sailors to go in with you, case you meet any places hard to cross underground. You'll go down on a rope ladder and mebbe use ropes inside too. To light yer torches, take some o' them live coals the pirates left." He pointed to the fire pit and a pot next to it. "And one more thing. Three pirates went into the cavern, but never came out. Prob'ly careless." A grin flitted across Ben's lips.

"One gets the feeling you would not rue another casualty." Mr. Pendleton's sharpness indicated his patience had ended.

Terry's patience had ended hours ago.

"Oh no, Yer Honor." Ben's somber tone would have fit with a funeral's dirge. "I hope the best fer the boy and his brother."

As Terry followed Ben Bolt out the cave, Mr. Pendleton's eyes were closed and his mouth moved, no doubt, in silent prayer. Terry tightened his jaw against making a silent plea of his own. God wouldn't like a hypocrite. But he hoped with all his heart that either the good man's prayers would be answered, or that lady luck would deign to smile.

CHAPTER 33

"Seems the pirates would've checked on their missing mates by now." Tom spoke slightly above a whisper from his far end on the ledge. He couldn't judge the time in the dark, but three or four hours could easily have passed since they'd disposed of the two men. "Let's see if the rope ladder's still there."

"We can't take chance," Dice whispered across Sara. "Wait maybe another four hours. Then we eat. Walk around. Warm up."

Tom didn't argue. He could stay perched on the ledge indefinitely, but he pitied Sara. She was shivering even though she was wearing both of her robes. He would take off his shirt and offer it to her, but Dice would object and claim that a "daughter of a samurai" wasn't like commoners. She could "endure the cold."

At the sound of distant voices, Tom stiffened. Speak of the devil—at least five or six fiends this time.

"Tom? Tom?" came from somewhere far away.

Had he lost his mind?

"I heard your name." Dice's words vibrated with hope.

"Would Ben Bolt know it?" Tom was sweating now. "Overheard it, maybe?"

"Tom, Tom. It's Terry! Where are you?"

"Here! Here! We're here!" Joy surging through him, Tom started to leap up, but Dice tackled him.

"Don't fall in! Let me get out," Dice ordered. "Then Sara. Carefully."

"Yes, yes!" Tom's voice cracked.

The minute the pair had scrambled out, Tom thrust his head through the hole, then hefted himself into the chamber. He headed for the faint glow coming from the tunnel, following Dice and Sara's shadowy figures. Right at the tunnel's entrance, a Navy man carrying a torch stopped them. Before Tom could muster up words, Terry stepped into the chamber.

"It's you!" His brother flung himself onto Tom.

Tom's legs gave way. Giddy with relief, he grabbed at Terry, who, while kneeling, was smiling and crying at the same time.

Tom was an eye blink away from crying himself. "I knew you'd never give up!" He regained his feet at the same time as Terry. "You're the best! The absolute best!"

Dice, who had continued out of the chamber with Sara, poked his head back in. "Five more men here. If you say safe, we get ladders out. Better than ship's ropes."

Terry gaped at Dice, then answered, "They're safe. They're Navy men, like the one in here." He turned back to Tom. "So, I take it he's one of the maroons Ben Bolt told us about."

"Ben Bolt told you?" Tom scowled. It wasn't a trick with the Navy backing Terry, but what did that diabolical creature have to do with anything?

"Yes, the scoundrel the pirates left. Come on, brother. Let's get out of here. I'll explain later."

Tom followed Terry up the ladders. Stepping into the tall grass, he sucked in the fresh air while squinting his eyes against the late afternoon sunshine. "Golly," he said, grasping Terry's arm, "I can hardly talk." He gulped in more air. "I've waited for this for so long, and now that it's happening, it's like a dream. A terrific, fantastic, unbelievable dream."

"I know." Terry gave a shaky laugh. "Like it's too good to be true."

"You're standing here. I can see that. So no more pirate horde. No years and years left on this blamed island." He shot his hands up toward the blue sky. "Rescued! Terry, you did it!"

Ben Bolt hobbled toward the group, smiling.

Tom clenched his fist. "What's the meaning of this?"

Bolt held up his hook with an innocent look of surprise. "Do I look like an enemy? Those nasty pirates left. Your brother had a gunboat and the Vice Consul of Nagasaki with him. Everything's negotiated. We're all right as rain."

"Impossible!" Tom hissed.

"You're found, ain't ye? You an' the Japanners? You're alive. Ye can thank me fer my gen'rosity."

Tom snorted and brushed past Bolt. He'd deal with the blathering monster later. Terry was pulling him forward and going on about the *William Parton*'s troubles, a vice consul named Pendleton, their passage to America on a ship called the *Retriever*, and a hundred other things.

Tom tried to take in all Terry was burstin' to tell him. But his rescue blocked out everything. At last, the nightmare was over. And it was over for Dice and Sara too, who walked a little ahead of him. A new warmth spread through him. Sara would say God did it. And for once, he'd agree—and shock her down to her toes.

When they reached his cave, the elderly man sitting there—undoubtedly Vice Consul Pendleton—rose on his cane and warmly shook Tom's hand. "What a grand sight you are!" His wrinkled face reflected kindness and dignity. "And healthy from all appearances despite what you must've endured."

"This day, sir, is the greatest of my life." Tom mustered a smile. "Thank you. I know you helped."

The vice consul pointed to Terry. "You'll be proud of your brother here. He worked toward your rescue with all his being and underwent a great deal to achieve it." Then he turned to Dice and Sara. "It seems you've been marooned also?" He actually translated his question into Japanese.

"Yes, shipwrecked," Dice answered, then bowed along with Sara.

"They have a long tale of endurance also, sir," Tom said. "I doubt I could've survived without them. And they speak English well. I hope you can help them too. It's dangerous right now for them to go back to their country, not because they're criminals, but because of Japan's laws."

"Yes, I know those laws against travel." The vice consul smiled at them. "You are most welcome on the *Retriever*. We'll find accommodations for you. The ship is sailing to Honolulu in the Hawaiian Islands, our next port, and from there to the west coast of America. You can decide how far to go while on the way to Honolulu."

When Bolt gave a disgruntled snort, Tom glanced at his face. Although no open hostility lay there, the pirate's stiff expression reminded Tom of a Halloween mask he once wore while disguised as a vampire.

"We belong in Japan," Dice said, a distant look in his eyes. "It is hard decision."

"This man's offer is your best chance to get away from here without having to hide in Japan," Tom cut in, suddenly scared for the two. "The frigate could take you back to its port, but disguising yourselves as masterless samurai sounds risky to me. I don't want to go away and leave you here either. I mean, more villains might find this place. My brother, this gentleman, the others with them aren't barbarians. You can trust them."

"We won't detain you if you wish to disembark in Honolulu," Pendleton added. "From there, you could eventually seek a way back to Japan, maybe when it becomes safer. But if you should choose to continue on to America, we would welcome your further companionship. I could also ask the captain to introduce you to the workings of the merchant ship, a knowledge that could be beneficial in your future and your country's place in the world."

Dice spoke in Japanese to Sara, who bowed. Not a bow of submission, but of happy agreement. Her eyes were sparkling.

"We will go with the ship to the next port. Maybe farther. Thank you." Dice turned to Tom. "I called you barbarian when we met. Now I call you most excellent friend, one like fellow samurai." This time he bowed to Tom.

Tom's heart filled to overflowing. "And you're my most excellent friend and will be Terry's too. Always. No matter if we're separated by an ocean." He bowed to Dice.

Mr. Pendleton stepped forward. "Congratulations to both of you for such splendid declarations." He shook Tom's hand and returned Dice's bow, after which he shook Dice's extended hand too.

Then the vice consul pivoted to Bolt, whose unwary scowl transformed into a smile—a smile through clenched teeth.

"Well, Mr. Bolt, you kept your word in revealing our friends' location. The search parties scoured this island with no luck. We would have been forced to give up the hunt for Thomas without you."

Tom couldn't believe his ears. Ben Bolt had *willingly* helped save them? That couldn't be right.

Then the pieces fell into place. Bolt had finagled a deal to avoid the noose, and it was working. Should he speak up? Dice and Sara hadn't yet. And if Dice had been willing to kill Bolt, they would still be hiding and marooned.

But Bolt had threatened Sara's purity. How could he overlook that? And he'd never forget the murderous look in the villain's eyes when he raised his knife in the shack. And the most recent foul act—Bolt's plot with the other pirates, returning evil for Dice's mercy.

Tom sucked in a breath. Sentenced as a pirate by Americans, the man would be shot or hanged—a quick death. But if left on the island in a type of solitary confinement, he'd have to think about his life while the years dragged by, possibly to the end of his days. Should that make a difference?

The vice consul had paused to run his eyes over the group, then continued addressing Bolt. "If these witnesses have no objection to my writing a letter attesting to your innocence—as far as known *by me*—I will write one here and now." He raised his eyebrows at Tom.

Tom looked at the wicked man, who didn't meet his gaze. His mind staggered between revealing the malevolence or allowing the monster a chance to become better.

Pushing aside his pulsing anger, he chose to remain quiet.

The vice consul turned toward Bolt. "But do we have paper?"

"There is one blank page at back of our Bible," Sara answered for him. "Are there Bibles where we are going?"

"Yes, indeed," Mr. Pendleton said at the same time that Terry and Tom chimed in.

Sara pulled the scarf off a small bundle she was carrying. It was the pair's worn Bible—the one possession she'd picked up on the way out of the cavern.

"Please use that last page if my brother approves. It can be left in the Bible, and Ben Bolt can have the book." She lowered her eyes.

Dice's jaw stiffened.

"I'm stayin' here," Bolt said quickly, "where I'll trouble nobody. Mebbe the good book'll learn me somethin'." He cast a sly look at Dice. "Learn me 'bout ne'er forgittin' a good deed."

Dice glared at the pirate, but then he adopted his usual veneer. "All right. Maybe so. You have many days, months, years, and more years, with such good book. Besides the Holy Bible, we give you all things in our cave. Also things in cavern if the men there"—he pointed to the seamen waiting outside—"will bring all things up." He cast a questioning look at the vice consul.

Pendleton nodded and called over to the two guards. "Tell the men to bring the supplies and ladders up from that cavern, if you please."

Tom detected a flicker of surprise on Bolt's face.

"Also, you will not be alone," Dice continued as the seamen started off.

"No?" Bolt wrinkled his brow.

"The monkey will throw many coconuts at you. But even with three ladders, maybe it is hard to bring your pet habu from the cove." Dice's face sported a smug expression.

"The snake died in its box on the shore. I kept the box to keep away two-legged varmints," Bolt rejoined.

Dice blinked, then actually laughed.

A samurai response, Tom decided.

"There are feathers out there for a quill," Sara said, pointing to where Tom had cleaned a duck to take to Dice for smoking.

Showing himself more than willing to help, Bolt hobbled outside to look over the feathers.

Sara picked up a split piece of coconut shell from among Tom's accumulated "dishes." "We can use ash for ink. A drop from shikuwasa lime makes it better, but we do not have one here."

"Ah, there's one in my larder." Tom arched an eyebrow at his brother, who was taking it all in. He moved the stone in front of the hole, and pulled out one of the limes left behind the day they had run for their lives. After spinning it in his hand to check for roaches, he handed it to Sara. "You can see how important Sara was to our team."

While the elderly man wrote in the propped-up Bible, carefully blotting Sara's concoction with his white handkerchief, Tom glanced around his cave. It had sheltered him from the weather and the bats. That had been good. But now, he was finished with its gloom, its dirt, its creepy echoes, and the tremors deep below the cave's floor. Thank goodness for that.

Then he eyed Dice and Sara as they stood behind Mr. Pendleton, watching him write. He wouldn't have chosen to be marooned in a million years, and especially not with foreigners. But Dice and Sara had been lifesavers, and in a word, they'd been kind to him—kind and thoughtful beyond what he could ever have expected. Who else would have provided food, taught him skills? Forgiven his poor judgment that endangered them? And because of them, he'd looked into the Bible.

After Mr. Pendleton handed Bolt his letter and treated him with a short lecture about the evils of pirating, the group left Bolt in the cave and climbed to the top of the ridge. Tom took a final look back at the empty hillsides, valley, and forests. How amazing that God had gone a massive step further than what he'd prayed, rescuing them from not only the pirates but the island itself. And on top of that, here was Terry next to him, safe off the vile *William Parton*.

When Tom and the others reached the beach and were waiting for a second boat, Ben Bolt caught up with them, dragging a kind of makeshift sled behind him. "Here be *payment* fer things in yer caves and the underground one too." He spoke loud enough for Mr. Pendleton to hear. He handed a large bag to Tom and slightly smaller ones to both Dice and Sara.

A minute later, the pirate leaned forward with eyes hard as flint. "Never come back," he warned, loud enough for the four of them to hear, but not the vice consul, who was in front of them, peering at the ship. "Do not jabber 'bout me or this island or treasure. If you be thinkin' there's more gold to be had—and *if'n* there are—you'd ne'er find the rock it's behind. All you be findin' is trouble, a bite worse'n a snake."

"No need to worry," Tom said. "You can keep the earthquakes and heat and bugs and bats and quicksand and whatever remains of the treasure—even if what you've paid here is a mere drop in the gold bucket."

Dice and Sara nodded their agreement.

Bolt eyed the bag he'd handed Tom as if about to reclaim it.

Tom held onto his bag with both hands. "Guess what you're getting in the caves is worth its weight in gold for a hermit. And we won't be returning to civilization penniless after our troubles here … with a man *known* to be a pirate, whose path will lead to death unless the book's words get hold of him like it has me. I know that path too well."

"So keep the bags," Bolt grumbled, "and better hope our paths ne'er cross." He cast a threatening look at Tom and hobbled away.

After the swift boat ride and his climb onto the *Retriever,* Tom knelt on the deck, his forehead touching the planks. The people standing by no doubt thought he was giving thanks to the ship for his rescue, like someone might kiss *terra firma* after a hot-air balloon flight. But he was bowing to his Deliverer, to Jesus.

When he stood back up, Sara and Dice were staring at him. Did they sense what had happened? Maybe, but if not, he'd tell them when the time was right.

Terry was watching him too, and half the crew, including— of all people—the young boy Jim, standing by Cook Salty and Doc Murdoch from the *William Parton.* The one good friend and their two supporters were somehow still with them. Jim had always stoically tried to ignore the crew's jeers, calling him the "ship's scullion," and laughing at his inexperience. But he was grinning now, like life had turned a wonderful corner.

Without a doubt, life had also turned an amazing corner for him and Terry. "Thanks, everyone!" he shouted. He threw his arm over Terry's shoulder. "Finally together! Alive and well, and on our way home. Does it seem real yet?"

"Now it does." Terry gave a wry smile. "It was all I wanted, all I dreamed about every hour of every day, even when finding you seemed impossible. I guess it's like they say, dreams can come true if you don't give up."

"And prayers can too," Tom added, lifting a brow at Terry's shocked look. "We have a lot of catching up to do. Your coming in time is like a miracle. Not a little one. A huge one."

"You *could* describe it like that. I'm still thinking on it. But I didn't expect to hear words about miracles—or prayers— popping out of *your* mouth."

The disapproval that leapt from his brother's face drew Tom

up short. He had hated pious words until he read the Bible for himself, and Terry had detested sitting in church as much as he had. "I'm still me," he said, moving to a more tolerable approach. "Still want to fish in our creek and hunt those stupid squirrels we never caught with Tuffy. No doubt I'll aggravate a bunch of people, like always." He quirked a quick grin. "I'm hoping to see Peg again—if she hasn't been spoken for. But being imprisoned on an island with two Japanese Christians, while under the threat of a pirate attack, finally got my attention—consider the odds of that situation. I'd never taken much time to think about really important questions before."

Terry glanced around, then leaned in toward Tom. "Talk about far-out odds. How about my staying with a disguised *preacher* inside the actual country where Christianity is the illegal 'Evil Religion.' Those odds are hard to beat too. So I've been forced to think as well—too much to my liking."

"You mean by Vice Consul Pendleton?"

"Right, Mr. Pendleton and his friends. He's one of the kindest persons you'll ever meet—maybe you noticed on the island—but he'll get the better of you if you're not watching."

Tom saw the vice consul beckoning the group. "Guess we better find out what the wily preacher expects of me." He rolled his eyes. "At least, we can pay both our ways unless there are rocks in here." He peered into the bag as Terry took a look too. "Nope. Sure enough, coins." He swirled the contents. "Some Spanish pesos and good old U.S. silver dollars, and lots of guineas."

Terry clapped Tom's shoulder. "Gold doubloons too." He beamed as they headed across the deck. "You don't have to pay my way on this ship. I'm part of the crew. But it's an awful good thing to have our way home covered after we reach San Francisco."

Mr. Pendleton held the door open and instructed everyone to take seats at a rectangular, fold-out table. "Supper for all of us will be delivered here so that you and I have a chance to relax a bit. This is Jim's and my stateroom."

While they were still taking their seats, the steward arrived with the food. The delicious smell of chicken, vegetables, soy, and rice filled the room.

Their host waved his hand over the dishes. "I imagine our maroons will appreciate a taste that's enjoyed in both Japan and America."

Tom joined with Sara and Dice in thanking the vice consul. It had been a coon's age since he'd smelled anything half as good. No more pigeon hearts, ground cattails, or gourd soup, but he avoided saying that out loud. Sara had done her best with what she had.

He eyed Terry, who still looked shell-shocked. "Eat well, brother. You're going to need the strength when I tell you my story. You're going to be flabbergasted. I guarantee it."

"Maybe I won't be any more than you'll be at mine." Terry's *heh, heh* held a trace of a challenge.

"We'll see." Tom fingered his bag from the pirate. "In fact, I have a gold doubloon that says you will be."

Mr. Pendleton, who was negotiating with the departing steward about hot tea and a dessert, turned and cleared his throat.

Tom set the bag down. "I reckon it's a duty to use the coins better, not for jesting. I'll lower the bet to my ... shirt." It was the only other thing available.

The vice consul's eyes twinkled as he took his seat. "I assume Terrence has to take the shirt if he loses."

Tom laughed along with the others, thinking that Dice and Sara would refuse to touch it if they were threatened with it as a prize.

"However," Mr. Pendleton continued, "that red shirt is very special. I assume you're the one who waved it at the whaler, Tom."

Tom winced. "Yes, afraid so, sir. That mistake caused a lot of trouble. Almost got us killed."

"Yet, it got you rescued."

Tom blinked. "How, sir?"

"The whaler's sailing master, who saw the shirt, gave us this island's correct coordinates. We had no other way of learning them, and we never would have located this scrap of coral without them."

Tom shook his head. "Now I'm flabbergasted. If Terry had agreed to a bet, I'd have to concede."

Tom glanced at Dice and Sara, both of whom had leaned forward at the news. He looked a moment longer at Sara, whose cheeks reddened when their eyes met. He offered a tentative smile, and she returned one before dropping her gaze.

He straightened on the bench. Why hadn't he claimed Sara as his "most excellent friend" too? Because, he realized with a start, Sara was more than that. Peg wouldn't approve if she knew, but this girl from Japan had wriggled her way into his heart. Deep into his heart. Maybe she and Dice would leave him in Honolulu. He sure hoped not. He hoped their adventure would continue together, uninterrupted for months … or years.

"Well, our food is getting cold. I'll ask the blessing," Mr. Pendleton announced, "so you won't have to wait any longer."

Tom tried to concentrate on the prayer, but instead, kept thinking how similar the vice consul was to his father—staid, yet with a dry sense of humor. And caring. His father had wanted him, his elder son, to be prepared for life, to grow up. He could see that now.

His last memory of his father was on the day his parents had stood on the dock, watching the ferry take Terry and him away for a stay at their grandparents' farm. His father couldn't have known they wouldn't all be together again for a very long time. Despite the letters Terry and he had sent home from several ports, they had to be beside themselves with worry.

But he thought, as the prayer ended, their parents would find their sons had learned a great deal. He would do his best to make their homecoming a cause for celebration. And, who knew? They might be welcoming Dice and Sara too.

The bosun cried, "Yo heave ho." The sea anchors' chains clanked. Sailors chanted and officers shouted. The thud of boots came from all directions. The groans of the ship's timbers joined with the belching of steam.

They were underway!

Going home! Terry and he were going home.

AFTERWORD

Readers familiar with Japanese history may question whether the Christian faith of the Japanese siblings and their ability to speak English have even a tiny shred of realism. After all, Okinawa submitted tribute to the Japanese Satsuma Domain in the story's time period, and Christianity was strictly prohibited in Japan. However, history tells us that Dr. Bernard Bettelheim, a Christian missionary and his family, backed by a British warship, managed to disembark at Naha in 1846 and take up residence in a Buddhist temple. He was not welcomed by the authorities or townspeople, but persevered in trying to share the Christian faith as well as offer medical aid and English lessons. The Bettelheims left on Commodore Perry's ship in 1854. This historical missionary's effort in Okinawa planted the idea for my fictional characters to learn English and become Christians in Naha before being marooned. Their acquisition of English was vital for communication with Tom on the island, and I was pleased to have them be the ones with the Christian faith, rather than the usual Westerner.

Although the story of *Isle of Darkness and Light* and all its characters are fictitious, another connection to real history involves my great-great-uncle, John Greer Walsh, the first American consul to Nagasaki. He served as honorary consul from 1859, the year the city opened for foreign residence, to 1865. At the age of thirty-four, he married Yamaguchi Rin. The couple had one daughter and lived the rest of their lives in Japan. When I was in Japan in the 1960s, I had the pleasure of getting to know the older grandchildren of the consul and his wife. They shared that they had good memories of their kind grandfather. If you have read the *Dragonfly Trilogy*, you probably recognized the fictitious Consul John Cardiff and Sumi Taguchi and hopefully cheered when they made their appearance in this story, married and with a baby girl.

Writing a story of survival on a remote Pacific island required many months of research. As Tom Ballard said in the story, "Last he heard, no teacher in the whole United States gave lessons on survival if marooned on a rock in the middle of an ocean." I did find that the Japanese island, Minami Daitō, has a spectacular underground cavern. The photographs of its chilling depth helped me empathize with Tom's horror of being stuck below ground in inky darkness—with bats!

This story was fun to write. The mix of American brothers, Japanese siblings, a Pacific island, Nagasaki, sail ships, pirates, and treasure hunters gave a rich trove from which to create a story of adventure, growth in understanding, and tested faith.

A NOTE FROM ELIZABETH ANN

Thank you for taking time to read *Isle of Darkness and Light*. I hope you became attached to Tom, Terry, Sara, and Dice—even as I did while writing about them. If you enjoyed this story, please take a minute to review it on Amazon. Offering just a sentence or two can have a big impact. Reviews are a story's lifeline!

* * *

Book One and Book Three of the *Brothers in Peril Trilogy*, open more doors into the brothers' adventures, trials, and triumphs. Both books are available on Amazon at this link (or just put my name in the search bar). www.amazon.com/s?k=elizabeth+ann+boyles

In the series' Book Three, **Fields of Shadow and Glory**, the Ballard brothers and their companions, Sara and Mr. Pendleton, have made it to the United States, but an old foe surfaces in San Francisco. Through the Civil War's chaos, this enemy sets a dangerous chain of events in motion. As the brothers and Sara face the darkness of a broken world, questions arise: Can mercy once again prevail over hatred? Can faith survive war? And what kind of love is worth waiting for?

Do you wonder how Tom and Terry got themselves into such a fix? Book One, **Entrapped,** traces their chain of missteps and the risky venture they undertake in their search for freedom and lasting friendships. You'll travel with the young men from Albany, New York, to their grandparents' farm, through Havana, around Cape Horn, into the Galapagos Archipelago, and across the Pacific. Sara and Daisuke make a stunning appearance too.

* * *

How about visiting the years directly preceding the *Brothers in Peril Trilogy*? The **Dragonfly Trilogy** dives into Consul Cardiff and Sumi's astonishing stories, in which they shine as the stars. Also, the delightful Mr. Pendleton shows up as their indispensable counselor and friend. The fascinating, but treacherous setting of 1859-1861 in Nagasaki, Japan, waits for you in the series' three novels, also available on Amazon.

DISCUSSION QUESTIONS

*Spoiler alert: These questions should
be discussed only after finishing the story.*

1. When you read the description of Tom's dilemma in the first chapter, what problem or possible danger on the island struck you as a critical one he might face?

2. Within a few chapters, contrasts in cultures become evident. Which different customs were most glaring to you?

3. Did anyone close to you come from a very different background with significantly different customs or beliefs? If you feel free to share, tell how you handled this and how it turned out.

4. Although the main characters have conflicting customs and beliefs, they also have several core desires and/or values in common. What similarities do you see?

5. What would you dislike most about your situation if you were in either Tom's or Terry's circumstances? Are there any advantages to situations like theirs?

6. In what ways do you see Tom growing and becoming a better individual while stuck on the island?

7. Terry, Sara, and Dice became more mature by the end of the

story, too. Choose the one you feel grew the most, and share why you picked him/her and what contributed to his/her growth. Of these three, who do you think changed the least?

8. In what ways did Sara's Christian faith appear genuine? How about her brother's?

9. Did Ben Bolt come across to you as a totally depraved villain? Do you think he gave out parts of the treasure purely from selfish motives or were his motives mixed?
How do you feel about his escape from the usual hanging for pirates? Right or wrong?

10. Of Mr. Pendleton's good qualities, which impressed you the most? Did any annoy you?

11. God's providential care is woven throughout the story. What evidence of His care especially caught your attention? Have you heard of, or experienced, a remarkable deliverance in answer to prayer that you would like to briefly share?

12. In addition to danger, what do you think were key reasons Tom turned to Christ?

13. Were the story's island and Japanese settings realistic?

ACKNOWLEDGMENTS

Throughout my years of writing, numerous people have kindly offered suggestions and encouragement. Here, I'll mention just those who contributed improvements specifically for *Isle of Darkness and Light* although I deeply appreciate every bit of the interest and help.

Thank you to members of the ACFW and neighborhood critique groups who read all or most of this book's manuscript and offered valuable advice: Kay Learned, Lee Carver, Kerry Dreher, Martha Ladyman, Suzanne Disheroon, Amanda Caudill, and Randy Oxentenko.

USA Best Selling Author, Lynne Gentry, not only read the manuscript, but also offered her endorsement, which I treasure.

I greatly appreciate the story's initial readers who contributed excellent suggestions as well as catching typos: Beverly Barlow, Kathleen Galahity, and Jan Johnson.

And last of all, a big thank you to my daughter Sherry and son Scott, who both listened patiently to my frequent book chatter and wholeheartedly supported my efforts.

ABOUT THE AUTHOR

Unique historical settings have always intrigued Elizabeth Ann, especially ones that feature a mix of American and other countries' cultures. Those settings provide a treasure chest for her fictional stories of adventure and discovery, often including a strand of romance.

She developed a love for the Far East when she lived in Japan, where she met and married her husband. She also spent many years teaching and building relationships with her international students at a Christian university in Dallas, Texas.

After her husband of fifty years took his final step into heaven, she moved to Colorado. She cherishes spending time at the foot of the gorgeous Rocky Mountains with her daughter and son, while entreating her three Texas grandsons to visit often.

Elizabeth Ann won the ACFW national Genesis award and the ACFW Virginia Crown award for historical/historical romance.

She would love to stay in touch through
Facebook.com/elizabethannboyles

Also, the welcome mat is always out at
elizabethannboyles.com